Liberty prepared to end the night without another word spoken between them. She stole a glance at Jarrett and their eyes collided for a heart-stopping moment. She blinked, his eyes telling her what words could not. Her pulse raced, her lips parted in an unconscious response to his passionate gaze. His eyes fell to her mouth and he groaned, unable to contain himself as he pulled her to him, his mouth devouring hers as he kissed her with all of the passion he had been holding inside for the past few hours. Liberty moaned, instantly aroused by his kiss, her body arching against his in complete abandon.

She knew he was frustrated but didn't care because his kiss also reassured her that he still wanted her and hadn't completely given up. She began to tremble with desire and pressed her body even closer to his as the kiss deepened, his mouth sucking her bottom lip until she began to quiver.

A car door slammed. Liberty jumped and her eyes popped open. Jarrett slowly released her, the tension in his body evidence that he too had lost control. Again their eyes locked until Liberty's fell. She swallowed before looking up again. He was no longer looking at her, but at the culprit who had interrupted their passion. As the car sped away, Liberty mustered the courage to speak first.

"Jarrett—" she began.

"Two days, Liberty. I can't wait longer than that," Jarrett interrupted, the coldness in his voice causing her to grit her teeth in consternation. The kiss had not softened his resolve.

He removed his arms from her and without another word, got back in his car. Liberty stared after him before sighing heavily. With great disappointment that he had no intention of coming inside, she unlocked her front door.

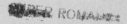

Also by Dianne Mayhew

Secret Passions

Playing with Fire

Impetuous

Dark Interlude

Stolen Moments

Encounter

DIANNE MAYHEW

ARABESQUE
BET
BOOKS

BET Publications, LLC
http://www.bet.com
http://www.arabesquebooks.com

ARABESQUE BOOKS are published by

BET Publications, LLC
c/o BET BOOKS
One BET Plaza
1900 W Place NE
Washington, DC 20018-1211

All Kensington Titles, Imprints, and Distributed Lines are
available at special quantity discounts for bulk purchases for
sales promotions, premiums, fund-raising, and educational
or institutional use. Special book excerpts or customized
printings can also be created to fit specific needs. For details,
write or phone the office of the Kensington special sales
manager: Kensington Publishing Corp., 850 Third Avenue,
New York, NY 10022, attn: Special Sales Department,
Phone: 1-800-221-2647.

BET Books is a trademark of Black Entertainment Television,
Inc. ARABESQUE, the ARABESQUE logo, and the BET
BOOKS logo are trademarks and registered trademarks.

First printing: June 2004
10 9 8 7 6 5 4 3 2 1

Printed in the United States of America

To the many wonderful readers out there who appreciate heartfelt romance with an edge of suspense and laughter. Also to my wonderful husband, Alex, for encouraging me when things got a little overwhelming.

ACKNOWLEDGMENTS

I want to acknowledge those closest to me for their support during the process of continuing the saga of Liberty Sutton. I want to thank my friend Jody Vaughn for her patience; my niece, Kelly Mayhew, for listening to all of my rewrites; my photographer, Doug Gillam; my friend William Massey; and my agent and friend, Jacqueline Coleman Young, for just making it happen.

Chapter 1

Soothing melodies from a hidden orchestra filled the air as a warm evening breeze fluttered against the sheer, snow-white curtains and soft white linen tablecloths. Romantic place settings just for two were surrounded with subtly lit candles that cast gentle silhouettes that created an enchanting atmosphere. The murmur of lovers' voices streamed from the cozy seating arrangements. Amidst it all, was the intense, sensuous gaze of the strikingly handsome Jarrett Irving. His expectant eyes were focused solely on Liberty.

Even after dating for nearly two years, he still caught himself admiring Liberty's beauty. She was an average height, about five seven. With her slender yet curvy figure, her height provided an added grace that he admired each time she moved. When she was near, his hands begged to caress her, ached to feel the softness of her smooth skin. His gaze fell on her full mouth, now pouting in her confusion. He wanted to lean in and kiss her until she had no thoughts but of him.

Say yes, he thought, hating the anguish that her continued silence brought him. As his gaze caught hers, he was captivated anew by her radiant brown eyes. He was always lost in their depth; her almond-shaped eyes were so serene and mysterious in their darkness. Her thick heavy eyelashes were fluttered low, effectively hiding her thoughts from him.

Liberty's heart thrashed wildly against her chest, the crazy rhythms drowning out every sound as she endured Jarrett's searching gaze. It was disturbing. She wanted to fidget. She forced herself to remain still. Yet she could not stop the emotions that were tearing her apart as his steady gaze slowly pummeled her resolve. Forgotten anxieties were returning and overwhelming her beneath his intense scrutiny. What could she say? How could she possibly answer him at this moment as his eyes were demanding? The potency of his charm made her want to melt and simply say, *Yes. I'll marry you.*

The reality of his question, the depth of its seriousness, immobilized her.

It was the anxiety of the past resurfacing. A feeling she could not deny. She had experienced love's painful betrayal and dared not chance it again. She had really loved once. And she had been hurt. She did not want to risk her heart again. As thrilling as it was to hear Jarrett ask her to marry him, it was just as overwhelming. Her moment of triumph, at last, and yet she felt dizzy with uncertainty.

It was true that their time together had proven to be an incredible experience for Liberty. He had not faltered as others before him had. Not even when she tested him. And she certainly had tested him during their courtship. He was the embodiment of the classic male every woman must surely want, Liberty believed. He was strong, secure, confident, loving, and charming. He was trustworthy and honorable.

Though she had taken her share of heartbreaks and had made her share of mistakes, she wanted to believe him when he claimed he would never break her heart. What she was most unsure of was herself. Liberty didn't know if she could prove to be faithful in the end. Old wounds died hard, so did old habits and old feelings. Even her recent triumphs could not erase the painful memories of her past.

As she sat there tracing the rim of her wineglass with her forefinger, she recalled two years earlier when she had first met Jarrett. She had been a completely different woman. She was willful, bitter, and full of distrust. She had been unable to believe in anyone, especially men. It had been a time when she was at her most selfish and impetuous. She had gone from one relationship to another, never once thinking of the person she left behind. She was a despondent woman and she had given up on love.

And then she met Jarrett and all at once, she realized that she didn't want to live her life without him. Yet, had it not been for the staggering turn of fate that gave her a new chance to have custody of her son, Liberty was sure she would never have fully come out of the near depression Anthony Anderson had caused in her after he abruptly left her and took her son with him.

Anthony Anderson was her son's father and had taken advantage of her naïve youth. In her blind infatuation, she had allowed herself to fall in love with his suave words and older charm. She had believed in him and staunchly thought that she was the love of his life. And why shouldn't she have believed it? she thought with a slight frown. After all, he had been the love of *her* life. Back then, she had wanted to marry him, to be the mother of his children. Well, she became the mother of his child but marriage was out of the question. He was already married.

Not only did he have a wife, but the couple had the

audacity to decide that they had the right to adopt her child as their own. Anthony had not even bothered to tell her of their intent. He had sent his wife and mother-in-law to tell her. And without so much as a good-bye, she lost custody of her infant son.

It had taken five tenacious years for Liberty to rein in her often volatile emotions and get her life on track. After she was hired at the public relations firm where Jarrett Irving was vice president of communications, she was immediately smitten with him. An innate instinct, as old as time, told her she would not get even close to the man without cleaning up her act. And she did, if only to get his attention at first. Soon, the new woman she became was the woman she really wanted to be and she never went back to being the pathetic child Anthony had helped create. With Jarrett's nurturing, she blossomed. Encouraged by the changes she exhibited with Jarrett by her side, she set out to prove that she had the right to be happy and to be with her son, never dreaming that fate would step in the way for her.

Just when she was prepared to take legal actions to get her son, Anthony had lost his wife and nearly lost their son too. She had never wished ill upon Anthony's wife, but it had proven to be a turning point in her goal to gain custody of her son and she was at last reunited with him.

And she was never going to allow anything or anyone to come between them again.

Her gaze fell from Jarrett's solemn face to his firm hands. He was tapping a slow, deliberate beat on the table with his fingers. One, two, three. Again. She stared, momentarily distracted, as she followed the rhythm of his fingers. Then her glance roamed back toward his face, still an inscrutable mask as he waited for her response. For his part, he doggedly stared into his coffee, now refusing to acknowledge her gaze. She felt dismay at that. It was such a contrast to the man she knew him to be. Open, honest, unassuming. How she wished she could have shared his belief that everything would be all right.

She didn't have his kind of confidence. Anthony had taken it from her when he had so easily stolen her heart, then her child, and try as she might, there had been nothing she could do about it until *he* changed *his* mind.

After finally being reunited with her son, Jamal, she wanted only to make sure that she never lost him again. And right now, marrying Jarrett would create an even bigger friction between herself and Anthony than the one that already existed. The two despised each other and made no attempt to temper their feelings.

Anthony's unreasonable selfishness had cost her five years of distress and loneliness. As much as she wanted Jarrett to be a part of her life, she needed Jamal even more and was not willing to suffer through another bout of Anthony's callousness. She was sure he'd try to take Jamal again if she married Jarrett. Jamal or Jarrett. It was a choice that was tearing her apart and she had no answers.

Her eyes glanced from Jarrett's fingers that had stopped strumming a steady beat on the table to his right hand that held a small black box. Within it, she knew, was the engagement ring he had planned to give her. His knuckles were taut, caused by his tight grasp on the box, the only sign of just how tense he actually was.

"Why don't you love me, Liberty?" she heard his muffled voice. Her eyes flew upon him again.

Taken aback by the accusation, a swift denial upon her lips, she wanted to cry out, *I love you beyond reason,* but held back the impulsive declaration. Her simple "I do love you, Jarrett" was all she could muster.

"And yet you can't give me a simple yes-or-no answer," Jarrett challenged, his eyebrows raised in an arrogant arch. She knew then that he was not only in misery but he was furious . . . and something else. Suspicion? *But why?* She gulped, unable to stand his scrutiny.

"Jarrett, I—" she began in a barely audible whisper, but he pushed from the table and abruptly came to his feet. His action caused her to pause. She stared up at him, confused. For what felt like forever, he didn't say a word, he just stared at her. Then, his face once again an inscrutable mask, he said stiffly, "I'm going to the restroom," and walked away.

Liberty stared after him, then reached for her water and sipped slowly. She needed a stiff drink, she thought, as the cool water eased her burning throat. She ached to scream, to call him back, to say what he wanted to hear. Instead, she carefully set the glass down and waited with outward calm for him to return.

Jarrett barely held his frustration in check as he left the table. He wanted to slam a door, break a window, slam Anthony's head against a wall. Unable to do any such thing, he shoved the bathroom door open with his foot and headed straight for the sink. He turned on the faucet, then splashed his face with cold water. He was hot and even the water didn't work to relieve his agitated state. He swore under his breath, glaring at his reflection.

At thirty-five, he was a good-looking man and took care of himself. He was tall, six one, and his dark complexion smooth. His features were not too fine or broad, clean cut. He had a firm mouth, a little more firm than usual right now, he thought, but he was angry. It was all he could do to keep from making a scene. He had always prided himself on being polished, cool-headed.

He had a great job, the vice president of communications in a public relations firm that had international holdings. He was doing very well for himself and even with his monthly alimony and child support checks, he had a lot to offer any woman. The fact was, his natural optimism returning, he was a good man, all around. From his looks to his career to his attitude, and Liberty was crazy to reject him, he thought without conceit.

With everything that he had to offer, the woman had taken his pride and crushed it like rotten garbage. He didn't feel so great right now and he was astonished that he could exhibit such weakness. He was behaving like a groveling idiot and it was not flattering to his ego not to know how to handle this rejection.

He had been married before, remembered the sadness it had once brought him when he and Dana had grown apart. He had sworn he would never marry again. Why should he? He had what most men wanted out of a wife, sons. Two wonderful boys that were becoming young men of whom he knew he would be proud. So why this burning need to marry Liberty? She wanted him, he knew that. Despite her rejection to marry him, he knew she cared for him. She had admitted that she loved him, it just wasn't enough to become his wife, he thought grimly.

He was sure of the reason. Anthony Anderson. She denied having any affection for Anthony, and Jarrett had to admit that he sensed no sexual tension between them, at least not on Liberty's part. But it made no sense. Love or not, Jarrett was certain that Anthony was the reason for Liberty's abrupt and very unflatteringly rejection. She hadn't said no, but if she were going to say yes, she wouldn't have had to think about it for so long.

He had gone from shocked dismay to cold anger before barely controlling his emotions. He wanted to shake her, demand that she tell him why, and no games. He wanted her to admit Anthony was the reason. Yet he dreaded to hear such a confession.

He sighed, shaking his head. He knew better than to shake Liberty or even attempt to touch her when he was angry. She was fragile, that he had learned, and easily heartbroken. She needed tenderness, and hadn't he offered her that? She needed patience; he had waited nearly two years to propose when he had wanted to from the moment he saw her with her son, loving the boy that she barely knew. She needed understanding, yet how much understanding could one man give? He leaned his elbows on the counter and laid his face in his hands.

Chapter 2

Why can't he see that I do love him? Liberty wondered as she watched Jarrett return. His walk was still stiff but she could see that he had calmed down, if only slightly. She knew by the tightening of his jaw and the gleam in his eyes that he was ready to argue his point further. She braced herself. She didn't want to lose him but she knew that she could not give in, no matter how persistent his approach.

Anthony would not be agreeable, she was certain, if she announced that she wanted to marry Jarrett. He would threaten to take her to court, claim full custody, and use every dirty trick he knew, and he knew a lot, to keep her from having Jamal. He would bring up her past, a time when she was weak and foolish and so very young. She wanted to groan at the memory of her behavior. *No,* she thought firmly, *I will not take a chance on losing my son.*

She continued to stare at him, waiting patiently as he returned to their table. As he sat, she considered him with an unwavering gaze. His shoulders were rigid, broad, and firm. His eyes seemed darker somehow, determined even. They pinned her. Staring into his steady gaze caused her breath to come in shaky light gasps. He didn't seem to notice. She was irritated that he could create such a reaction in her when he seemed so cool now, so detached. Then his words stole her breath.

He stated in a calm, low voice, "If you love me, Liberty, then marry me."

The statement did not surprise Liberty, but her heart still dropped with distress. She took a deep breath, branded by his words. She could not tell him about her qualms surrounding Anthony. His ego would never allow him to admit that Anthony could hurt them. Jarrett would not consider her rejection as a form of protecting their relationship, but instead he would see it as protecting Anthony, something she certainly was not doing. She licked her suddenly dry lips and leaned back in her own chair, attempting to appear poised despite her inner turmoil.

"Jarrett," she murmured, choosing her words with caution, "I do love you, so very much," she insisted. "But I need a little time . . ."

"Time?" he asked coolly though his jaw hardened, his teeth clenched. He caught himself, controlling his frustration at the look of uncertainty that she gave him. He relaxed his jaw and sat back and waited.

"Yes. Time. I just . . . Why can't you understand that I need a little time to think about it?" Liberty asked in a pained voice. He was not the Jarrett she knew. Certainly she had seen him riled up, particularly when Anthony was around, if Dana was late bringing over his sons, things like that. But this Jarrett was not the Jarrett she had come to know. He had never fought her with such stubborn determination before. She was not at all prepared to manage the situation and was doing a poor job as a result.

Had she but had a clue, perhaps she could have come up with a better response than that she needed time to answer his marriage proposal. Jarrett had given her no hint that he intended to ask her to marry him. Certainly they had talked about his divorce from Dana, how he felt about marriage. They had discussed how naïve she had been to think she and Anthony would have married so many years ago. In all of their discussions, not once had she concluded that he was ready to broach the subject of marriage in their future.

His gaze left her holding her breath. For long moments he did not respond, and then finally he leaned forward, his eyes unwavering as he spoke slowly, each word cryptic and distinct. "All right . . . how much time, Liberty?"

Liberty forced herself not to swallow or lick her lips in nervous reaction to his response. Her nerves were on edge. She didn't want to lose him but she could not risk Jamal. She hadn't really thought about how much time she would need. The proposal was so sudden. How much time would it take to make Anthony accept a marriage between herself and Jarrett? Forever? She sobbed inside, furious with Jarrett, furious with Anthony and the world at large. Jarrett's gaze locked with hers, refusing to shift or fall until he had an answer. Despite herself, she licked her lips and tried to appear calm.

"A few weeks," Liberty responded as coolly as she could. It didn't matter. His face broke with fury before his words tore out with such vehemence she nearly gasped.

"A few weeks!" he exploded.

Liberty jumped at the outburst and gave him a weary glance before looking around to see if anyone had heard or noticed. The many discreet stares were answer enough that they had. She looked back at him with a frown.

"I need a few weeks' time," she began reasonably, imploring him with her soft voice to understand. But he cut her off.

"Time for what? Never mind." Jarrett seethed, then took a deep breath. He pulled out his wallet and waved for the waiter.

She was getting angry with him. He was being unreasonable and bullheaded and he was not listening to her. She waited in stony silence for Jarrett to finish his business with the waiter.

"Sir? Would you like to see the dessert menu?" the waiter asked with a bright smile. It faded beneath Jarrett's cold stare.

"No. Just the check. Now," Jarrett added at the waiter's hesitant departure. The waiter nodded and hastened away.

"I'm not going to bombard you with questions. I'm not going to ask what difference now versus two weeks or three weeks or forever will make. But I will tell you this, if you don't want to marry me I would prefer to hear it now rather than later. If you don't want this relationship, you would be doing us both a favor if you would just say so, now," Jarrett chastised.

As he spoke, Liberty shook her head in denial, aching to interrupt, determined not to make a scene.

"That's not it at all, Jarrett. I believe you know that is not how I feel. I do want to marry you. . . ."

"Then say yes," Jarrett groaned instantly, his eyes momentarily hot upon her, the coldness gone, the urgency back.

"I can't. Not yet," Liberty whispered.

The heat left his gaze and once again he seemed a stranger.

The waiter's return found them both silent and sulking. He handed Jarrett his receipt and after receiving Jarrett's signature, he bid them good day and hastened away again. It was obvious in the waiter's subdued demeanor that he was uncomfortable with the pair. The tension between them was intense.

"I never took you for the type to play games, Liberty," Jarrett stated flatly. Liberty started, hurt by his accusation. "But," he continued before she could respond, "all that innocence, that uncertainty you exhibited, even after I discovered you had a son, even after I found Anthony with you . . . I still didn't see you that way. I should have known better. You play very well," he added harshly.

She was bemused. She knew that he spoke out of anger and rejection and wanted to hurt her, if only to assuage his ego. She forced a light smile to her lips, ignored his cold stare, and considered him with a gentle gaze. "I am not playing games, Jarrett. I just need a little more time. A few weeks is not that much to ask. You're . . . wait," she pleaded when he turned his head ever so slightly from her. "Listen please."

She placed her hand on his arm, imploring him to respond. Grudgingly he looked at her again and she continued. "You're asking for an answer to a decision that can affect the rest of my life, my son's life, and *your* sons' lives too. To expect me to answer you just like this is not fair. You, of all people, Jarrett, know how much I've been through and what more can be done to me if I am not careful with all of my decisions," Liberty added firmly. She slowly released him and waited for his outburst. When none came she stared straight ahead, her gazed fixed on the beautiful design of the sheer white curtains. There was nothing more she could say. Not yet.

Jarrett closed his eyes, mulling over Liberty's words. When he finally considered her again, he spoke in a voice so low she had to concentrate to hear him. "Liberty," he said very slowly, as if he were talking to a child. "It's not as if I'm a leech, some kind of loser that'll bring you and Jamal down into the gutter. You speak as if marrying me would be like marrying someone of the lowest character. I resent that very much," he added.

He paused. When she didn't respond, he continued, "When you're in love, you say yes. You're happy to be asked into marriage. When you're in love, Liberty, it's already there." He stopped, looking at her with disapproval. He cleared his throat, then leaning forward, said sternly, "Two days, Liberty. I'll give you until Sunday. If you care about me, about *us*, at all, it shouldn't take weeks to decide. What is there to decide anyway?" Jarrett scoffed.

She truly wanted to marry Jarrett, but she could not say yes, at least not yet. Not until she was sure Anthony would not attempt to take Jamal as he had been threatening to do. If he did try to take Jamal she would run with her son. It was an impulsive thought but she knew it to be the truth. She would run and that was something she could not ask Jarrett to do. He had sons of his own from his first marriage. Two boys, not much older than Jamal. They were good boys, no drama in their lives even during Jarrett's divorce from Dana Irving. It had been done by two mature, amicable adults and neither of them regretted their decision to end the marriage. They were, in fact, friends and comfortable with interacting in their ex's new lives. Liberty wished it were the case with her and Anthony.

She could not explain her fears to Jarrett. He would never understand. He would never consider her déclassé as a hindrance, he never had. He would assure her he could manage anything Anthony attempted to do. Liberty had learned during her fight for Jamal that status did matter, reputations did matter, and Anthony would use every bit of clout he had to best her. She had even met with lawyers who told her she didn't have a chance when she first attempted to get Jamal back. Why should anything have changed?

"Jarrett," Liberty murmured, her eyes imploring him to understand.

"I'm going to the car. Are you coming?" Jarrett demanded, ignoring her beseeching gaze. He didn't want her feeling sorry for him. He wanted her love, he wanted her to be his wife!

Their eyes locked yet again and this time Liberty could not read his mood at all. Knowing further arguments would get them nowhere and create only more anguish, she stood slowly.

Jarrett watched her in silence, waiting patiently, his blank gaze void of the turmoil he was feeling inside. Nonetheless, Liberty knew there was nothing more she could say. She would have to wait until Sunday before she attempted to discuss it further, to explain herself again. At the moment, she could not appease him, no matter how much she admitted she loved him. He didn't and couldn't understand. Not in the state of mind he was in. All she could do was allow him time, which ironically was all she was asking for herself.

She reached for her purse with as much dignity as she could muster and went to his side. She knew people were wondering what was going on. It infuriated her that he could be so indiscreet. Her very correct man was acting like a spoiled boy and she could not get over how she had never seen such behavior from him before. Perhaps he had learned it from her, she thought ruefully. For everything he was doing to her now she had done to him during their initial courtship.

It would have been amusing if the situation wasn't so serious. Jarrett had always been so considerate of her feelings. Was this the person he would become when he felt rejected?

Aware of the customers still gawking at them, she unconsciously gripped her purse against her bosom and with a high head followed Jarrett's brisk walk from the restaurant. She refused to sprint to keep up with him. When she finally did catch up, he was already standing beside his car. Although he was visibly upset by the outcome of their dinner, he held the passenger door open for Liberty and waited until she was buckled inside before closing it.

They did not speak a word the entire time it took to drive to her town house. The silence was heavy and strained. It was exhausting just being with him, she realized. And never had she felt exhausted in Jarrett's presence. Wouldn't Anthony be pleased to know that they were having very real problems now? she thought. She sat up suddenly rigid in her seat. No, Anthony was not to know anything about her conflict with Jarrett. He would not only find pleasure in her misery but he would provoke Jarrett at every turn and opportunity. If Anthony thought Jarrett actually wanted to marry her, he would bend over backward to keep them apart.

Therein was her solution. She suddenly realized what she had to do. If she could talk with Anthony, perhaps she could goad him into using his flippant remarks about Jarrett to her benefit. If she could make it seem that he put the idea of marrying Jarrett on her, her problem would be solved. It was a risk, goading Anthony, but it was the only thing she could think of to get him to accept a marriage between her and Jarrett. To somehow make Anthony believe it was his idea that she and Jarrett marry would be tricky. Anthony was never an easy man to manage, and he might even suspect what she was doing if she was not very careful.

But how? She frowned, drained by the idea of having to talk to Anthony at all, but to go to him with some pretense at peace, that would be sheer torture.

She dared a fleeting glimpse of Jarrett beneath the shield of her eyelashes. He was such a handsome man, incredibly well built, and under different circumstances she would have admired his strength, poise, and determination. Yet, it was those very qualities that were unsettling her. His stern countenance in particular was disturbing since he hadn't spoken a word to her once they got into the car. She doubted that there was anything she could say to lessen his hurt and she did not attempt to rationalize her response to him. There wasn't anything she could do until she spoke with Anthony. Until then, her dear Jarrett would simply have to continue to sulk and ignore her. She had two days and there was the smallest chance that she might be able to manage it.

Chapter 3

It took an enormous effort for Jarrett to concentrate on driving. He didn't want to discuss Liberty's decision, but he had a million things he wanted to say to her, a ton of questions he wanted to ask, and one answer he wanted to hear. Since she could not give him the answer he needed, or any real answer at all, he refused to say a word. A conversation would only create more frustration for him and he didn't think he could handle any more. Besides, he knew it was futile to demand an explanation from Liberty. She had made that perfectly clear.

He sensed her desire to speak. Stubbornly he kept his eyes on the road, refusing to acknowledge her or compromise his mood. She had hurt him and he wasn't about to soothe her, not when his heart was swelling with pain.

They reached Liberty's home in a quiet suburb outside of Charles County, Maryland. Liberty's townhome was the third house on a row of six. The residences were breathtakingly spacious, the landscapes colorful and well taken care of. It was a quiet town with neighbors used to a much slower lifestyle than Liberty had grown up with in Washington, D.C. She felt safe.

After parking the car, Jarrett, even in the distracted

state he was currently in, got out and opened the door for her.

Liberty stepped out, preparing to end the night without another word spoken between them. She stole a glance at Jarrett and their eyes collided for a heart-stopping moment. She blinked, his eyes telling her what words could not. Her pulse raced, her lips parted in an unconscious response to his passionate gaze. His eyes fell to her mouth and he groaned, unable to contain himself as he pulled her to him, his mouth devouring hers as he kissed her with all of the passion he had been holding inside for the past few hours. Liberty moaned, instantly aroused by his kiss, her body arching against his in complete abandon.

She knew he was frustrated but didn't care because his kiss also reassured her that he still wanted her and hadn't completely given up. She began to tremble with desire and pressed her body even closer to his as the kiss deepened, his mouth sucking her bottom lip until she began to quiver.

A car door slammed. Liberty jumped and her eyes popped open. Jarrett slowly released her, the tension in his body evidence that he too had lost control. Again their eyes locked until Liberty's fell. She swallowed before looking up again. He was no longer looking at her, but at the culprit who had interrupted their passionate make-out session. As the car sped away, Liberty mustered the courage to speak first.

"Jarrett—" she began.

"Two days, Liberty. I can't wait longer than that," Jarrett interrupted, the coldness in his voice causing her to grit her teeth in consternation. The kiss had not softened his resolve.

He removed his arms from her and without another word, got back in his car. Liberty stared after him before sighing heavily. With great disappointment that he had no intention of coming inside, she unlocked her front door.

She paused before entering the house. She had wanted him to come inside and finish what he'd started. Trying to squelch the desire he had ignited, Liberty stepped inside the house and closed the door. The lock had scarcely snapped in place before she heard Jarrett speed away.

Liberty swung the door open again. With a worried frown, she watched as Jarrett recklessly drove out of the parking lot until the car disappeared from view. She was just closing the door when her neighbor, Mrs. Wilkins, stepped outside and waved to Liberty.

Liberty smiled at her neighbor, forcing Jarrett's tumultuous departure from her thoughts. From the start, Mrs. Wilkins had been an interestingly friendly neighbor. With the manners of a woman used to having her way, Mrs. Wilkins had bullied her way into Liberty's home. She was a slight woman, slender and frail in her age. Liberty guessed her to be at least seventy. If it weren't for Mrs. Wilkins's arrogance and bossy behavior, Liberty would have been concerned for the older woman living alone. She was widowed, Liberty had discovered, and was quite content to be by herself.

Her silvery hair was pulled away from her face in an austere bun and her sharp green eyes were still alert and clear despite her age. Liberty doubted if Mrs. Wilkins needed anyone to fuss over her welfare. The older woman may have become wrinkled and shriveled due to her age, but she was nobody's fool.

Mrs. Wilkins stood on her front porch, her stiffly starched pale blue pantsuit more appropriate for a business meeting than a stroll in the neighborhood.

Liberty wondered too at Mrs. Wilkins's wardrobe. It was something she admired often. The old woman could certainly dress, Liberty thought with a grin. Jarrett's temperamental race from her home was momentarily forgotten.

"Well, he was in a hurry," Mrs. Wilkins called. Her voice, though it shook slightly, was clear and firm.

"Yes, he's tired," Liberty responded lightly. She wasn't about to tell Mrs. Wilkins she and Jarrett were bickering. It would only serve to have her lecture Liberty on how a young woman should behave with a man. Ah, she remembered clearly her first lecture from her mother on how young women had no idea how to allow a man to court them. That a man needed to be a man. On and on the speech had gone until Liberty wanted to put her hands to her ears and beg for mercy.

"Ah, yes, that would do it. Have a good night then," Mrs. Wilkins called, deceptively accepting of Liberty's explanation. Liberty, however, had no doubt that Mrs. Wilkins suspected the truth of the matter. She was grateful that her neighbor obviously was in no mood to hammer the point.

"You too, Mrs. Wilkins," Liberty answered, then slowly closed and locked her front door.

"Ms. Sutton. You're home so early," Tosha said, skipping lightly down the stairs.

Liberty stepped away from the door and considered Tosha with a bright smile. She liked Tosha. Introduced to her by Mrs. Wilkins, who was determined to have someone she deemed trustworthy to care for Jamal when Liberty needed to "get away," Liberty had quickly warmed to the young woman. She immediately became Jamal's babysitter.

She was young, barely nineteen. Looking at her,

Liberty thought Tosha could easily pass for fourteen or even younger. She was short and slim with long hair that she wore in a ponytail every day. Her demeanor and taste were very youthful, more in line with a preteen than a young woman. Her stylish jeans and T-shirt that fit like a glove were the fashion of the day, showing off her slight assets.

Neither Tosha's age nor her fashion bothered Liberty. She trusted Tosha with Jamal and that was the only thing that was important. She shrugged at Tosha's comment. She had told Tosha she would be in by eleven. She had not known Jarrett's intentions then.

"Jarrett and I were a little tired. We thought we'd call it an early night," Liberty responded easily. As with Mrs. Wilkins, Liberty had no wish to tell Tosha what happened to bring her home so early. Especially knowing how Tosha placed their romance on a pedestal. If only it were true.

"Oh? Well, Jamal's asleep. He was tired, too, I guess," Tosha added.

Her whimsical response brought another smile to Liberty's face. Tosha always had a cheerful effect on Liberty. It was interesting, how she was drawn to Tosha. She had never really had many girlfriends. In fact, Brenda was pretty much the only female she could call a friend. She was in fact Liberty's best and only friend. Unlike Brenda, Tosha was jovial and always in high spirits. And she was the picture of the latest fashion, too. Normally private and careful with social acquaintances, Liberty had surprisingly bonded with the girl.

"Was he?" Liberty asked breathlessly, already passing Tosha to head up the stairs. "Thanks so much, Tosha. I'll just peek in on him."

A quick glance at her son and she assured herself all was well. Smiling and always at peace when Jamal was with her, she headed back down the stairs where Tosha waited for her.

"All okay?" Tosha asked, no animosity in her question. She was used to Liberty's protectiveness over Jamal.

"Absolutely. He's sleeping like a babe," Liberty said, then laughed, adding, "He is a baby."

"A beautiful one, too," Tosha agreed. "Well, I'm going to get going now. It's still early so I'm going to try and catch up with some of my girlfriends. Have a good night." She slung her purse over her shoulders and hurried from the house, her heels tapping across the steps and down the sidewalk in a light sprint.

"Don't party too hard," Liberty called with a grin and waved good night to Tosha.

Locking her front door, Liberty walked from room to room switching off the lights, murmuring in amazement that Tosha had actually turned on every one. When she was done securing the house, Liberty paused in the middle of her foyer. She closed her eyes and took a deep breath. As she had moved about the house, images of Jarrett kept invading her thoughts. She knew she could never explain it to him. Her rejection was not how he interpreted it, still it was very real to him and there was little she could do short of seeing Anthony immediately. She shrugged. She had a plan and she had to set the wheels in motion. She didn't like what was happening to her and Jarrett.

She forced Jarrett from her thoughts with a slight shake of her head. She was not going to fret all night, that was for sure. She walked up the steps and made her way to Jamal's room. Her problems could wait a few moments, at least until after she spent a few minutes with her son.

Liberty walked to Jamal's bed, this time lingering over him. She smiled, amazed anew at the life she had brought into this world. He was her precious bundle of joy, she thought happily. He made everything she did worth it. And, he loved Jarrett. She leaned over and sweetly kissed his cheek. He didn't move as she gently pulled his blanket over him and covered him up to his neck. Standing, she hesitated, then gave him another kiss on his cheek before quietly leaving his room. A few minutes later she undressed in her bedroom. Pulling on her bathrobe, she sat in her window settee. Her gaze was pensive as she stared out her bedroom window into the dark, quiet street below.

Her eyes followed the trail of autumn leaves that were falling with soundless grace. As she sat staring at the burnt-orange leaves, no longer fighting the melancholy that had threatened to overwhelm her all evening, she allowed Jarrett to invade her thoughts. Once she had dreamt of the moment that he would ask her to marry him. She was twenty-eight years old, a single mom, and was finally beginning to feel she had a chance at a successful career. It was an eternity since the girl she once was had imagined the great Jarrett Irving loving her. And when her dream had come to reality, what had she done? Panicked, turned him away, allowing Anthony to sway her heart for fear of losing her son.

Jarrett would never understand. In fact, he would never believe the warmth that had spread through her from pure pleasure when he'd popped the question. She had wanted to fall into his arms, kiss him with all of her heart, show him with all of her soul just how willing she was to be his wife. Then she remembered Jamal. As quickly as she was warmed by Jarrett's proposal, she suddenly became frightened. She loved Jarrett but she could not only think of herself, not anymore. Certainly she believed that eventually she and Jarrett could and would marry. It was just that Anthony had to be cleared on it first. She felt foolish thinking that way, but she had been through a hard lesson, one that no sane woman could forget.

She was confident of Anthony and his mother-in-law's power to wreak havoc upon her life. Anthony and his mother-in-law. She grimaced in distaste at the thought of them. They were an obstinate pair. They could and would cause far more problems and pain than Jarrett could heal or manage. They had done so before when Tina was alive. What the Andersons wanted, the Andersons got. The Andersons had stolen off with her son with the legal papers signed and sealed before she knew just what had hit her. There was no way she was going to go through such emotional distress again. She wasn't willing to put Jamal through the trauma of another court battle for custody either.

Even if she didn't have concern over Anthony, his mother-in-law was not to be taken lightly. Tina Anderson's mother had been just as involved in claiming Jamal as her daughter and Anthony had been. Tina couldn't have children. When Anthony's indiscretion with Liberty was discovered, Tina's mother sought justice by taking Anthony's child from Liberty and giving Jamal to her daughter. In the process, she got the grandchild she had always wanted. Never mind that Liberty had no desire to give up her son. Liberty sucked her teeth. The memory of Jamal being taken from her was still painful.

If she told Jarrett her concerns, she knew he would

have blown them off as an easy fix. He would say that he had two sons just a few years older than Jamal. He had an ex-wife and an ex-girlfriend-almost-fiancée, who were both still involved in his life due to work or family.

His ex-girlfriend, Dominique, was on the board of his firm. Although she had proven to be a jealous woman, she had moved on once she knew that she would never have Jarrett. Dominique had created some problems for them at first, but Jarrett had easily put her out of his life and stopped any attempts she made to interfere with his romance with Liberty.

His ex-wife, Dana, had significant input on the up-bringing and decisions surrounding their two sons. Jarrett had managed to build a friendship built on mutual respect and love for their sons. In face, Dana had signed the divorce papers and never looked back. They were as compatible and amiable as two old friends. No jealousy, no egos, nothing to hinder their relationship with their sons as they moved on with their own lives.

It was no wonder that with his experiences to judge from, he wouldn't consider Anthony anything more than a mere inconvenience. He didn't have a vain, angry, egotistical man with a bitter mother-in-law goading him on. The fact was, Dana Irving and Dominique were not a problem. Anthony Anderson was.

As she sat staring out the window, Liberty's gaze fell on a burgundy sedan pulling into the parking lot. Liberty watched in surprise as Mrs. Wilkins got out of the car. The older woman had barely reached her front door when the car pulled off. Liberty glanced at her clock and thought how curious it was that Mrs. Wilkins had gone out so late. She still had on the pale blue suit and looked sharp as ever.

A smile curved Liberty's mouth as she thought about Mrs. Wilkins and how generous she had been when Liberty moved in next door. She had insisted that Liberty exchange phone numbers with her in case of emergencies. The older woman was truly an interesting and dear lady.

Although a little forgetful, Mrs. Wilkins portrayed the image of a woman once sleek and sophisticated. Liberty could see that in her youth she would have been someone many people would have looked up to and admired. It was a shame that she was all alone, Liberty thought.

Thinking of Mrs. Wilkins up in age and lonely made Liberty glum. She wanted to toss all caution through the window and call Jarrett now. But she didn't. She had to be logical and not allow her wild impulses to take control of her decisions.

If she had to lose Jarrett to ensure that she didn't lose her son again, it was a possibility she had to risk. A painful, unbelievably heart-wrenching sacrifice, she thought as she dropped the curtain and left the windowsill. If only she could stop the clock and time would indeed be her friend. All too soon she would have to meet with Anthony and put her plan into action.

Jarrett drove home barely attentive to his surroundings and the traffic as he followed the road. His head was swimming with disappointment and disgruntlement. He was no fool. He knew Anthony was the cause for Liberty's hesitation. *But why?* Did she fancy herself falling back in love with Anthony? He groaned trying to analyze all of the opportunities that Anthony had been given to get close to Liberty. How many times had Anthony been around to steal Liberty's heart? Jarrett slammed his fist against his dashboard. He had behaved like a fool, considering himself a gentleman. Look at what it had gotten him! All the while, as he sat back and bided his time, Anthony Anderson was making moves on Liberty. And she apparently had fallen for them.

Jarrett groaned again, closing his eyes in agony. He had tried to give Liberty the space she needed to learn to trust again. He knew she was fragile, wary of love and needed him to trust her. He had hoped that by being patient, giving her time to breathe and think about what they were doing, she would see him for the man he was and learn to trust him. Instead, he got the cold reality that nice guys finished last. It was losers like Anthony Anderson that always seemed to land on their feet. Jarrett's eyes darkened. He despised Anthony Anderson!

A car horn brought Jarrett's car to a screeching halt. In his sulking, he had nearly run a red light. Giving the other driver an apologetic look, Jarrett reversed his car and cautiously backed out of the intersection. Glancing around, he was thankful that there weren't too many cars on the road, especially for a Friday night. When the light turned green he slowly proceeded, his mind immediately drifting back to Liberty.

He loved her; he couldn't pretend that he didn't. He didn't want to ignore his feelings, either. He wanted her more than he had ever wanted any woman. It hurt like crazy to think he could really have lost her to Anthony. He had been open-minded with Liberty in an effort to give *her* time to cope with her tumultuous emotions and to get over the hurt she had experienced. He'd thought that by allowing Liberty the time she needed to bond with her son and patch up her problems with his father, he and Liberty would be able to settle into finally experiencing a loving bond with each other. He never imagined it would work against him.

When he discovered that Anthony Anderson and his wife, Tina, had conspired and successfully taken away Liberty's son while she was still recovering in the maternity ward, he had been full of fury at the injustice of what they had done. He discovered that Liberty wasn't even aware that Anthony was married until after she got pregnant, that she had fancied he loved her and planned to marry her. The man was heartless and Jarrett had sworn he would help Liberty get her son back no matter what. Anthony had caused Liberty many years of pain. Jarrett had patiently, lovingly done his best to give her back the faith in love she so rightly deserved. And now he had lost her.

No, he thought gravely. He had not lost her, at least not yet. She wanted time and he was going to give it to her. She would accept that marriage was the right thing to do, that they belonged together. Anthony was another matter. Jarrett was going to see to it that Anthony realized he had no authority over Liberty, Jamal's father or not. Jarrett wasn't going to just sit back and allow her son's father to dictate their future. He loved Liberty Sutton and they were going to be together.

Calmer, yet still bristling from the disastrous dinner, Jarrett sped his car into his driveway, pulled out his passkey, and headed for his apartment. He barely had the key in the door when he heard the telephone ringing. A rush of anticipation shot through him. It was Liberty calling him, he was certain. She had changed her mind.

Anxious to reach the phone, he nearly tripped over the carpet as he rushed inside. He snatched it breathing heavily into the receiver. Before he could say hello, he heard voices behind him. He looked at the front door and rolled his eyes. He had forgotten to close it. Two men walked past his door and down the hall, talking loud and laughing even louder. Frowning, he realized he was just holding the phone, then said, "Hello?" as he walked to the door and shut it.

"Hello?" Jarrett repeated, confounded by the silence on the other end. He dropped his keys on the mantel, then headed for his bar to pour himself a drink.

"Oh, Jarrett I wasn't sure if you could hear me. I'm so glad to catch you," a familiar sweet voice murmured.

Jarrett shut his eyes for a moment. Disappointed that it was not Liberty, he forced himself to exercise patience for Dominique. *What does she want?* he wondered as he sat on his camel-brown leather chair. He loosened his tie, put one foot on his coffee table, then asked, "What's up, Nikki?"

He knew he sounded cold when he spoke. It wasn't his intention but he could barely contain himself. Everything had gone wrong this evening, right up to the phone call from the wrong woman. He sighed. He didn't want to take his anger out on Dominique. Whatever she was, she didn't deserve to be punished for his inability to get Liberty to the altar.

"I wanted you to be the first to know . . . I'm engaged," Dominique said, her voice hesitant and nervous, but the *I'm engaged* part came out in a rush of excitement. It was an emotion that Jarrett resented. He took a long swig from his drink, then muttered, "Congratulations." She should be congratulating him at that moment, not the other way around, he thought, feeling sorry for himself.

"Yes, well, thank you. I wanted to call you and make sure you heard it from me. After all, we never really talked after what happened with you and that girl that used to be your secretary, but—"

"She was never my secretary, Dominique. You know that," Jarrett added.

"Whatever she was, she certainly worked for you," Dominique insisted.

"We've been through this. More than once," Jarrett said, an edge of impatience and warning in his voice.

"And I'm not trying to rehash it, I promise, Jarrett. It just hurt so much how you hooked up with her and left me out there, looking the fool." Dominique complained.

"Didn't you just say you're engaged?" Jarrett suggested softly, the calmness in his voice hiding his growing irritation. He ran the glass over his forehead, its coolness comforting his skin.

"You're right. And I'm just so happy," Dominique conceded. "I didn't call to argue. I only wanted to let you know that there are no hard feelings and that you and your secretary, I mean girlfriend, are going to be invited to my wedding. I hope you'll come," she added, her enthusiasm not fooling Jarrett for a moment.

Dominique had not changed one bit, Jarrett mused.

"That's really big of you, Nikki," Jarrett said, his voice almost teasing in his amusement.

"Don't be like that, Jarrett. I'm serious. I want you and Liberty to come. It's a turning point in my life and I'm excited," Dominique insisted.

Jarrett laughed then. The suggestion that he and

Liberty would go to Dominique's wedding was an irony she couldn't begin to understand. And besides, he could imagine the wedding, Dominique's beautiful gown, the sucker who was going to marry her completely clueless that his new wife had invited poor Liberty so that she could throw innuendos and nasty barbs at her. He wasn't about to put Liberty through a day of discomfort. He owed Dominique nothing.

"We'll see. Who knows? Liberty may want to actually come. She may want to be there to get some wedding ideas since I asked her to marry me too." He paused long enough to allow Dominique to digest his announcement. She responded in a sputter of words.

"You didn't! How could you, Jarrett? My God, she's an uneducated ghetto-fabulous hussy. You don't marry women like her, Jarrett," Dominique hissed.

"Funny, I was just thinking that of the sucker who's going to marry you," Jarrett snapped.

"He's no sucker. You're the fool. What has this woman to offer you? Nothing. I worked long and hard to be where I am. I have a college degree. And I'm not worn out from dating every fool that crosses my path. You can't marry her. You've got to be kidding. Tell me you're kidding," Dominique pressed on. She was emphatic and giving him a headache.

"I'm not kidding. Liberty is everything I want, Nikki, and that is all that matters. I hope this guy feels that way about you. I can't imagine why he would," Jarrett said, shrugging as he spoke. "But I'm glad you found someone else. Maybe now you'll be happy. Have a great wedding. Enjoy your life." He hung up the phone. He stared at it before he downed the rest of his cognac.

Dominique was getting married, he thought dully. Well, good riddance. A slight smile curved his tired mouth at the thought that at least he didn't have to worry about Dominique interfering with him and Liberty ever again. Liberty's image invaded his senses. So what if Liberty hadn't said yes? What he told Dominique was true. Liberty was going to marry him. She loved him. Besides, Liberty had once accused him of being stubborn and relentless when he wanted something. Now was not the time to change his attitude. He refused to accept anything less than marriage from her and he was certain she would eventually agree that there was no reason they should not marry.

Exhausted, having indulged in more liquor than he had intended, he stood and forced himself to go to bed. He lay on his bed still fully clothed. He loosened, feeling the warmth of the cognac spreading through him. He prayed he didn't have a headache in the morning to remind him of his intake. He opened his eyes to stare up at the ceiling. He stared into the lines until his eyes grew heavy and he could no longer resist the desire to sleep and, if for only one night, forget about his frustration with Liberty Sutton.

Chapter 4

Liberty went through the day in a slight daze. Her first action was to call Anthony even though she resolved not to the night before. She needed to set the wheels in motion. Unfortunately, he wasn't home. Disappointed, she was forced to idle away the hours. She couldn't call Jarrett, not yet.

Jamal awakened, demanding breakfast, then proceeded to spend hours on a Nintendo game that Jarrett had bought him just a few days earlier. When Jarrett first bought the game, Liberty determined she would only allow Jamal to spend an hour a week playing, but today she was just too distraught to worry about it.

As evening rolled in, she tired of reading and turned on the television. Switching through the stations, she repeatedly found that all of the programs were uninteresting. She was restless.

She was behaving like an idiot. She and Jarrett would marry. She had a plan now and it was just a matter of time before she would have Anthony convinced that he wanted her to marry Jarrett. She smiled, amused at the game she was about to play. It was his own fault, of course. Did Anthony think she would remain single forever, to suit his demands?

She got up and went to Jamal's room. He was still

engrossed in the game, his tiny fingers repeatedly pressing the buttons on the controller. Waiting patiently for the game to come to a break, she watched him from the doorway and thought with amazement how much he looked and even behaved like Anthony.

Anthony was a handsome man, in both form and face. She never worried about Jamal in that department. As for character, she frowned, offering up a quick prayer that Jamal would be a better man than his father.

As if on cue, Jamal noticed her and grinned.

"Do you want to play, Mommy?" he asked.

Liberty beamed at him. It was incredible how the simple title of Mommy coming from his lips could still touch her. She had feared those first few months that he would never be comfortable calling her that, but to Anthony's credit and even Tina's mother's, Jamal had gotten comfortable and used to calling his true mother Mommy.

"Nope," was Liberty's easy reply, although she was a tumultuous fit of nerves inside. She walked fully into his room, sat on the bed, and considered him. Jamal paused from his game, watching his mother with a new curiosity before finally saying, "Mommy, stop watching me."

Liberty laughed, realizing that he must have been very uncomfortable beneath her examination. "I'm sorry, baby, I just love watching you so much. Do you know how much I love you?"

"This much?" Jamal asked, then spread his arms wide and grinned at her.

Liberty bent over and swept him into her arms and smiled. "More than that much. Too much to ever, ever show you."

"Let me go, Mommy, I'm playin' Nintendo," Jamal

protested. Liberty sighed but released him. Jamal was every bit a traditional boy. He was rough, independent, and had very little interest in hugs and kisses. He seemed to understand her need to hold him often, but he always squirmed after only moments to be released. She took what he was willing to give, happy that he gave of himself at all.

"Jamal, before you play, Mommy needs to ask you a question," Liberty began cautiously.

Round curious eyes stared up at her.

"It's about Jarrett," she started and noted with approval that Jamal instantly broke into a smile. "Do you like Jarrett?"

"Uh-huh," Jamal answered easily.

"Do you think . . . Would you like Jarrett to live with you and me?" she asked, holding her breath while Jamal stared up at her as he tried to understand her statement. In those moments she could see Anthony and hoped his answer would not come out as his father's would.

"Sure. Will he play Nintendo with me then?" Jamal asked.

"I think he would love to play Nintendo with you. But, Jamal, Jarrett will be here all the time, even at night when you go to bed. You do understand?"

"Mommy." Jamal laughed, sitting back in his seat as if to dismiss the conversation. "Of course, married people have to stay home at night."

"All right," Liberty whispered and watched as Jamal picked up his controller and started playing the game again.

Wearily, she came to her feet and went back to her room. She certainly would have to start looking at Jamal a little more differently. He was, after all, in school and very much more aware of things than she had realized. Though she hadn't mentioned marriage, Jamal assumed that his mother and Jarrett would marry.

"Mommy?" Jamal called, running into her room.

"Yes?"

"We don't have any more cereal, can we please get some cereal?" he asked.

"Cereal? It's almost six o'clock, Jamal."

"But tomorrow I won't have any in the morning. Pleeeease."

Liberty shrugged and Jamal squealed with delight. "Go put your shoes on and meet me downstairs," Liberty ordered, then slipped into a pair of shoes. A few minutes later they were on their way to the store. It took Jamal all of five seconds to choose his box of Fruity Pebbles.

On the car ride home, as the trees passed by in a blur of brilliant autumn colors, Liberty allowed her thoughts to trail to Jarrett. She had gone after him with a resolve born of innate desire, nothing more. She had never expected to be truly loved by him. She never dreamed that years later he would still be around with such a significant role in her life. Though her intent was to seduce Jarrett when they first met, she had come to realize he was more than an affair for her. Thus, she had worked hard to get him and keep him, too. She couldn't allow Anthony to ruin this for them.

She pulled into her driveway, halfway expecting to see Jarrett's car. He wasn't there. She wasn't sure if she was relieved or annoyed. She was being unfair, she knew. He wanted his answer and he wasn't going to come around until she called him and said yes. She sighed, wishing she and Anthony had already spoken. It was unfortunate indeed that she had not been able to reach him earlier. He was conveniently not around when she really needed to deal with him.

She parked her car, reached for her keys, and with a content gaze watched as her son, as usual, awoke with a stretch and a sweet yawn immediately after she turned off the engine. His round baby-brown eyes blinked at her and he raised his arms to her, his silent request to be picked up. Liberty was happy to oblige him, even if carrying him of late had proven to be a bit of a burden. How could she resist such a sweet face?

Taking Jamal into her arms, she grabbed her purse and the box of cereal from the backseat. As she hurried to unlock the door, Jamal snuggled his face into the crook of her neck and wrapped his arms even tighter about her. Liberty smiled and was deep in motherly bliss when a figure appeared from the house beside her.

Her eyes caught his and her smile froze. He was an older white man, perhaps in his late forties, early fifties. His brown hair was edged with a blue-gray tint. His face was hairless, no mustache or beard or even sideburns. It was an oddly old face, almost no wrinkles, yet she could see he was not young. He was short and stocky. His rigid stance indicated he was not at all happy at the sight of Liberty. His eyes seemed to burn her. They were dark, perhaps green or gray, she couldn't tell from the distance. But they were steady and unmoving as they contemplated her.

Liberty swallowed, uncomfortable beneath the man's disapproving gaze. She turned away, not giving her usual pleasant hello. The man did not move. He was standing right in front of Mrs. Wilkins's house. His eyes remained on her even as she turned from him. He stood on the sidewalk, watching her until she had finished fumbling with the lock and keys and gone inside.

In the house, Liberty locked the front door and leaned against it for a moment. Her brief encounter with the stranger was alarming. She sat Jamal on the floor, right in front of the door, as she peered out the window to see if the stranger was still standing outside. She gasped and took a step back. He was still staring at her front door.

"Mommy?" Jamal inquired, his sleepy eyes looking up at her in confusion.

"Go to your room, baby. Mommy's fine," Liberty whispered, as if the strange man outside could hear her.

Jamal gave her another inquiring look. Then, remembering his new Nintendo, he got up and raced up the stairs to his room, anxious to play the game again. Liberty took a deep breath and once more pulled back the curtains to inspect the stranger. She expected to discover the man still standing on the doorsteps, watching her as if he could see into her house even after the door closed.

A thorough survey over the expanse of her neighborhood gave no sign of his presence. It was almost as if he were a mirage, a figment of her imagination. She released a shaky sigh. His stoic stance, penetrating gaze, and sudden disappearance left her completely unnerved. It had been as if she had intruded on him. Although she was new to the neighborhood, within the few weeks she had moved there she thought she had met and seen who all of her immediate neighbors were. Her confidence that she was fairly familiar with her surroundings was completely shattered by this man's unexpected appearance. As the rhythm of her heart soothed to a more normal pattern, she wondered who the man was and why he was standing in front of Mrs. Wilkins's home.

Had he come to visit Mrs. Wilkins? They were, after all, both white and Liberty didn't have many white neighbors. In fact, she thought, narrowing her gaze, the man did have a certain resemblance to Mrs. Wilkins.

She had never noticed anyone visiting her neighbor. She had assumed from the woman's behavior and closeness with the people in their community that she was alone in this world except for whoever had dropped her off the night before. Whoever he was, he didn't appear neighborly or approachable. One thing was for sure, Liberty was determined to steer clear of the man and from now on, stay alert of her surroundings.

Her anxieties over Jarrett and Anthony were temporarily set aside as she double-checked that all the doors and windows were locked. Feeling a little safer, she was on the first step of the stairwell when the vision of Mrs. Wilkins came to mind. Fleetingly she had thought of the woman, but now she wondered with a worried frown if the woman was all right.

Liberty struggled with her conscience. She wanted to ignore her instincts, to shrug off the worry and move on, but she couldn't. She couldn't let go of the nagging suspicion that all was not normal with the man's presence. And poor Mrs. Wilkins was all alone and defenseless. Such a person, if he wanted to, could create havoc with an elderly woman. It was true too that she had never seen this person. Had he not watched her with such concentration, she may not have been so apprehensive. She was a city girl. She knew how dangerous people could be. Wouldn't she want her neighbor to check on her welfare if someone or something suspicious occurred at her home?

Sighing in resignation, Liberty walked back down the stairs and went to her front door once more. She peered out the peephole, then cautiously opened the door. Seeing that the street was quiet, she stepped just outside onto her small patio. Forcing back her fear, she glanced up at the window belonging to Jamal. He would be all right. She would only be a moment. She made a swift perusal over the neighborhood. Feeling confident that the man was truly gone and with determination bred as much from curiosity as worry, she hurried to Mrs. Wilkins's front door.

She knocked, timidly at first, then louder and louder. After several minutes had passed, she released a deep breath and hung her head in defeat. Mrs. Wilkins had not answered. She took a step back and stared the house up and down, hoping for signs that Mrs. Wilkins was inside. The silence was heavy. That disturbed Liberty even more.

Disconcerted, she looked from left to right, giving a cautious inspection over the neighborhood again. Still, no one was outside. She ran back to her house, locked the front door, and hurried to the telephone. She had to call for help. Picking up the phone, Liberty hesitated. She didn't want to be rash, irrational, or hysterical.

She decided to call Mrs. Wilkins's home first. She dialed her neighbor's telephone number and waited patiently through six rings before the voice mail picked up. She hung up and dialed again and again. No answer.

Liberty was hesitant to call the police. She could be wrong. She wanted to be wrong, she thought desperately. Mrs. Wilkins could simply not have been at home. The man could have been a visitor frustrated that she wasn't. It could have been as ordinary as that. He hadn't done a thing, she tried to reason with herself. He had just stood there and that was enough. She groaned. Certain something was not right with the man's presence, Liberty decided that she needed to confide her fears in someone and get rational, unemotional advice. She thought of her best friend, Brenda Smith.

Brenda answered the phone, her tone dry. In all of the years that Liberty had known her, Brenda always appeared uninterested in just about everything. Even when Brenda finally fell in love and married, she was nonchalant about it. She and Liberty were as opposite as any two women could be. Liberty was bold and brazen in showing off her good looks, Brenda was serene and conservative with eyeglasses that were almost a shield against anyone who might want to probe too deeply. Brenda was taller than Liberty, thinner, and less shapely. Liberty always felt that with a little effort, Brenda would have been a beauty with a score of men after her. Brenda wanted none of that and went through great pains to prove it.

With all of their differences, it was curious that they were the closest, most loyal of friends. Liberty trusted Brenda explicitly and knew, even when Brenda was abrasive and harsh in her opinions, that she truly cared for her. So what that Brenda was rarely cheerful and certainly not someone you call late in the evening?

Ignoring Brenda's tone, Liberty released a flurry of words, so fast that Brenda had to cut in and insist that she slow down.

"Okay, okay." Liberty breathed and began again, her words chosen carefully, her pace slow. "I just encountered the strangest man, Brenda. He looked so mean."

"Encountered how? What happened?" Brenda demanded, suddenly alert and attentive.

"I went to the grocery store to get more cereal for Jamal. When we came back, there was a man standing in front of my neighbor's house. You know Mrs. Wilkins? I've mentioned her to you before," Liberty insisted.

"Yes. Go on," Brenda responded.

"Well, he was just standing there, looking mean and crazy or something. I don't know. But the look he gave me was creepy. I think he did something to Mrs. Wilkins. She's not answering her door."

"Something like what?" Brenda inquired, her voice calm although she had sat upright at Liberty's words.

"I don't know. Maybe he was trying to rob her and hurt her in the process. Maybe she's seriously hurt, Brenda," Liberty whispered.

"Oh, come on! You've been watching too many movies, Liberty," Brenda scolded.

"No. I hate to think it but I can't shake it. I think it's serious. I'm scared, Brenda," Liberty admitted.

"How ironic," Brenda drawled, humor lifting her voice. "There you are, a city girl just newly moved from a pretty scary neighborhood, if I dare say so. And now, in the heart of the suburbs, you realize fear? I can't help but find that amusing."

"You wouldn't think it was so amusing if you had seen that man as I had. And besides," Liberty added defensively, "I had no reason to fear the people from my old neighborhood. I grew up there, remember? At least there I knew exactly what was going on."

"Uh-huh. Well, I was scared there, that's for sure. I hated coming over. I'll tell you this, I won't visit you if you ever decide to go back. So you'd better shake off your fear of the suburbs—"

"Brenda! It's not fear of the suburbs, just a little white man with a long stare and beady eyes," Liberty interrupted.

"Same thing," Brenda suggested. They both smiled into their phones. Then Liberty sighed.

"I don't know what to do. I already called Mrs. Wilkins but I'm not getting an answer. Should I go back and knock on her door again maybe?" Liberty wondered, a furrow creasing her forehead as she worried over the older woman next door.

"No, I wouldn't advise it. Have Jarrett do it. In fact, where's Jarrett? Have you told him what's going on?" Brenda asked.

"No, Jarrett and I had a fight," Liberty confessed.

"A fight? About what?" Brenda cried, surprised. Jarrett was so easygoing, so perfect for Liberty, Brenda thought. She prayed Liberty had not finally succeeded in pushing the man away.

"About nothing. He wants to get married."

"Oh, yeah, that's nothing," Brenda commented dryly before adding, "I thought that was your goal, Liberty."

"It was. Or at least it was what I thought I wanted. I'm afraid, I guess," Liberty said slowly.

"Afraid of marriage? Not you, Liberty. Besides, if Carl and I could get married, anyone can," Brenda added.

"What do you mean? Everything is okay between you two, isn't it?" Liberty asked, suddenly concerned.

"Of course. Carl is so used to being direct, years of training in security has done that to him, and then here I am, too direct for my own good as well. So I only meant that with our extremely independent personalities, our marriage was nothing less than a miracle. You and Jarrett will be fine. There's nothing to fear, take it from this newlywed."

Liberty could hear a smile in Brenda's voice and was pleased that her friend was happy. Brenda, unlike herself, was so serious about everything and everyone. Very little humor came out of her, and certainly pleasure was never a goal Brenda aspired to reach. It was a miracle to Liberty as well that Brenda found love and actually married.

Liberty wished she could feel as confident and nonchalant about Jarrett and her future as Brenda felt about her life with Carl. But they didn't have a kid lurking in the background or a custody problem that could be an end-all to their relationship.

"It's not marriage that frightens me, Brenda. I'm afraid that Anthony won't like it if I marry Jarrett," Liberty murmured.

Brenda's response was heated as she sputtered in an indignant voice, "Anthony Anderson does not own you! Who cares if he doesn't like it? He's lucky that you didn't take him to court for full custody of Jamal after that stunt he and his wife pulled on you. Oh, please, Liberty! This is your life. Marry Jarrett and be happy."

"I know, I know. But it's not that simple, Brenda. You've always kept your life simple, free of drama. I'm not you and I know Anthony. I don't trust him. I can't risk losing Jamal again, not even for the love of my life." Liberty sighed. Brenda didn't respond.

Throughout the conversation, Liberty had been sitting with her forehead resting in the palm of her hand, her elbow supporting her arm as she talked into the phone. As they paused, she glanced up. A shadow moved across her window. Liberty released a stifled scream.

Brenda jumped to her feet, suddenly wishing she was at Liberty's house. She felt completely useless across town as she was.

"Liberty! What is it?" she whispered as if someone were listening to their conversation.

"A shadow. That man. I'm sure of it. He was peeping in my window," Liberty whispered, coming to her feet and walking lightly to the front door.

"Be careful, Liberty. In fact, just listen to me. I want you to hang up the phone, call the police right now. Carl and I are on our way. Oh, and call Jarrett, for goodness' sake!" Brenda ordered, trying to remain calm herself, although her heart was pounding in panic for Liberty. A man, anyone for that matter, peeping in a window was such a violation.

"Okay, I will, I will," Liberty whispered, then did as she was instructed.

Chapter 5

Liberty knew she had become unnerved and even somewhat irrational from the moment she saw the man outside, but she was confident that she had not imagined the shadow. Someone had passed by, if not actually paused in front of her bay window. She was certain it was the stranger. As odd as it sounded, they had connected. It was as if in those brief moments when they appraised one another, he had read her mind and knew her. Yet she had never seen him before. It was unsettling.

She waited anxiously for Brenda or the police to arrive. At Brenda's request, she started to call Jarrett. Before she could dial the last digit of his phone number, she slowly placed the receiver down. She didn't want to call him yet. Though she would feel safer with him near, they still had the rift between them and she would simply trade one sense of unease for another. Or, he would be worried and insist she and Jamal leave immediately with him. She didn't want to or need to leave. If she was going to get Anthony to insist she marry Jarrett, she would need to appear in control, and running away from home was not in control.

Jarrett would weaken her resolve. She would be inclined to simply allow him to take over and bask in his strength. And that would be a mistake. He would certainly press the issue of their marriage if she told him she was afraid of a stranger, a potential perfectly harmless stranger. She needed to be sure her instinct was right before she involved Jarrett. She breathed a sharp sigh. If only she knew that Mrs. Wilkins was in the house and unharmed.

She glanced at her watch. She had been waiting merely minutes, but it felt as if hours had passed. Where were they? Pacing back and forth, from her foyer to the kitchen to her living room, Liberty found she could not sit still for more than a few moments before she was on her feet again. She held her hands together in an attempt to remain calm. One thing was for sure, she decided in frustration, if she ever needed help she knew not to expect the police to rush over. Molasses was faster than they were, she fumed.

When she finally heard a car pull up, she jumped to her feet, nearly bumping the coffee table as she hurried to the window. It was the police in two patrol cars. They did not have on their sirens or even the swirling lights, but they were a very welcome sight.

She released her breath. She had not felt secure since she saw the stranger. Now she exhaled in relief, the tension slowly ebbed away, and her veins felt as if cool liquid were calming her. She had been so distraught from her encounter that the impression of the stranger had become a permanent and very unwelcome image in her head.

As if on cue, the police officers got out of their cars at the same time. They looked directly at Liberty's house, then Mrs. Wilkins's, then they approached each other. They spoke a few words before moving to Liberty's front door. She hastened to it and swung it open before they had an opportunity to knock. The officers took a wary step back, surprised by her sudden presence, their hands poised above their gun holsters.

Liberty gasped, alarmed by their movement. She threw her hands into the air, her eyes wide with disbelief. Again the officers glanced at each other and were about to tell her she need not hold her hands up when a car sped into the parking lot and came to a screeching halt.

Carl barely put the car in park and turned off the ignition before his wife flung open her door, jumped out of the car, and raced to Liberty's side. She had become frantic the moment she saw Liberty standing in the doorway, her arms in the air. Aghast at the sight that greeted them, Brenda prayed that Liberty had not lost her mind and gone after some poor stranger who just happened to be in the neighborhood, thinking he meant her harm.

"Hold it right there, ma'am," one of the officers warned Brenda, reaching for her as she brushed past them. Brenda gasped, offended that the officer had touched her. Her husband was a law enforcement officer himself with a private firm, but he had certain authorities and she would not be accosted. With a haughty glare, she halted immediately and shook herself free, then waited with all the dignity of a queen for the officer to speak.

The officer suppressed his displeasure beneath Brenda's derisive gaze. He turned his attention back to Liberty, who incredibly continued to keep her hands in the air. His annoyance dissolved and was replaced with humor. Did the woman think she was under arrest? His eyes twinkled with amusement although he carefully held back a smile.

"Liberty Sutton?" the other officer asked, closely examining Liberty's face. It was taking an even greater effort for this officer not to laugh as he too wondered at Liberty's position.

"Yes. I called about my neighbor," Liberty responded breathlessly, barely able to breathe or speak beneath the officers' scrutiny. She risked a glance at Brenda, noting her friend's exasperated frown, but didn't say a word or lower her arms.

"Ma'am, you don't have to keep your hands in the air," the first officer finally informed her, with a smile that curved his mouth.

Slowly she lowered her arms to her side. Brenda snorted, indignant, as she stood in silent support at Liberty's side. Their good humor swiftly fled as both officers considered Brenda with disapproval.

"May we step inside a moment?" one of the officers finally asked.

"Of course," Liberty said promptly, immediately overwhelmed by their entry. She said nothing as she leaned against the still open door and considered them expectantly.

"I'm Officer Proctor. This is Officer Thomas. We received the call regarding a disturbance at your neighbor's house."

"Yes. I mean . . . well, I don't know just what kind of a disturbance. I guess I can't say there was a disturbance, just that I saw a strange man standing at her front door. I think he was up to something; maybe he was trying to break in. I'm not even sure if she's home, her car isn't here, but . . . I just don't know," Liberty explained.

She felt completely ridiculous. Her words were not making any sense to them at all and she knew it. It was difficult to explain a feeling about something rather than state simple facts now that she was actually dealing with the authorities. Yet, she was convinced that she was not mistaken, she was positive something was wrong next door.

"Excuse me, Officers, I'm with the young ladies," Carl said, pushing past Liberty's half-closed door to enter the house. The officers allowed room for Carl to walk to be at his wife's side, measuring him with suspicion the entire time.

"What took you so long?" Brenda murmured, giving him a nudge against his side with her elbow. He gasped at the not-so-gentle prod and scowled almost comically at her.

"I had to park the car. One of us had to act like we're sane," he mumbled. He sidestepped her before she could nudge him again. Her glare stung just as much but he didn't say another word. He crossed his arms in front of his chest and waited as his wife turned her back to him and swept past the officers to stand at Liberty's side. He rolled his eyes heavenward. She could be extremely unreasonable when she wanted to be. Although he was baffled by just what was wrong. *Where in the world is Jarrett?* He glanced around for him while the officers continued to talk to Liberty.

"I see, ma'am. You didn't actually see or hear anything? Is that what you're telling us?" Officer Thomas asked. His eyebrows shot together in a curious curve.

Liberty's eyes focused on his eyebrows and she found herself frowning as she responded in turn, "Well, yes. But I think something is definitely wrong next door. I haven't been able to reach Mrs. Wilkins all evening, definitely not since I saw that man outside her house," she added firmly.

"Definitely," Proctor muscd.

"I saw nothing, but I'm definite—" Liberty started.

"You saw nothing, heard nothing but—" Thomas interrupted.

"What is this, a Laurel and Hardy act? She said she saw a strange man, Officers. She saw something," Brenda snapped, her disapproval apparent in the narrowing of her gaze.

"Ma'am, if you'll please refrain from interrupting," Thomas said.

Brenda rolled her eyes in defiance but restrained herself from further comment.

"So you think someone broke into your neighbor's house?" Proctor inquired, glancing momentarily at Brenda, then back at Liberty. He wasn't about to allow the haughty woman with her domineering presence to take over his investigation. He kept his gaze on Liberty, studiously ignoring Brenda.

"Maybe, I don't know. It's just that I haven't seen her since I saw the stranger in front of her home. I called Mrs. Wilkins as well as knocked at her door. She hasn't answered. So yes, maybe he broke into her home. I really couldn't tell." Liberty was uncomfortable and glanced at Brenda for support. Brenda's words had been harsh but firm with the officers, and Liberty knew it made them at the very least listen with less amusement. She was thankful that Brenda had arrived when she did.

"How do you know that something's wrong? You didn't see anything happen, you said. Is it unusual, in your opinion, for Mrs. Wilkins to have guests, perhaps?" Thomas inquired, growing more annoyed with each word Liberty spoke. The woman made no sense. Now they would have a pile of paperwork about nothing. He was tired and ready to leave. He was about to state his intention when Brenda interrupted Liberty before she could respond.

"She just answered that question, Officer. She doesn't know. But I know one thing, whatever she saw scared her enough to call me and my husband over and to call the police. You are the police, right? So why aren't you next door checking on . . . What's her name, Liberty?"

"Mrs. Wilkins."

"Yes. Mrs. Wilkins. Why aren't you checking on her instead of wasting time with us?"

"Go check out the house, Thomas," Officer Proctor ordered. Thomas gave his partner a disbelieving scowl, glowered at Brenda, and then with a shrug left Liberty's house to search out her neighbor's.

"Can you describe the man you saw, ma'am?" Proctor continued after Thomas left.

"Yes, I absolutely can," Liberty said firmly. She watched as Officer Thomas walked up to Mrs. Wilkins's front door.

"And can you tell me what you saw him doing, ma'am?" Officer Proctor continued to probe, also glancing at his partner.

"He wasn't really doing anything," Liberty answered honestly. Her eyes fell back on Officer Proctor with a hint of uncertainty. "I just was worried about Mrs. Wilkins."

Officer Proctor raised his eyebrow at the confession. Liberty felt compelled to add, "I told you, I had . . . have a feeling. Nothing else."

Officer Thomas knocked on the door several times. Each knock got progressively louder as he made the same efforts Liberty had undertaken not even a half hour earlier. Brenda and Liberty's eyes fell on the officer, both waiting for someone to answer the door. Again the officer knocked on the door and Liberty was sure the entire neighborhood could hear him. As he stood there staring at the door, Liberty held her breath, hoping Mrs. Wilkins would in fact answer. Brenda gave Liberty's elbow a gentle, reassuring squeeze. The moments passed in silence.

Officer Proctor returned his attention to Liberty, his eyes even more narrow after Liberty's comment. "Just what was this 'doing nothing' that he did when you saw him? Why were you worried about her, Ms. Sutton?" Proctor probed further, his words edged with suspicion.

The fact that Ms. Sutton had not actually witnessed a crime, merely suspected that one had been done, annoyed the officer. The young woman at her side was obviously there for support and could create more problems, if her interference thus far was any indication of her nature. She couldn't be a lawyer, as the black suit, somber hairstyle, and aggressive stance had initially suggested. If she was, he was certain she would have made that fact known from the moment she arrived on the scene. Rolling his eyes heavenward, he grimaced at the thought that the two women were more than likely just paranoid and easily panicked. The young woman could have misjudged the stranger's presence as being more than it was. So far, Thomas had given no indication that the lack of response from the door could be anything other than that the woman was not home. This Liberty Sutton was going to come up with better answers than she had done so far. He could fine her for calling out a false alarm, he thought, somewhat appeased by the idea.

"How many ways can I say the same thing?" Liberty blurted. When the officer did not respond, she sighed and answered more cautiously, "He was just standing there, watching me, looking very suspicious. It was as if he wanted to . . . wanted to remember what I looked like," Liberty insisted.

A smile curved Thomas's mouth then, surprising both Liberty and Brenda. "Could it be, Ms. Sutton, begging my pardon, that he just thought that you are a very attractive woman?"

"No," Liberty said flatly, then adamantly shook her head. "No," she repeated. "No conceit intended, but I know when a man thinks I'm attractive. He had no attraction for me. Not even curiosity. It was something even calculating in his gaze, and I tell you it was not normal," she added emphatically.

"And?"

"And nothing. He was just a suspicious person."

"Yes, but suspicious how?" Proctor insisted, not relenting even as he felt Brenda's impatience with him. He chanced a glance at the neighbor's house again. Officer Thomas had long since given up on getting an answer from Mrs. Wilkins's door. It was obvious that no one was home. The house was dark, not even the outside lights were turned on.

"He was suspicious in how he watched me, for a very long time. He looked . . . I don't know . . . agitated. Something was definitely wrong with his behavior. He was an older man, about your age, I guess. He was short and, well, he just looked so suspicious when he left Mrs. Wilkins's house," Liberty finished, defiance in her voice. The officers thought she was crazy. They didn't give any credence to her concern. They might as well leave, she thought with a wave of frustration.

"No answer?" Officer Proctor asked Officer Thomas upon his return, his attention no longer on her.

"Nada. What do you think?" Thomas asked, glancing at Liberty as if she had the answers. His gaze clearly expressed his opinion that Liberty was a nuisance. Liberty flushed, thinking if she were a white woman, her color would be beet red beneath that gaze. Instead, she felt a rush of embarrassment beneath their sulky regard.

"It depends on what she actually saw," Proctor responded. He was doubtful now that anything had happened next door or that the stranger had meant anyone ill.

"Oh, for crying out loud," Liberty muttered. She took a deep breath before speaking again. "I told you, I didn't really see anything, it just was . . . The man was acting so strange," she added, realizing for the first time that Mrs. Wilkins was probably not even home.

"Strange how?" they asked in unison, their gazes having followed her sudden fervent search over the parking lot.

Liberty hesitated, then shrugged and said with a bit of uncertainty, "He stared at me . . . for a long time. And while I was on the phone with Brenda—this is Brenda"—she pointed at Brenda—"I saw a shadow outside my window."

The officers looked at each other, then Proctor sighed and took a few steps back, saying, "What kind of a shadow?"

"I don't know. It was just for a second," Liberty answered.

"But she screamed. I heard her," Brenda chimed in, nodding at Liberty in agreement.

"When I went to check the window, the shadow was gone and no one was there, of course. But I know what I saw. And I'm sure that it was that same man trying to see what I was doing," Liberty rushed on.

"I see," Officer Proctor said calmly. "The shadow

you saw could have been anything, ma'am. May I ask how long you have resided here?"

"A few months, almost four," Liberty replied.

"So you haven't really been here long enough to know what is normal behavior or isn't," the officer concluded. "Frankly, Ms. Sutton, I'm afraid you haven't given us enough reason to break into your neighbor's house and check for problems."

"But she could be hurt. She's old and lives alone," Liberty protested.

The officers considered her in silent contemplation for a few moments. Finally, Proctor sighed regretfully and said, "We'll check out the grounds and see if we see anything suspicious."

Liberty was dismayed at their lack of concern. Even if she was mistaken and no crime was committed, they could show a little compassion for an old woman's welfare. Fighting the instinct to roll her eyes and slam the door in their faces, she said as graciously as she could, "Thank you, Officers. That will make me feel much better."

Brenda seethed the moment they walked away. "Oh, you were just too nice to those idiots." Liberty's eyes followed them, her anxiety overpowering her aggravation with the officers.

"I know, but I really want them to check things out. Maybe I'm overimaginative right now because of me and Jarrett, but I can't shake the feeling that something's wrong over there," Liberty murmured. Her gaze continued to follow the officers as they began looking closely at the grounds, peering inside Mrs. Wilkins's windows and then disappearing around the side of the house. It was only then that Liberty stepped back inside her house and closed the door. As she did so she turned around and stared directly into Brenda's inquisitive gaze.

"And just what's happening with you and Jarrett?" Brenda demanded, her chin lifted as if she was daring Liberty to deny she had just slipped about her problem.

Liberty glanced at Carl, then back at Brenda. "Nothing, Brenda. I already told you that he wants to get married and I want to wait. It's not a big deal," Liberty answered hastily. She didn't need a lecture from Brenda, not now. And she certainly had no intention of telling Brenda how she planned to get Anthony involved. She could almost hear Brenda's assertion that it was a lame idea.

"I think it is. Carl?" Brenda turned to her husband.

"Huh?" Carl asked, pausing from his idle flipping through Liberty's *Black Enterprise* magazine. He had grown weary of standing in the background, trying to decipher just what had gotten Liberty so riled up that she would call the police. He was, in fact, in agreement with the police that Liberty had probably panicked needlessly, but he kept his opinion to himself. She would know soon enough and then her fears would be alleviated and he and Brenda could go home. He looked up at his wife, unruffled as he waited for her to speak.

"Can you go upstairs? Maybe check on Jamal? Liberty and I need to talk, alone, sweetie. Okay?" Brenda added, giving Carl one of her rare but beautiful smiles. Carl smiled back, happy to do anything she wanted when she looked at him that way. Her earlier harshness was forgotten instantly.

"Of course. Take your time," he answered. He was relieved in fact that Liberty hadn't asked his expert advice. Setting the magazine aside, he walked to

Brenda, kissed her on her cheek, then hurried upstairs.

The moment he was out of sight, Brenda turned her attention once more on Liberty. Liberty had been watching in amazement as Brenda ordered her husband around like a child and he responded, happy to do her bidding. Oh, if she could get Anthony in check with just one tenth of that measure, her life would be at peace. The problem was Anthony was not her man and she did not want him to be.

"Wow, I can't believe you have him so docile," Liberty gushed, grinning at Brenda.

"Don't even try to change the subject, Liberty Sutton. You hinted at problems with Jarrett on the phone. And just a few minutes ago. Now I want you to talk to me. What's wrong with Mr. Perfect?"

"Oh, Brenda." Liberty sighed, then without any warning, she burst into tears.

Brenda was shocked. She immediately came to Liberty and wrapped her arms about her. No longer the stern mother, she became the protective sister.

"Oh, hon, it's all right. You go right ahead and cry if you need to. It's just you and me and I'm not tripping," Brenda said, consoling her. Slowly she guided Liberty's sobbing form to the sofa and helped her to sit. Brenda hurried to the bathroom, grabbed Liberty's box of tissues, and rushed back to her friend's side. Liberty pulled a few tissues and unabashedly blew her nose. A few moments later she had tapered off from full-blown sobs to uncontrollable sniffling.

"I'm sorry, Brenda, I didn't mean to do that," Liberty apologized between sniffles.

"I know but it's all right, it happens," Brenda said.

At her words, Liberty wiped her eyes and covered her nose with the tissue before staring in amazement at her friend. It occurred to her how much Brenda had changed in the past year. There was a time when Brenda was so no-nonsense that Liberty was afraid to show or share any emotions with her without fear of being ridiculed. Now her friend was a stranger to her, but a nice one. Liberty smiled at Brenda and batted her eyes to control herself from releasing further tears.

"I can't believe how understanding you're being. You were never this nice. I don't even remember how we came to be friends. You've changed so much." Liberty laughed, though she was serious about Brenda's dramatically changed attitude.

"Yes, I know. Carl's mellowed me out, believe it or not. I give him the blues but he loves me and I feel . . . I feel much better, Liberty. Happy. Sexy. It's funny," Brenda said, her voice soft and full with love. "He and I are like gloves and hands, cheese and crackers, you know? Peanut butter and jelly," she added with a wide grin, and Liberty laughed.

"I get it, I get it."

"In bed he is wonderful, too. Great. Fully in control of my body and my mind. He—"

"Okay, okay, too much information." Liberty laughed. "But I know what you mean."

"I think you and Jarrett are like that, too," Brenda stated softly.

"No, I think we love each other, that much I believe. But we are not a perfect match, not by far. I have so many issues I could be a case study for how not to screw up your life," Liberty muttered.

"Hardly! You've done wonders with your life. Girl, you better not forget where you came from or where you were. Less than six months ago you were in that ragged little apartment of yours, with all that gross pink furniture, partying wild and out of control, acting like there was no tomorrow. And look at you now," Brenda said with a sweeping wave over Liberty's nicely furnished home.

Liberty's gaze followed Brenda's and she nodded in agreement. She had come a long way but she was still, deep down inside, unable to hide that she was Liberty Sutton, the girl whose heart and spirit Anthony Anderson and his family had broken. True, she had fought her way out of a depression. But her problems had not gone away just because she had a new home. And Anthony, he was a pistol, a real bastard to say the least. He was so full of veiled threats and innuendoes that Liberty never knew what he was up to. She only knew she didn't want to risk losing her son. No, she was going to ensure her future with Jamal, and no hope for a great love story was going to ruin her rights to be with her son.

"Thanks, Brenda. I needed that, I really did," Liberty said. "I have a confession, though," she added in a humbled whisper.

Brenda waited, her silence giving Liberty the time she needed to speak. Finally Liberty murmured, "I still feel . . . alone. I'm scared to death of doing something wrong, first with Jamal and now with Jarrett. I don't want to lose him but I can't allow my needs to be more important than Jamal's. Not this time."

Brenda chose her words carefully before responding in a firm voice, "I'm not sure what needs you have that you're putting to the side, Liberty. I'm guessing your need is Jarrett. In what way things are different now than when he helped you to get Jamal, I can't fathom. But I know this, being a mother, a loving, gentle, considerate, and beautiful mom, which you are, does not mean you have to sacrifice your entire hap-

piness. Whatever is going on, whatever has happened
to get you so tearful, I believe you can work it out. I'll
never know Jarrett the way you do, of course, but I believe he's a good guy and he'll work with you. But like
I've always said, Liberty, if you don't speak up, how
can anyone listen? Think about that," Brenda added
in a hush as Carl and Jamal came down the stairs,
their laughs loud as they entered the family room.

Liberty quickly wiped at her face and put the Puffs
aside. Brenda gave Liberty's hand a quick squeeze before she and Liberty stood up and greeted the pair.

"Hi, Jamal. Wow, you're getting so big," Brenda
gushed as she distracted the pair from approaching
Liberty.

"I know. That's why I beat Uncle Carl on Mario,"
Jamal stated proudly.

"Really? Well, you'll just have to show me how to
play so I can beat Carl, too." Brenda laughed, then
raced up the stairs.

Jamal hastily ran back upstairs behind her, excited
that she wanted to play his Nintendo with him. Carl
sighed heavily, dropped his shoulders in defeat, and
followed Brenda after she gave him a stern look from
the top of the stairwell. He hated playing games, but
Brenda obviously wanted to get them away from Liberty. He was no imbecile, he could see that Liberty
had been crying. Over her neighbor? he wondered.
He followed his wife back to Jamal's room, leaving
Liberty alone.

Talking with Brenda hadn't solved anything, Liberty
realized as she stared after them. Momentarily she listened to Jamal's adorable laugh. A smile softened her
gaze. No, indeed, Brenda had not solved her problem.
Well, other than for a brief moment she had released
a flood of tears, and with it a wave of anxiety did seem

to melt away. She could hear Jamal squealing in his room as he played his game with Brenda and Carl. That brought another smile to her face, and it also made her think even more about Jarrett.

She went into her living room. She plopped onto the sofa, tucking her feet under her, and stared at her floor.

Jarrett was the love of her life. Brenda was right. They belonged together. Without him she could very well still be wandering about trying to find herself. He deserved some of the credit not only for helping her obtain more, but for helping her get partial custody of Jamal. She sat listening to the laughter upstairs, very aware of how easily things could change based on the incident of her neighbor's strange visitor. She also was very aware that she didn't want to miss the chance to be with the man of her dreams, a man who just so happened to fully return her love.

Jarrett meant the world to her and she was being a fool to allow him to slip away. She could manage Anthony. She would not allow his ego to stop her happiness. And besides, Jamal loved Jarrett and Jarrett loved Jamal. She couldn't expect a better situation. She would not make him wait until after she spoke with Anthony, she would tell him now. Tonight.

Giddy with elation at her newfound confidence, she reached for the telephone and dialed his number. She would tell him how foolish she had behaved, that she loved him, that his proposal was all that she had dreamed of since she met him.

Yes, yes! She would marry him.

Chapter 6

Jarrett's day began badly.

He had indulged in far more liquor than he was used to drinking. His head hurt and he was annoyed with himself for not thinking about the consequences his actions would have the next morning. If he hadn't been so busy feeling sorry for himself, he would not have consumed so much. He opened his eyes and squinted in pain. The sunlight hurt. He forced himself out of bed long enough to close the drapes, then returned to the firmness of his mattress. The sunlight blocked out, he released a grunt of relief.

Even in his hungover state, the night before was as fresh as the moment. He recalled everything, right down to Dominique's annoying call. Why had he mentioned that he asked Liberty to marry him? He couldn't care less about making Dominique jealous. He only knew he would be embarrassed if Liberty rejected him and his proposal. The possibility, and the why behind it, upset him even more.

Wretched and brooding in his misery, both from Liberty's rejection and his head, he lay in bed most of the day, glancing at the telephone every so often. He lay still, listening and waiting in hope that Liberty would call. She didn't. *Is she sulking too?* He doubted it

By the evening, his frustration with Liberty had grown again and he was ready to confront his problem. He shrugged off his despondency and got out of bed. He showered, dressed, and left his apartment, one destination in mind the entire time: Anthony Anderson's house.

In his car, he hesitated and looked at his reflection in his mirror. He knew instinctively that it was a poor decision to approach Anthony. It wasn't that he was at all worried about Anthony's response or feelings. It was Liberty he was concerned about. She would be furious. It was just the sort of behavior Liberty hated.

A frown creased his eyebrows at the thought of Liberty's reaction. It was actually the sort of behavior she *claimed* she hated. He grunted in disgust. It didn't matter. He was through with Anthony's interference. So what if the man was Jamal's father? It gave him no right to continue to meddle in Liberty's love life. He had given in to Liberty's every whim, understanding her traumatic loss of Jamal, but enough was enough!

He reassured himself that over the years he had tried to be a gentleman and solve any problems they had with mature reasoning. But Anthony wasn't mature and the man was too obtuse to handle with traditional civility.

Jarrett pulled into Anthony's driveway, too distracted with his pondering to notice that the car had driven over the well-manicured green lawn. He had attempted to give Liberty autonomy in managing her relationship with Anthony. She considered Anthony her problem and she wanted to deal with him in her own way. As far as Jarrett was concerned, she had proven that she couldn't manage. It was time he took the matter into his own hands, he reaffirmed.

His resolved renewed, he flung open the car door,

not even bothering to shut it, so focused he was on his plan to meet Anthony man to man and put an end to Liberty's uncertainty. Hurrying across the lawn, he was at Anthony's front door in a few strides. For just a moment, Jarrett hesitated. Liberty could very well never forgive him for interfering, she was so fearful of losing her son again. Didn't she know he would never let that happen?

His knock was loud and sharp and not easy to ignore. His dark brown eyes sparkled dangerously as his impatience grew when no one responded. He didn't believe for one moment that Anthony hadn't heard the knock. He scowled, then rung the doorbell repeatedly.

Moments passed as he knocked with more persistence. His desire to kick the door down was strong. Anthony's cowardness only infuriated Jarrett. For a moment he could invision himself beating Anthony to a pulp. But that wouldn't do. He wasn't an animal and Liberty would definitely never forgive him if he actually harmed her son's father. Jarrett released a long agitated sigh, ran his hand over his head in defeat, and then stepped down the stairs and glanced back up at the house.

It was almost serene in the quiet of the evening, yet he could see that there was a light on in one of the upstairs windows. With a quick glance around him, it was only then that he noticed Anthony's car was gone. In his haste he hadn't taken heed to the empty driveway. Glancing up and down the street, he was thankful that it was clear and unperturbed by his noisy intrusion. No one seemed to notice his rude behavior. Sighing at his undignified performance, he promptly returned to his car, turned the ignition key, then sped off the lawn and away.

He allowed his instincts to direct him and did not hesitate once he realized he was headed toward Liberty's home. They needed to talk, he decided, although he had promised her two days to get her thoughts clear. It wasn't even twenty-four hours since he had seen her. He glowered, glancing at himself in his review mirror. He prided himself on being dignified, reasonable, and self-assured. It had gotten him far and now he was struggling to get a grip on his wayward emotions. He knew that had Anthony been home and opened the door, they would have fought. He also knew that had he done so he would probably have lost any hope to win Liberty. He gritted his teeth and shook his head, amazed at how difficult it was for him to maintain his stoicism. Liberty had him that messed up. He was whipped, as the young boys would say. He shook his head at the thought.

Had she any idea how crazy she was driving him? How did she expect him to get any sleep, to work or function at all with her "*I need time*" invading his every thought?

And Anthony did not fool Jarrett for a moment. He had no doubts that the man still desired Liberty. Jarrett had even bluntly told Liberty what he suspected. She refused to acknowledge it, insisting it was in the past and forgotten. It was exasperating, her patience and concern for Anthony's feelings. How long was she going to allow Anthony to call the shots? When was she going to stand her ground and put that snake in check? She was so busy being patient and concerned about Anthony's feelings that she was completely oblivious of Jarrett's. That had to stop.

She had sworn her caution with Anthony had nothing to do with her feelings and everything to do with her fear of losing Jamal. As Jamal's father and with his being so fully entrenched in Jamal's life, she didn't want any friction between the two of them. Fine. Except it was causing friction between the two of *them* instead.

So it came full circle. Now she needed more time to decide if she loved him enough to marry him. As if he was such a fool that he couldn't read into the situation. Anthony Anderson was written all over her doubts. She was going to admit it tonight. He was going to make it all crystal clear for her. He wanted to believe that she was simply being naïve and playing right into Anthony's hands. He refused to accept that it could be otherwise. Regardless of what it was, she was going to face the fact that either she was in love with Jarrett or she was still in love with Anthony. She had a choice and he was going to see to it that she decided, tonight, once and for all.

He grimaced. The thought that she could potentially turn him away in preference for Anthony if he pushed her too far pierced through his veins and caused his head to pound even more. What if she chose Anthony? He reached into his glove compartment and pulled out a bottle of aspirin. He took two.

Jarrett arrived at Liberty's house feeling more chagrined than bolstered as he came to his own conclusions. He pulled into the first available parking space and became worried slightly at her reaction to find him at her door. He had promised her two days. Instead he was at her house ready to broach the subject again. And what if Jamal was awake? Jarrett knew he would never get Liberty to discuss anything with Jamal around. He was behaving like an idiot. He got out of his car, unsure of himself in a way he had never experienced.

Shoving aside his uncertainty, he swiftly knocked at

Liberty's door. In his need to reassert himself, his un-relenting knock was unintentionally loud until Liberty swung open the door.

"Have you lost your . . . Jarrett!" she gasped. She stared into his steely dark eyes, stunned to see him.

Jarrett noted the shock, then dismay that seemed to shadow Liberty's gaze. He was disappointed with her reaction. Without waiting for her to invite him in, he walked past her and entered the house. A subtle glance around gave no signs that Anthony was present. "Expecting Anthony?" Jarrett demanded once he finished his inspection and turned his full attention back to her.

"Why would I be expecting Anthony?" she asked softly, her silken voice deceptive.

It hurt her that Jarrett was still so focused on An-thony; it also annoyed her how he appeared at her doorstep: unshaven and disgruntled. If she didn't know him better she would wonder if he somehow thought his appearance sexy. Jarrett was usually not one to not take his appearance lightly. She could only conclude that he was really distraught and really didn't trust her. She didn't like that thought. And to think, she had been about to call him.

She closed the door and locked it. She wasn't sure if Jamal had heard Jarrett's arrival. She hoped he had not. Jarrett was obviously there to argue over Anthony and she did not want her son around to hear it. She was also certain that Brenda and Carl were aware that someone had come in. How could they not be after the way he had banged on her door and barged in-side? Perhaps they thought it was the police coming back for more questions.

She stood perfectly still, reluctant to show her dis-may even as her eardrums throbbed from her wildly beating heart. He had that affect on her, he always had, and she guessed he always would. She tried to ignore her sudden need for him and crossed her arms. She knew from experience that she should at least appear poised and patient as she waited for Jarrett to speak.

"He's around a lot these days, right? I got to admit you played me well, Liberty. How could I have missed what was happening right under my nose? Tell me, please, just when did you decide that you wanted Anthony?" Jarrett demanded.

Liberty gasped. She was surprised and hurt by his accusation.

Once they were out, he knew he could not take his words back. He hadn't planned to say any such thing; it was a mistake that he tripped over with each word. He only wanted her to say once and for all what it was that she wanted out of their relationship. He wanted to kick himself for his stupid accusatory approach. His face remained a mask though he was already regretting the outburst. It wasn't what he thought at all. He had just become so furious at how coolly she watched him that a foolish part of him had wanted to provoke a reaction. As he watched her in turn, he feared he had provoked a far deeper emotion than he had desired. In fact, if she threw him out then and there, he knew he could not blame her. How could he?

Liberty was nowhere near as angry as Jarrett believed. Her initial shock at his words simmered to rueful understanding. He was being defensive, attacking her to assuage his hurt. She had been guilty of the same in the past.

She knew that she had to be careful how she responded, even more careful how she broached the subject of getting married. He would think it was a pity response when she said yes, rather than her true desire. And if she knew Jarrett, pity was the last thing he wanted or would accept from her.

Liberty allowed a sweet smile to spread her mouth and she gently raised her hand to caress his cheek. "Jarrett," she murmured, "just listen. I do not want Anthony. He is Jamal's father, yes, and—"

"And you can't upset Jamal's father, right?" he interrupted gravely. "So Anthony gets to decide your future. In the meantime, he has the perfect opportunity to try and win you over, Liberty. While I'm left on the outside, the poor, blind fool. Is that it?" Jarrett added, his voice growing more boisterous with each word.

Liberty shook her head in denial, aware that Brenda and Carl most likely had heard everything. They must know she was not alone. She put a finger to his mouth, quieting him as she tried again.

"That's not it at all. Just hear me out. I—" she whispered, her hand still softly against his lips.

He stepped away from her and ran his hand from his forehead to his head in a frustrated gesture. Liberty dropped her hand, feeling her own frustration rise as he turned from her. "I don't want to hear it, Liberty," he groaned, his back to her momentarily. Struggling to get his emotions in check, he turned to face Liberty once more. She appeared so vulnerable, so hurt, but he wasn't going to allow her sad gaze to break him. Couldn't she see what Anthony had done to them?

"You're hurting me every moment you put our relationship on hold. Have you any idea how that makes me feel? I love you. I'm tired of hearing Anthony this and Anthony that. Do you think I don't know that Anthony is the reason you can't find the guts to just say yes, you'll marry me? What do you expect me to do? Wait forever?" Jarrett bit out, walking back to her until he stood just a breath away. She did not back away even though she could feel the heat from his body.

She raised her eyes to his, wondering at his silence. Her breath caught at the familiar gleam she saw in his dark eyes before he pulled her to him and kissed her so thoroughly she felt faint. His mouth released her for only a moment before he groaned and kissed her again. Liberty trembled in his arms, her body weak as she curved into the fold of his body. She knew she should pull away and reassure him that he had to wait no longer, but it felt so good in his arms, she didn't want to let go. The pressure of his lips suddenly stopped and Liberty slowly opened her eyes. Jarrett was staring at her in confusion.

"I'm sorry," he grumbled before releasing her abruptly.

Liberty felt shunned. What had he expected, that she wouldn't respond? Why not? Because of Anthony? She resented the idea. She watched him with a look of composure that she did not feel. His words hurt her where his kiss had filled her with joy.

In a strained voice, she asked in turn, "Do you have any idea what it feels like to know that another person, a person you despise even, could take your child from you? Do you have any idea how it feels to know that you think I could so stupidly, so foolishly go back to that same callous person? So what do you expect me to do, knowing how you feel when it's all said and done? My son's father will always be a part of Jamal's life, Jarrett. Kissing me won't change that."

Jarrett paused. Her words were like a douse of cold water. She watched him as his expression slowly smoothed over from anger to irony to guilt. As he tried to form words to apologize, a loud knock at the front door caused both of them to fall silent. She hesitated only a moment, reluctant to turn from him when she was just getting him to understand their situation. Another knock and she dropped her gaze and started for the door.

Jarrett's chagrin fled. Liberty's haste to answer the door caused him to scowl. He grabbed her arm, keeping her from the door as he bit out, "Expecting *him?*"

For a second she was confused, then her eyes narrowed. He was truly behaving childishly now.

"Oh, Jarrett." She sighed, exasperated. Shaking off his hold, she hurried to the door, pausing only to peer through the peephole before flinging it open. As she opened the door, Brenda and Carl hurried down the stairs. Their footsteps slowed tremendously at the unexpected sight of Jarrett. Contrary to Liberty's concern, they had not heard Jarrett's earlier arrival above the commotion of Jamal's Nintendo game.

Jarrett looked at the couple, taken aback at their presence. He wondered why Liberty had not mentioned she had company in the house. Had she done so before? Left out the fact that she was not alone when she spoke with him? he wondered. He felt a rush of embarrassment, uncomfortable with the idea that they had heard the heated exchange. He gave Liberty a questioning look, but she was not paying attention. She was looking expectantly at two officers standing almost shyly in front of her door. Jarrett's frown turned to worry. He stood protectively by her side, his arm circling her waist as he stared at the officers.

"What's wrong?" he asked no one in particular. At his words, the officers noticed him for the first time.

"You were right to be concerned about your neigh-

bor, Ms. Sutton," Thomas said hastily, his voice ringing with dismay. Proctor grimaced at the sound of
Thomas's apologetic words.

"Is Mrs. Wilkins all right?" Liberty asked, ignoring
their embarrassment. She assumed this discomfort
was due to the bad news they were about to give her.
And from the look on their reddened faces, she knew
that the news was definitely not good.

"Mrs. Wilkins? The lady next door?" Jarrett asked,
determined to find out what was going on.

"Yes. I think something happened to her," Liberty
answered him, glancing at him only a moment before
giving the officers her full attention again. Brenda
and Carl came to stand just behind Liberty and Jarrett.

The officers ignored all of them except Liberty. Officer Proctor spoke first, his gaze consoling. "Well,
we're not sure yet if the woman we found is this Mrs.
Wilkins, although she certainly fits your description."

"Found? Where?" Liberty probed, her gaze wide-
eyed and fearful.

"She was found on the floor just inside the kitchen,"
Officer Thomas said, his gaze thoroughly scanning
Brenda's, Carl's, and Jarrett's faces as he spoke.

"Well, is she—" Liberty began when her son's voice
interrupted her.

"Mommy, what's wrong?" Jamal asked as he pushed
his way between Brenda and Carl to tug at his
mother's arm.

"Jamal, baby, let your mother talk to the police.
Everything's okay. Here, we have him, Liberty,"
Brenda said quickly, pulling Jamal gently away from
his mother.

Carl effortlessly picked Jamal up and quickly carried him up to his room. He knew Brenda didn't want

to leave Liberty's side and she would give him all the details he needed later.

"Is she . . . was she badly hurt?" Liberty asked as soon as she was sure Jamal was out of hearing range.

Gravely, Thomas nodded. "I'd say," Proctor agreed.

"But she's alive?" Brenda demanded, knowing that was what Liberty wanted to know.

"Yes. But I think she may have a concussion or something. She was breathing, but she's not fully conscious. We've already called the ambulance," Proctor answered carefully.

As if on cue, the sirens could be heard in the distance.

"Just what happened? What's going on, Liberty?" Jarrett asked, his hold firm on her arm, partially to keep her steady, partially to keep her from leaving his side.

Before anyone could answer him, two more police cars sped into the parking lot with the ambulance following. The second police car had barely parked when a woman, not much older than Liberty, jumped out of the car and raced up the stairs to Mrs. Wilkins's door.

Liberty and her household watched as the woman ran up to Mrs. Wilkins's open front door, her face tear-streaked, her demeanor barely contained hysteria. Stepping outside of her house to get a closer look, Liberty and Jarrett stood side by side and watched as the woman began to weep before she had even gone fully into the house. One of the newly arrived officers went to her side and guided her back to the car, murmuring softly to her. The paramedics raced past them and went into the house, followed by Officers Thomas and Proctor and two other nonuniformed officers.

Liberty took a step forward as if she was going to Mrs. Wilkins's house as well. Jarrett's firm hand on her shoulder stopped her. She realized what she was doing and turned to him, her eyes wide with concern.

Brenda stood to Liberty's left and gave her a quick hug, despite Jarrett's continuing hold. "It's going to be all right, Liberty. At least you had the brains not to ignore your instincts. At least it wasn't . . . well, worse," Brenda said consolingly.

"Can someone please tell me what the hell is going on?" Jarrett demanded.

He was ready to burst with frustration. He had been so distraught with his own issues and fear of losing Liberty that he had failed to notice what was going on around him.

"Well?" he pushed, curious now by her wariness to answer him.

"I saw a strange man outside Mrs. Wilkins's house and I called the police," she said evenly. But he wasn't fooled. Her gaze faltered, she quivered even as he held her, and he was certain it had nothing to do with the cold.

"I see," he murmured. "Was this before or after you called Brenda to come over?" he asked as casually as if he were offering her a cup of coffee. He felt her stiffen, saw her quick glance at Brenda, then felt her soft sigh.

"After," was her whispered answer.

"And did you call anyone else?" he asked, suddenly very still, waiting with bated breath for her response. He released her so that he could stand directly in front of her. She was frowning, seeming genuinely confused.

"If you mean you, Jarrett, I was just about to when you banged on the door," she answered truthfully. His eyes narrowed. He crossed his arms over his chest and took a deep breath to steady his rising temper. He was not a temperamental man, at least he had never been until he met Liberty. What was she doing to him?

"I'm confused. You called Brenda, the police, then me, in that order. Right?" he demanded.

She nodded, wishing she had called him first now, knowing he was feeling even more rejected than before.

"Did you call anyone else?" he exclaimed, unable to suppress the indignation he felt that she had not contacted him first.

"No," she said calmly. "I did not call Anthony, if that's what you're asking."

"Why not? You called everyone else," Jarrett muttered. He saw her eyes sparkling and couldn't tell if she was laughing at him or angry. His voice had grown husky from worry, anger, and hurt. There was nothing to laugh about. He wanted to get in his car and leave her standing there. He wanted to hold her and make sure no harm came to her. She was a pain in his side and he was unwilling and unable to turn away. He loved the maddening woman.

"Jarrett," Brenda interrupted softly, finally braving his frosty stare, "Liberty's neighbor was attacked and she may have seen who did it. Don't you think you're being a little unfair?" she asked almost too kindly.

He felt patronized but refrained from saying so.

"Yeah. Maybe. I'm just . . . Why didn't you call me first, Liberty? You could have been hurt," Jarrett chastised, his gaze falling back on Liberty.

"We've been arguing," Liberty hastened to reply, sobering instantly at his comment.

"So what?" Jarrett said, refusing to accept her answer.

"I didn't want to worry you. I don't know," Liberty admitted in a stammer.

"Don't you know me yet?" Jarrett asked. "No argument could keep me from wanting to protect you, Liberty. Nothing can keep me from wanting you," he added, his voice barely above a whisper as he pulled her into his arms again. She buried her face in his chest and welcomed the warmth of his hold.

"I know . . . I should have known. I . . . It was just so much going on and I was confused. But not anymore—" she began, again ready to tell him she wanted to marry him. That her answer was yes, their argument a moot point as he held her so passionately against him.

"Ms. Sutton?" a female voice called out. Liberty looked up. The caller was the same woman who had run up to Mrs. Wilkins's house just minutes earlier. Although she appeared to have been crying, she was poised as she stood waiting for Liberty to acknowledge her. Liberty gently pulled herself out of Jarrett's embrace and faced the woman.

"Yes?" she said, eyeing the tall, beautiful woman with open curiosity.

"I'm Elizabeth Wilkins. Your neighbor's granddaughter," the woman said.

Liberty was astonished and her eyes told on her. She had always assumed Mrs. Wilkins was a kindly old white woman, with no family. But this woman was a young, black woman, claiming to be her granddaughter of all things. Certainly light but not white. Her hair was about Liberty's length, her complexion a few shades lighter, her eyes almost the same as Liberty's. They could have been sisters or at the very least cousins.

"I'm sorry about your grandmother," Liberty said with a hint of sadness in her voice, her confusion gone.

Elizabeth smiled winsomely. "So am I but the officers seems to think she'll be fine. It looks like she fell and hit her head. She probably knocked herself out."

"Or someone did it for her," Liberty blurted before she could control her words. At Elizabeth's wide-eyed gaze, Liberty regretted her hasty response. "I just mean . . . Didn't they tell you about the man outside her house?"

"No," was the flat answer.

"I called the police because I saw a stranger outside your grandmother's house and I knew something was wrong," Liberty explained.

"Oh?" Elizabeth murmured, her eyes narrowing slightly.

"He must have been trying to rob her," Jarrett suggested, wrapping his arm about Liberty's waist once more. He was carefully considering the young woman claiming to be Mrs. Wilkins's granddaughter. She was a beautiful woman with remarkably lovely eyes that he found vaguely familiar. He was sure though that he had never met this Elizabeth woman, or he would have remembered. As beautiful and serene as she appeared, he wasn't comfortable with her talking to Liberty. He couldn't pinpoint why.

"Well, I just wanted to thank you for calling the police. If you hadn't, Grandmother may have . . . well, it could have turned out much worse," Elizabeth whispered.

"Of course. I couldn't have done anything less."

"And you think it was a robbery?" Elizabeth asked, glancing from Liberty to Jarrett, then back to Liberty again. Jarrett felt as if Elizabeth knew or saw more than she was letting on. He held his opinion to himself. She would be gone soon enough, then he and Liberty could talk.

"We don't know. But I saw something . . . someone earlier," Liberty whispered, her eyes wide with fear as she turned to Jarrett.

"Ms. Wilkins. May we speak with you?" one of the officers called. Liberty paused.

"Of course," Elizabeth called, glancing at the officers. She looked at Liberty, her eyes keen before she nodded. "I thank you again for what you've done. Perhaps we'll see each other again when my grandmother is well?"

"Yes, that would be nice," Liberty said politely, but like Jarrett she found Elizabeth Wilkins presence disconcerting, at the very least.

"If you'll excuse me," Elizabeth asked, then hurried back to the waiting officers.

"I wish you hadn't told them what you were thinking. They know too much." Jarrett grimaced, nodding his head in the direction of the officers standing around Elizabeth Wilkins.

Liberty nodded, her gaze wide-eyed and unsure.

He pulled her to him and held her closely around her waist. He was worried. Liberty had no idea, none of them had any idea of what mess this night could be creating. He was very unhappy about the events of the evening.

Brenda heard the exchange and frowned. She was in agreement with Jarrett. The last thing she wanted was for Liberty to be involved in all this.

"Maybe we should go inside, Liberty, Jarrett," Brenda suggested, holding the door open for them to enter.

A crowd of curious onlookers and neighbors had formed around the vicinity of the crime scene. Jarrett protectively drew Liberty even closer. She shivered, but did not draw away from him. In fact, she drew closer, feeling secure in his arms.

At Brenda's suggestion, Jarrett gazed into the crowd. He had heard somewhere that oftentimes, when a crime was committed, the criminal could be found within the crowd. He didn't want the burglar, if it was a burglary, to see Liberty talking with the police. Gently, he insisted that Liberty go back inside, agreeing with Brenda.

"I'm not ready to go inside yet," Liberty protested.

Jarrett stared down at her with worry and asked, "What about Jamal? He's got to be worried sick with all of this activity outside his house. You need to go to him, Liberty. At least until things quiet down," he added at her continued hesitation.

"Jarrett's right. The best thing you can do, Liberty, is be close to Jamal," Brenda chimed in, her eyes locking in silent agreement with Jarrett. They were both worried about Liberty.

Liberty didn't resist any further. She was tired and frightened and upset by Mrs. Wilkins's fate, no less so after meeting the kind but odd granddaughter. Besides, she did want to be near her son, although she didn't want to leave from Jarrett just yet. She lowered her gaze, nodded her head, and agreed to go to Jamal.

"I'll just check on him. Who knows? Maybe he's asleep," she added with a poor attempt at a smile.

"Sure, maybe," Brenda offered. "I'll fill Jarrett in while you check."

Chapter 7

Liberty sat in the dining room at the request of the officers; they wanted to create distance, if just a little, between herself, Jarrett, and Brenda. She was overwhelmed as the officers asked her question after question. She was utterly devastated over Mrs. Wilkins. She wanted to help but it was beginning to feel like an attack on her memory and her credibility rather than an effort to discover who had felled Mrs. Wilkins.

She was feeling harassed. It was almost as if she were on trial—not an eyewitness to a crime. They asked her to repeat what she saw, what time it was, what happened, had she seen Mrs. Wilkins earlier? what was Mrs. Wilkins doing last? what was Liberty doing? how was Mrs. Wilkins behaving when last seen? was Mrs. Wilkins distraught? how did she know something was wrong if she didn't actually see the crime committed? and on and on. And to cap it all off, Liberty was barely allowed to respond, let alone to take a breath from one answer to another.

She just wanted it all to be over with. She could only imagine how much worse this interrogation would have been if something worse had happened. To her great relief, Mrs. Wilkins by all accounts, despite her age, had a good chance of coming out all right.

Jarrett maintained a constant vigilance of Liberty from the living room. He did not like how the officers surrounded her, nearly blocking her from his sight. He had insisted that Liberty tell them to leave and that she would answer their questions downtown with her own lawyer. Liberty had blown it off as if she could handle the officers. Looking at her now, he knew he was right. He heard at least three questions asked to her in several different ways. Every so often their eyes would meet and it was during those chance glances that he could see her discomfort. He would have pre-ferred to hold Liberty's hand and console her while the officers questioned her. But the officers had in-sisted he step aside.

She had put herself in the middle of an awkward position. He stared at Liberty, purposely shaking off his own guilt. He could not have predicted the future, and how could he have guessed she would go to Brenda before calling him if she was in trouble?

His attention was abruptly distracted when the of-ficers began moving. Finally they were satisfied with the information they had obtained from Liberty. Liberty stood slowly, weary from the long day and what was fast becoming an even longer night. She noted that Brenda had fallen asleep on the couch and was resting her head on Carl's shoulder. Jarrett was still standing with his arms crossed over his chest. He laid his head against the wall, appearing asleep although his eyes were slightly open. At seeing Lib-erty rise, he pushed away from the wall and headed toward her.

Liberty offered Jarrett an exhausted smile that was supposed to reassure him as she escorted the police-men out. For a moment, she leaned her forehead against the locked door in sheer exhaustion. She sensed Jarrett's nearness before she turned around. *Does he have any idea of the strength and warmth he exudes?* she wondered.

"Come here," he said, the gentleness of his gaze softening the command. She didn't need any coaxing. She fell into his arms, needing the comfort that his warm embrace offered. His strong biceps and firm chest reassured her that the worst was over. After a few moments had passed, he slowly released Liberty and double-checked the lock on the door. He wasn't taking any chances tonight. He had just turned from the door and was reaching out to hold Liberty once more when the telephone's shrill ring stopped him.

He frowned and glanced at the clock. It was just past eleven o'clock. His frown deepened.

Brenda stirred, awakened by the constant ringing of the telephone. A quick survey of the room and she realized Carl had let her sleep through the interrogation, and that was exactly what it was, she thought matter-of-factly. The officers were gone now and Carl was suppressing another yawn, his eyes closed in a polite attempt not to notice the silent exchange between Jarrett and Liberty. Brenda carefully pushed away from Carl's resting head and came to her feet. The unanswered phone had stopped ringing.

"Liberty? Are you all right?" Brenda asked, glancing from Liberty's distraught face to Jarrett's scowl. Carl opened his eyes at her question, at last feeding his curiosity. He was surprised by the aghast expression on Liberty's face. Just moments earlier, the two had looked like a pair of lovers that couldn't wait to be alone.

"Yes. I'm fine. I just don't want to talk to anyone," Liberty answered calmly. She didn't look at Jarrett as she spoke. He would think it was a lie and she didn't want to fight, not now.

"Maybe it was a wrong number," Carl said helpfully. Brenda shot an evil glance at him.

"It wasn't a wrong number," Jarrett said firmly, his eyes on Liberty.

Her refusal to answer the phone told him everything he didn't want to know; she expected to hear from Anthony. Why? was the question, but he would wait until Carl and Brenda were gone before he demanded an answer. It could very well be the police too, he reasoned, wanting to believe that he was wrong.

The phone rang again. Jarrett asked patiently, "Do you want me to answer it?"

"Please," Liberty responded in a soft murmur. Any other response would have drawn Jarrett's suspicion. She had nothing to hide, she had done nothing wrong. She squared her shoulders and raised her chin defensively. She knew Jarrett noticed but she couldn't help it.

Brenda caught the change in Liberty's expression. She knew something was going on beyond her understanding, just what, she wasn't able to interpret. Feeling protective, Brenda cautiously went to Liberty's side, showing her support.

"Are you all right?" Brenda whispered.

"Yes, I'm fine," Liberty insisted. Brenda ignored her and urged her to take a seat. Liberty agreed. As she sat down, she kept her gaze on Jarrett.

Keeping his eyes on Liberty, Jarrett reached for the phone. "Hel—."

"About damn time!" an irate masculine voice cursed even before Jarrett had finished saying hello.

Jarrett scowled, his concern forgotten the instant he heard Anthony's voice. "It's late, Anderson."

"So it is," Anthony snapped, riled that Jarrett answered the phone.

"What do you want?" Jarrett asked calmly.

"I *want* to talk to Liberty," Anthony hissed.

Jarrett's eyes darkened in disdain, his dislike of Anthony more than he could bear. Then he saw Liberty and Brenda watching him and in a flash his frown smoothed into a mask of control. With deliberate steps, he approached Liberty, his eyes never leaving her as he handed her the phone. His voice was flat. "It's Anthony."

Liberty sighed, having suspected so the moment Jarrett had said hello. She was not at all prepared to talk with Anthony in the wake of her neighbor's attack and her subsequent interaction with the police. And she certainly didn't want to talk with him with Jarrett hovering over her like a hawk out for a prey. Extending her hand, she kept her gaze on Jarrett, a feeling of shock running through her at the unexpected touch of his fingers as she took the phone. She lowered her gaze, not wanting him to see just how easily he affected her. Knowing Jarrett, he would imagine she was actually expecting to hear from Anthony.

"Yes, Anthony?" she answered the call, her tone sounding bored even to her own ears.

"See lover boy is still hanging around," Anthony instantly retorted, resenting her dry tone, hating Jarrett for being there instead of him.

"Jamal's in bed, Anthony. What do you need?" Liberty responded coolly, refusing to rise to the bait of his words. She raised her gaze to Jarrett, doing all she could to remain unflinching beneath his expectant gaze.

"Good. I would expect his mother to see that the boy gets into bed at a decent hour," Anthony goaded her.

Liberty didn't respond and waited patiently for him to state the purpose of his call. She was beyond exhaustion. Not only had she had a very trying day but she was tired of going back and forth with Jarrett. She was not going to allow Anthony to make her any more defensive. She swore silently.

"Liberty?" Anthony asked harshly, confused by her silence. He was highly frustrated to come home and find his mother-in-law worried because someone had come to his house like a madman and ravaged his lawn with his car. He was no fool. Who else but Liberty would pull a stunt like that, especially since, as his mother-in-law had informed him, she had called and found out he wasn't home just that morning? She was reckless and selfish and petty, he thought. Now she was portraying an innocent. She might have Jarrett Irving fooled with that calm act, but he knew better.

"I'm here, Anthony." She sighed in exasperation.

Jarrett lifted his eyebrows at her words and she knew he suspected she was talking in code or riddles to confuse him.

"I thought you hung up for a moment."

"I'm still here and I'm busy. What do you want?" Liberty bit out each word, her agitation growing with each passing moment. *Is he drunk?* Liberty stared at the floor rather than hold Jarrett's heated gaze. Of all the possible moments Anthony could have called, he chose to do so while not only was Jarrett there, but

Brenda and Carl as well. She wanted to just hang up the phone and forget he existed. Of course, she couldn't.

Jarrett's patience was gone. His eyes had narrowed at Liberty's cryptic response to her son's father. Whatever Anthony was saying, Liberty was definitely careful with her responses. He had never been a fool and he was sick and tired of behaving like one for her, for Anthony!

"What does he want?" Jarrett demanded.

Liberty shrugged, giving him an uncomfortable frown.

Jarrett's eyes narrowed, then he leaned forward and said firmly, "Give me the phone."

Liberty hesitated. She didn't want to give him the phone, to listen to him ask stupid questions about her and Anthony. Knowing Anthony, he would goad Jarrett further, agree with anything Jarrett accused him of just to cause trouble. She wasn't going to give him the phone. Just as she made the decision, Jarrett firmly took the phone away from her, ignoring her protest.

Furious with his action, she glared up at him. He was acting like a child, as if she were a child. Well, she was no child and she was going to tell him so. Before she could snap in response, Brenda stopped her with a calming hand on her arm.

"Carl and I are going to leave. You're in good hands now," Brenda said breathlessly, smiling at Jarrett. She for one was glad that Jarrett was taking the matter into his own hands. Liberty allowed Anthony to get away with far too much. It was time she stopped fearing the man and put him in his place. She was definitely on Jarrett's side in this silent fight. She smiled at Liberty and added for her ears only, "Let it go. He loves you. Call me later."

Liberty's eyes narrowed, Brenda didn't wait to give her time to make a sassy reply. She hastened Carl up and out the door before he could fully say good-bye.

Liberty walked to the front door and locked it once again. The entire time, she could hear every word Jarrett spoke.

"It's pretty late to be calling for Jamal. Liberty asked what you want. So what do you want?" Jarrett was demanding, his eyes following Liberty as she moved around the house, checking the windows and locks. Liberty shot him an annoyed warning and mouthed the words "Who do you think you are?" to Jarrett. He raised his eyebrows before turning his back to her.

Anthony was caught by surprise when Jarrett took the phone. His first impulse was to hang up, but then he decided he was going to enjoy rattling Jarrett. If Jarrett thought he was going to cow Anthony into retreat, he was gravely mistaken. He considered his response carefully.

"Ah, hey, man, did I upset the love nest? I wish I could say I'm sorry, really, bro, but I got . . . no, make that we've got a problem," Anthony drawled.

"And that is?" Jarrett queried.

"Liberty, what else?" Anthony said mockingly. "I'm just getting back home and was wondering if Liberty had missed me as much as she . . ."

"Cute," Jarrett said, his tone deceptively calm. The veins in his neck were suddenly taut at Anthony's comment. His eyes narrowed even more. Liberty could only imagine what Anthony was saying. She should have snatched the phone right back from him, she thought.

"Not really. What she's done is not cute at all," Anthony raged, forgetting his plan to goad Jarrett in his own growing anger.

"And what was that?" Jarrett probed gently. But he didn't feel gentle. He wanted to slam Anthony against a wall and beat him senseless. He grimaced, again surprised by how volatile he'd become since falling in love with Liberty. Where were his senses? He shook his head as if to clear it and concentrated on Anthony's answer.

"What? She didn't tell you about her little visit over here?" Anthony said sharply. "I take it she must have missed me. After all, the way she came flying over here, driving over my lawn in her hurry to greet me, what else could I think? Of course, all she had to do was call. I've always got time for her," Anthony added purposely, his voice turning silken. He was in a fierce mood. After his mother-in-law told him what happened earlier he was of a mind to give Liberty some of her own treatment. He wasn't even sure what prompted him to make the call rather than storm her home. Not that he knew Jarrett would be there. He was glad he hadn't come over now. "The fact is, I get the impression she wants to see me or *something,* because she came flying over here and banging at my front door."

"I see," Jarrett said calmly. At first, he nearly slammed the phone down on the receiver, but as Anthony spoke, the scene he described became vaguely familiar to him. Anthony thought that Liberty, not Jarrett, had visited him earlier. Jarrett was now amused.

"No, you don't see," Anthony fumed, annoyed that nothing he had said seemed to penetrate Jarrett's calm. It was like talking to a brick wall. He had no idea just how upset he had gotten Jarrett. He added, "I'm talking about your woman wrecking my place and causing my mother-in-law to nearly have a heart attack!" Anthony accused, his voice almost high-pitched in his outrage. "She ran her car all over my lawn leaving tread marks and a mess behind. And my mother-in-law said she was banging at the front door earlier. She got scared and was about to call for help. But by the time she reached the phone and looked out the window again, she only saw a car speeding away. We both know damn well it was Liberty. Why she's tripping I do not know, but I assure you both, when I get done with her, she won't trip like that again," Anthony ranted and threatened.

Anthony had been cool, as he had planned to be, but as he spoke, his temper rose and he could no longer maintain his reserve. The mere fact that he was explaining himself to Jarrett infuriated him.

Jarrett grimaced at Anthony's words. He was threatening Liberty and it was his fault. He was surprised that Anthony's mother had seen anything. It had happened so fast that he hadn't thought about the consequences. But Jarrett had known someone was home. Of course it was the man's mother-in-law. Giving Liberty an apologetic glance, he held a smug smile in check.

Liberty was curious at Jarrett's changed disposition. He appeared relaxed almost. She considered him with a questioning look. He looked rueful, almost abashed, and she wondered at it. "What is it?" she murmured, watching him closely. He shrugged in response.

"Your mom was mistaken. Liberty's been here all evening. Trust me on this," Jarrett said, keeping the amusement out of his voice as he spoke.

"Jarrett, I can handle Anthony without you, thank you," Liberty whispered fiercely, putting her hand out for the telephone. Whatever Anthony was accusing her of, she had a right to know and deal with him herself. Jarrett's eyes flickered over her face as he ignored her hand and waited for Anthony to respond.

"I've no reason to trust *you*," Anthony scoffed, annoyed at Jarrett's audacity.

"Fine. But it was me your mom saw. We need to talk. Name a date and time," Jarrett said evenly. He didn't want to admit that he had been the one acting like a madman on Anthony's lawn, but Anthony's threat left him no choice. He couldn't allow the man to believe otherwise.

"You make it sound as if you want to fight me, man," Anthony complained, ignoring Jarrett's claim that it was he and not Liberty that took a wild ride over his lawn. He was no fool and he knew Liberty well. She was volatile and irresponsible and he was not going to be scolded by her lover!

"Never that, just talk," Jarrett assured him.

"Well, I don't want to talk to you," Anthony cried pettishly. "I want to talk to Liberty and set her straight."

"Liberty's done nothing wrong. Like I said, it was me your mom saw," Jarrett said calmly.

As he spoke, Liberty tried hard to comprehend the meaning behind his comments. Anthony's mother had seen Jarrett? Where? And why would it matter to Anthony? She paused from her fidgeting about in the kitchen and stared at Jarrett in incredulity. Could Jarrett have gone to Anthony's house? Anthony would be furious if that was the case.

But it would explain a lot. The late night call, Jarrett's insistence on speaking with the man, and the guilty way he was watching her now. She narrowed her eyes, watching him and listening. Anthony was obviously bashing her. At first she was amazed that Jarrett was defending her about whatever they were discussing. She had expected him to throw accusations himself, to accuse Anthony of chasing her or stopping her from being with him. Instead, Jarrett was keeping the wolf at bay. Nevertheless, she was curious over just what Anthony's mom saw Jarrett doing and where Jarrett was when she saw him.

"Ever the devoted lover, huh?" Anthony said scornfully. "Whatever the case, you still don't know Liberty like I do and you never will . . ."

"I disagree, but you think what you like. I came over and you weren't in. It wasn't Liberty," Jarrett said firmly. He wasn't about to allow Anthony to provoke him into a yelling match. He was determined to keep his cool, regain the composure that he seemed to have lost in the last twenty-four hours.

"I tell you what, you just tell Liberty if she wants to start acting up I can revisit the issue of custody," Anthony stormed.

"And I'll be right at her side to see that the issue is revisited thoroughly," Jarrett stated casually as if unaffected by Anthony's threat, although he was instantly alarmed. It was Liberty's worst fear that Anthony might try to gain full custody of Jamal and he knew she would never forgive him if Anthony was to follow through with his threat.

"You do that, because she'll need all the help she can get if I keep having issues with her. You tell Liberty she should be on her best behavior or she will have a problem. And you tell her that this is not about the rejection, like she'll think, it's just about my son's welfare."

Jarrett's head snapped up quickly. His gaze was as dark as a panther on the prowl and she knew Anthony had hit his target. Liberty shuddered, suddenly alarmed. Just what had Anthony said to shake Jarrett so much?

Jarrett was frowning. Rejected? Just what did that mean? Before he could question Anthony about the comment, the galling man hung up the phone. Jarrett knew that for once he had been the aggressor. He had kept Anthony so riled up that the man could hardly think straight. In the end, somehow Anthony had managed to turn the conversation around so that Jarrett was left on the defensive.

He was thoughtful as he watched Liberty. Jarrett set the phone back on the receiver. His mind was racing, repeating Anthony's comment about "rejection." Anthony's belief that Liberty would think he was upset because she rejected him clearly supported Jarrett's suspicion that Anthony had gone after Liberty. He was certain that Anthony had tried to seduce Liberty. Jarrett would have been angry with the realization if it weren't for the fact that Anthony's claim also exonerated Liberty. Still, he swore beneath his breath.

Liberty hadn't and would never tell him if she was having problems like *that* with Anthony. Why couldn't she just trust him and tell him that Anthony was giving her a hard time? She had to handle everything herself and in the process put their relationship on hold. Of course, he also suspected Liberty would have kept such an event from him out of worry about what he would do to Anthony even if he hadn't proposed marriage. It wouldn't be the first time he had wanted to put an end to Anthony's interference. She had expressed before her concern that he would hurt Anthony in a fit of rage, and where would that leave them? She was right. The more he thought of Anthony's desire for Liberty, the angrier he grew and he knew that if Anthony was in the same room with him he would have no control of his emotions.

"Well?" Liberty asked finally. She closed the dishwasher and turned to him, her face expectant.

"Well what?" he asked, turning away from her. He wasn't ready to talk yet. He had to compose himself before he blurted something foolish in his bewildered state. The long, steadying breath Liberty took told him that she wasn't about to let him ignore her.

"What's going on? Did you go to Anthony's house?" Liberty said accusingly.

"Yes."

Jarrett's simple answer took her breath away. She had suspected it was the situation; she wasn't an idiot. But she couldn't believe that *he* was.

"Jarrett." She sighed in resignation and shook her head in dismay. Before he could say another word, she brushed past him and hurried up the stairs, moving faster and faster as she distanced herself from him.

How could he! she fumed as she ran up the stairs. How could he take such a chance? He had no right at all to meddle with her relationship with Anthony. He was Jamal's father. She couldn't change that. Angrily, she swiped the emerging tears away from her eyes. She wasn't going to cry like some weakling child. She breathed deeply to collect her thoughts before she spoke to Jarrett again. She was having an awful day, she thought in exhaustion.

She hadn't planned to go to Jamal's room but that's where she found herself moments later. She watched her son, relieved to see that despite the commotion below, he slept soundly in his bed. She stood in the doorway, her gaze spanning the room, loving the way it was softly silhouetted by the moon's light.

It was so peaceful. A direct contrast to her raging emotions. She clasped her hands together and brought them to her heart. She was trembling. Just hours earlier she had been fully prepared to deal with whatever would come and tell Jarrett she wanted to marry him.

She knew she couldn't say yes to Jarrett now. Not tonight anyway. Not only was she angry with him for going to Anthony, probably prepared to accuse them of having an affair, but now she suspected Anthony would definitely try to take Jamal from her if she said she was going to marry. Jarrett had ruined everything. He had successfully brought her worst nightmare to light with his arrogance, impatience, and sheer bull-headedness, she thought in exasperation. Of course he hadn't discussed it with her first. He had wanted to confront Anthony, catch him off guard probably, and prove to himself that he had all the answers. She wished she could turn the clock back by three days, five weeks, a year, six years, anytime but now. Then she gazed at Jamal and knew that regardless of the future, to have him in her life was worth every fight she had gone through.

She softly stepped outside her son's bedroom and carefully closed his door. Padding softly down the hall, she went to her room and sat heavily on the edge of the bed. Whatever exchange Jarrett had with Anthony, good or bad, she had no choice but to be angry. How dare he try to take control over her in such a way?

He was certainly not the man she had come to know. She wanted to yell at both men, rant and rave at how they were driving her crazy. She heaved a sigh and came to her feet. She didn't want any more drama and she wasn't going to allow Jarrett's jealousy or Anthony's bullying to lull her into asininity. She started down the stairs, bracing herself to face Jarrett again, thinking in stubborn defiance that she would not give Jarrett the answer he wanted, at least not tonight.

Jarrett sat on the bottom step and rested his head on his arms. He rubbed his head, cursing himself for his adolescent behavior. He knew his interference had very possibly pushed Liberty from him. Anthony was constantly trying his patience and Jarrett was finding it more difficult each day to control his emotions. Liberty's response to Anthony didn't help either. Couldn't she see the game Anthony was playing? He was trying to come between them, draw a wedge, and it was working. Jarrett released a groan and lifted his head. He stared up the stairway, wondering if Liberty intended to stay upstairs all night and if he should just leave. It would be like Liberty not to come back downstairs, not to face him.

He wanted to go up the stairs and insist that she talk to him. He also knew that Liberty was always on the edge when it came to Jamal. He controlled his impulsive need to run up and confront her. Instead, he could only hope that she would return. Her son's relationship with her was just as important to him as it was to her. He understood, having sons of his own.

A few minutes later he heard Liberty's soft footsteps on the carpeted stairs and unconsciously held his breath in wary expectation. As she descended the stairway, he got up and waited to meet her. He didn't say a word as she approached him. Their eyes locked. Although he was just standing there, she saw the caution on his face, the guilt in his eyes, and she was once again confused. She paused beneath his gaze and finally offered a smile. He released his breath with a slow exhale. At least she was still able to smile.

"Still annoyed, Jarrett?" she asked gently, pausing only a moment to thoroughly look at him. Then she passed him and went to sit on the sofa.

He nodded his head in agreement. "Yes. I'm annoyed. But we both have reasons to be. Tell me, Liberty, you say that you wouldn't be upset if you were at my house and my sons' mother called and I could barely talk because you were there. Tell me that it would not have bothered you just a little if Dana had me in check the way Anthony has you, Liberty," Jarrett demanded, daring her to deny that she understood his feelings.

"Anthony does not have me in check," Liberty retorted, her mirth destroyed by that accusation.

"No? Then what is it? Does he have a weak heart, some ailment I don't know about?" Jarrett demanded sarcastically.

"You know he doesn't," Liberty said. "You're right," she added slowly. "I would have been bothered if you were having the same . . . communication with Dana that I have with Anthony. But then it's different and you know it is."

"How so?" Jarrett shot a mocking eyebrow up at her statement.

"Dana's sweet. She's a woman. She doesn't hate *me*. And she needs you to keep paying child support. The shoe is on the other foot in your case. And more importantly," Liberty added quickly when he started to interrupt her, "I wouldn't have taken the phone from you and tried to live your life for you, Jarrett. That I have never done. Never," she said softly.

"Oh, so that was it? I spoiled your conversation with Anthony? Is that the problem?" he demanded as he sat next to her, so close that Liberty felt trapped between him and the arm of the sofa. He was being unreasonable. He knew it. She made him feel so out of control. He was almost helpless with his need to hear her say that he was wrong.

"No, Jarrett. Conversation with Anthony was not the problem, you are. You're the problem," Liberty hissed, frustrated with him, overwhelmed with all of the events of the day. She could no longer control a flow of silent tears.

Jarrett sat back, startled by the unexpected sight. They were intense and she fiercely wiped them away. Contrite that he had caused her to cry, he tried to make amends by pulling her close to him, to embrace her and ask for forgiveness. Liberty resisted and pulled away. Coming firmly to her feet, she took a few steps away, drying her cheeks with both hands as she glared down at him.

"I don't want you to hold me, Jarrett. I just want you to trust me," she cried, her voice stricken with emotions she had been trying to control for hours.

Jarrett looked up at Liberty. He realized just how shaken she was. It hit him then that she wasn't just crying because of her problems with him. She was also troubled by the incident next door. He sighed, watching her, and it occurred to him that from the day he met her, she always put on an act that she was tougher than she was. She wanted to be a woman that could handle anything. She didn't want him to think her vulnerable, sometimes naïve even, although it was just those untainted qualities that he loved about her. And she needed him to be understanding just now.

Again he berated himself for being a blind, lovesick idiot.

He looked down at his hands in vexation. He should trust her, as he had once asked of her with him. He looked back at her; for a moment her vulnerability was fully evident, in the tremor of her mouth, the wideness of her eyes, the imploring of her hands as she clasped them together. She was beautiful and sweet and he just wanted to protect her, to forget Anthony and Jamal and Mrs. Wilkins. To forget everything but their love.

Coming to his feet, he stepped in front of her and stared deeply into her brown eyes. His eyes softened as his gaze swept over her face and rested on her mouth. Before Liberty could anticipate his intentions, his mouth captured hers. He enfolded her in the circle of his arms and pulled her firmly against him. Holding her in a sweet embrace, he left no room for escape as he kissed her with a desperation that told of his need for her, his fear of losing her. He kissed her until they were breathless and still he did not stop. He needed her as he had never needed a woman. She had claimed his heart from the start and he was willing to do anything to keep from losing her.

As he kissed her, the confusion that had enshrouded Liberty over the last few days vanished. A soft moan escaped her as she relished the strength of Jarrett's closeness. His kiss washed away her frustrations. Like a healing balm, it drove away all thoughts of her neighbor, of Anthony and even Jamal, as her body molded into his hold. Feeling her surrender to his kiss, Jarrett groaned in sweet agony. He wanted her desperately but he was also very aware of her sensitivities and knew he needed to be gentle and patient with her. Not to mention that Jamal was home. That meant that making love to her on the sofa was out of the question.

He resisted the impulse to sweep her off her feet and hurry into her bedroom just a few feet away where they could make love without fear of waking Jamal. Instead, he held her close, basking in her softness as his mouth explored the depth of her sweetness. He wanted to crumble with her to the floor, to taste her sweetness right there. When she sighed softly and gently massaged his tongue with her own, he knew he wouldn't be in control much longer.

Liberty's body ached for release as Jarrett held her closer. She felt every hard muscle, every part of his body as if they were welded together, so complete was their connection. Mind and body were one, and she forgot that she was ever angry with him. His firm touch reminded her just how much she desired him, just how much she had longed to be near him again. She felt like satin in his arms and melted against him, needing his strong arms to soothe her, to coax her body until she was on fire with her need to wrap herself about him. Her arms came up and wrapped possessively around his neck. She pulled him closer, allowing his mouth to fully explore hers as she deepened their kiss.

When he finally pulled away, she was gasping for air. He gazed into her eyes, his face a mass of uncertainty as her eyelashes shadowed her eyes and successfully hid her thoughts from him. He was speechless as he watched her. It was so easy for him to get lost in Liberty's arms and to forget his own frustrations. When he held her a flood of emotions enveloped him. He loved her and needed her to love him. He wanted her so much it hurt. Refusing to ask even one question that would ruin their lovemaking, he easily lifted her into his arms and carried her from the living room into her bedroom.

Liberty did not resist. With the heel of his foot, he closed the door behind them. Softly, he laid her on the bed and proceeded to deftly undress her. When he was done, she lay naked and yielding before him, her arms welcoming him to enfold her. He did not hesitate. He undressed himself and put on a condom. He made love to Liberty, slow and passionately, then rose to wild heights that left Liberty panting in breathless pleasure. It was as if Jarrett's body had spoken all the words he could not form. And she forgave him. When they were done, they lay in each other's arms, quiet and sated.

Liberty was the first to move. She leaned on one elbow, pulling the sheet over her as she stared down at Jarrett. A sweet smile played over her mouth. He was lying with his hands tucked under his head, staring at the ceiling, his face thoughtful, his eyes unfathomable.

"Jarrett?" Liberty whispered, watching him carefully.

"Yes," came his low reply.

"There is nothing happening between me and Anthony," Liberty said flatly.

He turned his gaze to her then and smiled warmly.

"I know that, Liberty. I know."

Neither spoke for a short while, then Liberty scooted down in the bed until she was facing him. With a gentle hand, she stroked his firm, chiseled jaw and with a gaze full of longing, she murmured, "I never meant to cause you so much frustration. I realize how my request to wait must have sounded to you and I'm sorry."

"Don't apologize, Liberty." Jarrett sighed, interrupting with his own need to make amends. He grabbed her hand, holding it firmly. He sat up and placing his finger under her chin, forcing her to keep her gaze on him. "I don't need an apology just because you're not ready. I just don't want Anthony to come between us." Jarrett paused, then said firmly, "Anthony doesn't love you, Liberty. And even if he does, he doesn't love you the way I do. Do you understand?" he added, his gaze worried as she considered him with a deep frown.

Liberty nearly laughed at the ridiculous idea that she could want or could be fooled by Anthony. It was even funnier that a man like Jarrett, so smart and savvy in business, and with so much to offer any woman, could be worried about a loser like Anthony. He was nothing to her, just an accident from her past. Nothing more.

She loved Jarrett and wanted very much to be his wife. Though she knew without a doubt that Anthony would attempt to block her marriage to Jarrett by using Jamal against her. She just wished that Jarrett did not misinterpret her need to wait.

Liberty didn't respond, she simply nodded and held Jarrett closer to her. She had planned to tell him her answer was yes. She had gone back and forth on the decision because of one incident and interference after another. Now she was certain that the only choice she had was to talk to Anthony and somehow get him to believe it was his idea to marry Jarrett . . . or at least that she get married.

Jarrett continued to hold Liberty, cradling her gently in his arms, completely unaware of her intent. She cuddled against him, trying to assure him with the warmth of her body that she was his. Her soft satisfied purr was like music to Jarrett's ears as she closed her eyes. She felt content and confident as she lay against Jarrett's solid frame. In the morning, she was going to see to it that Anthony never interfered with her and Jarrett again. Anthony would have to understand, whether he liked it or not; she just wished she could make him like it.

Chapter 8

Anthony awoke with a raging headache.

After his unrewarding conversation with Jarrett the night before, he had taken a bottle of Hennessy to bed with him and drunk straight from the bottle. He had awoken with a sharp pain reminding him of his hotheaded behavior the previous evening. He was immediately annoyed that he had allowed Liberty and her man to provoke him into drinking himself into a stupor.

He stood and walked to his window to close the curtain. His gaze swept across his lawn and he recalled his agitation the night before and swore. His lawn was ruined, at least where Liberty had trampled his flower bed. Liberty. She should be thanking him, kissing his feet in fact, for allowing her to have partial custody of Jamal. Instead she behaved like a spoiled brat. Who did she think she was?

He had given her custody of Jamal, something he did not have to do, he thought with pompous righteousness. He had allowed Jamal to know Liberty, with worry, he admitted, but he had chosen to acknowledge that Liberty Sutton was Jamal's mother. He had even encouraged the boy to trust that sap boyfriend of hers just to make Liberty happy. And how did she repay him? With constant insults and now this deliberate vandalizing of his property. The only thing that kept him from calling the police on her was their son. And she was treading a thin line with that situation, he thought with narrowed eyes.

He pulled on his robe and went downstairs. As he entered the kitchen, he spotted his mother-in-law. She was picking her purse up from the table and wrapping her shawl about her shoulders when he walked in. She looked up at him and their eyes momentary locked. It was a glint of mutual distaste they witnessed.

"Leaving, Mom?" he grumbled, instantly shielding his gaze by looking toward the empty coffeepot. He disliked her nearly as much as he had disliked his wife during their last few years together. But with Tina's death two years ago, he needed his mother-in-law around, at least until he married again. He didn't need the hassles of raising a kid alone, and good ol' mother-in-law was as perfect a babysitter as he could expect. So he tolerated her and her money.

"My charity club is meeting. I'm late. I'll see you this afternoon," was her short reply. She had no love for her son-in-law, either. Had it not been for him, her beloved Tina would still be alive. She believed that and always would. He had hurt Tina, pushed her away, and caused her to recklessly leave home with their son. But she wasn't going to walk away from her grandson, not for Anthony or Liberty. She was going to stay with Anthony until she died, to make sure that boy knew that Tina Anderson had loved him, regardless of any story he heard from his mother. With her chin lifted and her eyes narrowed, she considered Anthony's disheveled appearance with obvious repugnance before releasing a deliberate sigh. Then she hurried from the house without a backward glance.

After she was gone, Anthony looked around the

kitchen in mild confusion. What did he want? he wondered. He wasn't hungry. The idea of food made him feel sick. His head was pounding. The baleful run-in with his mother-in-law didn't help, either. He needed a concoction to relieve him of his misery. Grudgingly he went back upstairs and looked in the medicine cabinet. Finding his bottle of Tylenol, he popped it open and took two. He started to replace it, then with a throbbing head, decided to carry the bottle back downstairs with him.

The moment he reentered the kitchen, his eyes fell on the coffeepot again. Coffee. Bending to peer in the lower cabinets, he groaned as he fumbled in search of the coffee grinder. Triumphantly, he pulled it out and hastily made himself a fresh pot. After pouring a full cup, he settled at his dinette table.

He eyed the newspaper left unread on the table but his thoughts were elsewhere. He mulled over what to do about Liberty and Jarrett. Obviously he could not ignore Liberty's latest insult. She was out of control. Whatever had gotten into her yesterday was not going to be forgotten or accepted. And he did not for one moment believe that Jarrett had caused the commotion at his house yesterday. That man never lost his cool, Anthony thought resentfully. No, Jarrett wasn't the type to lose it or cause a scene. It had to be Liberty.

He glanced at the clock and frowned. It was early, just past seven A.M. His mother-in-law was crazy to attend any meeting so early, he thought with a frown, the movement causing his head to ache more. He had barely slept after hanging up the telephone with Liberty and Jarrett. The Hennessy didn't help, either.

Since his realization that Liberty no longer desired him, his pride had kept him from further attempts

to woo her. He had only made mild, insignificant attempts to engage her in provocative behavior. Most
were unsuccessful or went completely unanswered,
she was so love-struck with Jarrett. He felt nothing but
contempt for Jarrett Irving.

Jarrett certainly thought he was in control of things.
But if Jarrett wasn't careful, Anthony would eagerly
take Liberty back, even if for just one night, he
thought with a smile. After all, Liberty was still beautiful, more beautiful than she had been when first
they met several years ago, Anthony decided. She had
matured and he suspected she was probably a better
lover now too. He frowned at the thought, resentful
that Jarrett Irving had captured her heart when he,
Anthony, was free at last. He could just imagine Liberty in Jarrett's arms. They were probably laid up right
now. His eyes narrowed.

How ironic that Liberty didn't even want him now,
after all she had done in the beginning to keep him.
He remembered with regret how he had turned from
her when she first told him she was pregnant. He had
been bitter, believing she was trying to trap him into
marriage. Of course, she had no idea that he was already married. She had been so innocent, he thought
with a wistful smile. He had left her without ever looking back, though. He wasn't about to give up the
lifestyle he had with Tina. Then Tina had gotten the
idea that they should get custody of Jamal. After all,
the baby was Anthony's and Tina was unable to have
children, her small frame always having been a health
risk. He had agreed, ruthless in his efforts to keep
Tina happy, when she discovered that Liberty Sutton
existed. He had thought he was fine with the results,
completely void of any feelings toward Liberty. Then

Tina had the accident and suddenly Liberty was back in his life.

And she was different.

And she was more beautiful than ever.

And she didn't want him anymore.

When he lost Tina, he had wasted no time going after Liberty with more gall, more determination. She rejected him. He had no doubt that it was all due to Jarrett. She fancied him to be a good man. Anthony had no such opinion. In fact, Anthony was sick of the man's interference. It wasn't as if they were married, he thought coldly. He had never actually thought about it, but surely Liberty wanted to get married. She certainly had wanted to marry him, even if that was many years ago. Didn't she wonder why the man hadn't proposed yet?

No, Jarrett didn't want to marry Liberty, Anthony decided. He fancied himself more of her bodyguard, some kind of savior rather than a husband. After all, she had a kid, and he was too uptight to get beyond that, Anthony decided with a smirk spreading across his unshaven face.

He sipped his coffee and glared at the newspaper on the table, left untouched since his mother-in-law had brought it inside. He thought how he was going to see Liberty as soon as the hour permitted. He was going to set some things straight with the girl, as he still thought of her. And he was going to see her without that nuisance Jarrett around.

The doorbell rang. A quick glance at his watch informed him it was barely seven-thirty; it was way too early for any visitors. Curious, he came to his feet, slipped on his house slippers, and walked with dragging feet to answer the door. He looked out the peephole, then stood back on his heels in disbelief. It was Liberty.

He chuckled at the coincidence of her appearing at his door just as he was thinking of visiting her. Headache forgotten, he swung the door open and grinned down at her. She was standing at his door, her hair pulled back in a demure ponytail. She wore a beige tank top and jeans. But what was most intriguing was the house slippers on her feet. He laughed out loud.

"You were in such a hurry to see me, you couldn't put on shoes, huh?" he suggested, stepping aside to allow her to enter into his home.

Liberty glanced at her feet and flushed. She hadn't thought about putting on shoes. She had told Jarrett she had to make a quick run and would be right back. He had groggily agreed to watch Jamal until she returned. She couldn't tell him that she was going to see Anthony, to end his antagonism, to fix everything so they could officially become engaged. Jarrett would not understand why she needed to do it and she could barely explain it to herself. She only knew that it had to be done.

"Well?" Anthony asked, a hint of impatience in his voice. With a wary glance, Liberty cautiously stepped inside. With effort, she kept from cringing when he shut the door and locked it behind her.

"Come on, you've been in here before. What's with the coyness all of a sudden?" Anthony asked, peeved by her visible discomfort.

"I'm not coy. I just am not comfortable," Liberty sputtered as she followed him into the kitchen. As if he weighed a ton, Anthony sat down with a heavy thud in his seat. Ignoring Liberty's uncertain stance near the entry of the kitchen, Anthony picked up his paper as if he had been reading it before she entered. When Liberty did not speak or move, he raised his eyes and considered her with a mildly curious gaze.

"What's wrong with you? And why are you here without Jamal anyway?" Anthony demanded, his eyes unconcerned and unfriendly.

"I came to ask you to please stop irritating Jarrett," Liberty finally blurted. She could have bit her tongue she was so upset at her outburst. That was not how she intended to communicate with Anthony. She needed to drive the conversation in such a way that he was goaded into commenting that she should just marry Jarrett. Now how was she going to do that? She fumed inwardly. Outwardly, she considered Anthony with a bold gaze, trying to hide her agitation. She would have to simply play it be ear and trust in herself to steer the conversation.

"Irritating Jarrett?" Anthony guffawed, laughing so hard that Liberty scowled.

"That's right, Anthony. You do everything you can to make him think there is more between us than there is or ever will be," Liberty accused, her anger replacing her unease at coming to Anthony's home and her awkward opening.

She had never come to his house without Jamal present before and it was unsettling. There was no sign that Tina's mother was around either. The few times she had been inside Anthony's home, Jarrett was usually waiting in the car. But neither Jarrett nor Jamal was around, and she recalled how when Anthony had first come back into her life he had been a bit . . . unmanageable.

Now he watched her curiously, his dismissal of her complaint apparent in the slouch of her shoulders as he sat. "Anything your boyfriend thinks about us is his own doing," he said at last, sitting up straight and considering Liberty with an arrogant appraisal. "Ever think it was something you were doing? Maybe you're still attracted to me and he can sense it. Ever think about that, Liberty?"

Liberty recoiled, so disgusted at the thought that she could not hide it in her expression. She wondered now how she could ever have been so in love with him. He was handsome, she could not take that from him, but he was also sly and cowardly. How could she have missed the slick look in his eyes when first they met? Why hadn't she noticed his weakness, his inability to stand up like a man? Oh, he could bully a woman, of that she had no doubt. She had experienced it firsthand. But he never could be the man that Jarrett was.

Anthony didn't fail to notice her disgust. He stood up with a compressed mouth, his sudden movement causing Liberty to take a wary step back. Her action brought a mocking smile to his face and he purposely approached her until she had backed up completely to the wall, shaken by his fierce stance.

"Have you changed so much, Ms. Sutton, that now I'm repulsive? Me, the guy you wanted so desperately to marry? Remember that, Liberty?" His eyes narrowed as Liberty cringed, her discomfort undisguised as she swallowed and stared up at him. "I haven't laid a hand on you, so why are you running? Is it guilt, Liberty?" Anthony asked huskily, his faces only inches from her own as he questioned at her.

"I have nothing to be guilty about," Liberty murmured, trying to regain her composure.

"I see. Then what? Do you still want me, Liberty? Are you fighting old desires whenever I'm near?

Come on, you can tell me. It's just us," Anthony coaxed, his face so close he could have kissed her.

"I don't want you," Liberty said firmly, standing as straight as she could without touching him.

"Sure you don't," Anthony retorted, then put his hands against the wall, barring her between his arms. "My mother saw you, Liberty. She saw you driving crazy over my lawn and banging at the front door. I don't know what game you're playing, coming here then and even now, but it won't work. Besides," he added in a voice suddenly seductive and sensual, "if you want me back, all you need do is say so. It isn't as if I'm attached anymore."

"What an incredibly insensitive and vain thing to say," Liberty retorted, then pushed him aside, surprised at how easily he moved away from her. Taking a few steps away, she continued. "I was not here last night. Your mother-in-law was mistaken, as I believe Jarrett informed you. In fact," she added coolly, "I believe he admitted that it was he that came over. Right?"

"Like I believe that. He's not man enough to face me and you know it," Anthony said sharply.

"Now who's trying to fool who? You know Jarrett has no fear of you. It's only my constant interference that holds him at bay," Liberty goaded, too upset at how close he had been to control herself.

"Yeah? Well, maybe I need to keep that in mind the next time you come over to get Jamal," Anthony warned, his anger so distinct he turned an unhealthy shade of red. Liberty gasped.

"Don't bring Jamal into this, Anthony," Liberty cried,

"How the hell can't I? He's my son and you're confessing that you're dating a dangerous nut, how am I supposed to react?" Anthony retorted.

"Jarrett isn't dangerous and you know it. He's . . . harmless," she added deliberately.

"So harmless that you have to keep him at bay from me, remember?" Anthony chided, his head suddenly pounding again.

"I didn't mean it like that," Liberty muttered, feeling at a loss. Nothing was going as planned. She had been stupid to think she could get Anthony to make her life easier in any way.

"Yeah? Well, he did claim to come over but you and I know it was you, don't we?" Anthony asked.

"It wasn't me."

"Stop lying, Liberty. Tina's mother saw you," Anthony insisted, his eyes narrowing as he watched her.

"She did not see me, because I was not here. Frankly, I doubt that she saw anyone," Liberty added defiantly. At his stern look she added more cautiously, "Whomever she saw, it wasn't me. As a matter of fact, I spent the entire evening with the police."

Anthony straightened at her confession, worry creasing his forehead. "What?" he asked sharply. "The police? Where's Jamal?" he asked in a flurry of words, all efforts to goad her forgotten as worry sobered him.

"Relax." Liberty waved away his concern, walking farther away from him until she stood on the other side of the breakfast table. She considered him with a cool gaze. She hadn't intended on telling him about the incident next door, but it seemed she had no choice.

She explained in a casual tone, "I witnessed . . . at least I believe I saw the suspect in a crime yesterday. My neighbor, Mrs. Wilkins, was attacked."

"Attacked? What the hell kind of neighborhood did

you move into, Liberty?" Anthony demanded, staring at her with wild, angry eyes.

"A good one. Unfortunately, Anthony, these things happen. I can't control where," Liberty said defensively.

"I knew it, I knew it!" Anthony stormed, pacing back and forth. Then he paused and stared at Liberty. "Everywhere you go, whatever you do, there's drama. I should not have allowed Jamal to know you."

Liberty gasped again. How could he blame her for some stranger's action? "I've done nothing wrong, Anthony. Nothing. I witnessed a crime. I didn't commit it."

"Always the victim, huh, Liberty?" Anthony snorted. He paused, then with a worried frown asked, "And does this person know you saw him or her?"

Liberty hesitated, afraid to tell Anthony everything after his reaction to her first confession. Carefully she responded with a soft "I'm not sure."

"I'm getting my son." Anthony swore, immediately fearing for Jamal's safety.

Liberty had barely finished her sentence when Anthony left the kitchen and started for the stairs to get dressed. Liberty panicked and ran up to him, grabbing his arm before he could start to ascend the stairs. He looked at her impatiently.

"Jamal is fine, Anthony. You can't think to take him," she whispered, her voice pained at the mere thought of losing Jamal even for a second. "Please."

The fear in her eyes made Anthony pause. He watched her, realizing just how much indeed Liberty had changed. Once upon a time she would have been in a fit of hysterics, screaming and hitting at him as if she had lost her mind. Now she only begged for mercy in a voice only the coldest of men could ignore.

Sighing, he turned around and sat on the bottom step.

"I need to know Jamal is safe, Liberty. Where is he now?" Anthony asked coolly, his elbows on his knees, his hands clasped together in agitation.

"With Jarrett."

"Ah, of course, the hero. And you think my son is safe with him? Never mind, I know that's what you think," Anthony snorted, hating how much Liberty trusted Jarrett. She had never given him that type of trust. But then, Anthony realized ruefully, he had never given her a reason to trust him that way.

"Jarrett loves Jamal just as sure as he loves his own sons. He would see that no harm comes to him," Liberty said protectively. Why couldn't Anthony and Jarrett get beyond their unreasonable dislike of each other? She needed them both to be more civilized. What was she supposed to do, be the referee forever, single forever?

"I believe he cares about Jamal. I don't have a problem with that. What I do have a problem with is how I barely see my son, Liberty. And when I do, all the boy talks about is what Jarrett bought him, where you and Jarrett took him shopping, this and that, and I want to know, who the hell is raising Jamal, you or Jarrett Irving?" Anthony blurted, allowing his resentment toward Jarrett to surface fully.

"All three of us. Jamal knows you're his father, Anthony. And I don't dispute that Tina was his mother, if not biologically so. I never speak badly of her. But he knows that I am his mother and that Jarrett is my . . . boyfriend—"

"Your lover, you mean," Anthony interrupted harshly, then added scathingly, a cruel look in his eyes, "If he was half the man that you think he is, he would have married you by now."

Liberty paused. She couldn't believe it. She had nearly forgotten her purpose for her visit when he threatened to take Jamal. And now he had said it, the words she needed him to say. She felt such joy she could have kissed him. She knew better than that of course. He would crush her joy like a pesky fly. She had to tread carefully. She swallowed, trying to look upset, although she was joyous at how easy he was making things for her.

"Whatever," she responded, deliberately trying to sound as if she were offended by his statement. "Jamal knows he can trust Jarrett. I trust Jarrett. He doesn't have to marry me for that," she added clearly, stating each word very carefully. Anthony's eyebrows shot up but he didn't say a word. She continued, faltering somewhat by his lack of response. "Besides, wouldn't you rather that Jamal know Jarrett as the only man in my life than to have an unknown number of men coming and going from my home, confusing our son?" Liberty asked.

She waited for his response, forcing herself not to hold her breath. She prayed fervently that he would bite. She wasn't sure what the right way to do it was, she just needed him to feel that he was pushing her into getting married or that it was at the very least not Jarrett's idea.

Anthony considered her. His eyes widened as he stared. She was beautiful, especially when she was being protective of Jamal. He stared at her half-open mouth, and wondered if she would respond if he kissed her. Could he wipe Jarrett from her thoughts, even for a moment? Did she really feel so confident now that she didn't want to marry anymore? He stood up and tilted his head to the side, a wide grin showing off his white teeth.

Liberty did not like the look that lit up his eyes as he slowly came to his feet, his full height overwhelming her. He gazed down at her and said, "Do you mean, the way it used to be when we first broke up, Liberty? The way men were in and out of your life like a timepiece: this man tonight, another man tomorrow night?"

Anthony's words were like a double-edged sword and Liberty gasped, appalled that he would throw her past at her. "I was never that bad," she grumbled, humiliated. It was his fault, she thought bitterly. He had taken her son and she was left devastated. She was fighting the pain and that was all.

"Really? I recall that you were 'that bad.' In fact, I'm worried that that old Liberty may return." Anthony bit closer, his gaze searching as he whispered, "Careful, Liberty. I think I see the old you lurking behind your dark eyes. But no worry, we can go just go upstairs and I'll take care of you. Your superhero need never know. And even if he did, it wouldn't matter. He won't marry you, right?"

Before Liberty could guess what he planned, he grabbed her to him, slamming her body against his hard chest, and held her still as he planted a hard kiss on her unsuspecting mouth. His mouth was like fire against her own and she panicked, resisting his kiss to the end. When he was done, he released her so abruptly she stumbled a little. Furious at his insult, Liberty slapped him before she could compose herself. Anthony looked shocked, not expecting her to react so vehemently against his touch.

"I see I was right. You haven't changed that much," Anthony muttered, his cheek smarting from her stinging slap, his pride wounded by her reaction. When he kissed her it took every bit of control he had not to take it further. He had forgotten how sweet she was, how wonderful she felt in his arms. What he couldn't recall was the coldness. She had been stiff as a rod against him, every inch of her flesh telling him he was not who she wanted. He was baffled, unable to accept that she could have so completely forgotten how much she craved to be in his arms.

"Don't ever do that again, Anthony!" Liberty gasped, wiping her mouth as if the most distasteful thing had just been there. Anthony's eyes mocked her, finding her appalled performance infuriating.

"Sure I won't." He laughed. Choosing to ignore the slap, he walked back into his kitchen. He took a sip of his now cold coffee and gagged.

"Anthony, I didn't come here for this . . . I just want peace between you and Jarrett."

Her voice implored him to look at her. He turned and considered her with a smile dangling at his mouth as if he was about to laugh.

Taking a deep breath, she murmured, "He wants to marry me, Anthony. He wants to marry me," she repeated softly. He didn't say a word. His silence stretched on and Liberty finally sat at the table, folding her hands in her lap as she waited for his response.

"Right," he drawled at last, a knowing smile on his lips. "I'm supposed to believe now that he does want to get married?"

"He does," she insisted, frowning at him.

"I see. And I take it you are waiting for my blessing? Is that why you came over?" he asked, his voice hard as he glared at her.

"I came over because I want to call a truce. To end

all of this . . . this childish behavior. I want you to stop hurting my chance at happiness with Jarrett—"

"The way you hurt mine with Tina?" Anthony accused.

Liberty wanted to slap him again at the comment. She refrained and turned her back to him in anger.

"Funny, I didn't think you were old enough to be senile just yet. As I recall, Anthony Anderson, you only told me that you were married to a woman unable to bear children after I became pregnant. And as I recall, Anthony, you wanted only what was good for you, not me. You led me on, made a fool out of me, and stole my son. Now you have the audacity to accuse me of interfering with your chance for happiness with Tina. I never had a chance, Anthony. Any *un*-happiness you suffered was by your hands, not mine!"

"All right! Calm down. You're right and I was a dog. I admit it. I just need a minute to digest this marriage thing," Anthony groaned, then sat down at the table.

Liberty was trembling but sat down as well. She was so furious. Even though he had admitted that what she said was true, she couldn't believe how what he had done could still cause her to become so agitated.

"You just said yourself that Jarrett should marry me," Liberty said quietly.

"I didn't say that," Anthony hissed.

"You did. You said if he was any kind of a man he would marry me. Well, he wants to marry me and I agree with you. We should be married."

Anthony glared at her, his eyes narrowed. She was up to something but he couldn't figure it out. So she wanted to marry Jarrett and like a fool he had practically insisted on it. He watched her in frustration, unable to think of some way to take back his comments about her boyfriend.

"I just need you to be fair," Liberty said softly, sensing that he was weakening. "You don't have to like it, but it would be great if you could be understanding and not create unnecessary conflict. Can you do that, Anthony? Can you stop calling and irritating Jarrett? Can you let me be happy, please?" she implored him.

"I can't determine your happiness, Liberty. I can't tell you who to marry either. I admit, I'm a little surprised. After all, I thought Jarrett was just another rebound. No one marries their rebound lovers," Anthony added coldly.

Liberty looked up at him and with a hint of a smile she said, "He's not a rebound lover, Anthony. He's the real thing and I love him."

"Then marry him. Go ahead. I can't promise you peace. But I can promise that if you two have problems and traumatize my son because of it, I'm taking him back, if I have to go through every court in the country," Anthony warned, his gaze roving over her as he spoke. And to add insult to injury, "And if you get lonely when Jarrett's on one of his road trips, I'll be happy to bed-sit for you."

"You're everything Jarrett isn't, Anthony," she sputtered in frustration. He had a way of twisting his words just so to keep her agitated. "The biggest favor you could have done was leaving me when you did. I see there's not going to be any difference in your attitude. So let me give you my own warning," Liberty bit out, appearing more calm than her thundering heart proved her to be. "If *you* cause any more havoc in *my* life I just may take *you* through every court in the country until I get *you* out of my and Jamal's life. And should you get lonely once Jamal is out of your life, be assured that *I* won't be there to comfort you."

After her daring statement, she turned to leave,

knowing that if she could kick herself for losing her temper she would. She should not have allowed him to provoke her.

Anthony jumped to his feet and hurried after her. Before she could take two steps he had caught her by the arm. He swung her around to face him and with eyes narrowed into slits of rage, he spat out, "Don't you ever threaten me again. Your boyfriend doesn't scare me and neither do you. I gave you Jamal and I can take him back. Trust me, Liberty, I'm the last man you want to challenge. I would think you would have learned that by now!" Anthony hissed.

His eyes were dark and lethal, sending shivers through Liberty. He was serious and she realized that challenging him had been a mistake. She had no doubts that he would try to take Jamal back just to put her in her place. Up until now, she had been careful to keep a semblance of peace between them. Perhaps she had grown too cocky with Anthony, she admitted to herself, but he had pushed her until she had no choice but to fight back. And she wanted to marry Jarrett. Anthony was the one always hurting her, yet he had an irrational belief that everything was her fault. How could she get him to see how wrong he was?

Liberty tried to yank her arm free but Anthony's grip was fierce and steadfast and she could not shake him this time. Taking a deep breath, she murmured, "I'm not threatening you, Anthony. I am just stating that if you try to hurt me I will fight back. I'm not the little girl you knew six years ago, Anthony, and I feel it's only fair to warn you."

"You were never a little girl. Not then and certainly not now," he began, his voice barely a whisper as his gaze roamed over her body, clearly showing how he saw her and still desired her. Then he added, "And while we're being fair, I feel that I should warn you, come here again like this and I won't be responsible for what happens."

"What?" Liberty stammered, trying to pull away as he moved to kiss her again.

"You heard me, Liberty, or do I need to give you an example?" Anthony chided and before she could respond he pulled her fully to him, crushing her body against his as he bent to kiss her again.

Liberty struggled to release herself, incensed that he had again stolen a kiss from her. She fought against him until Anthony finally released her, his breathing ragged as he stepped away from her. As he stared at her disheveled appearance, her mouth slightly parted in shock and still moist from his kiss, it was all that he could do not to toss her over his shoulders and take her to his bedroom. She may have forgotten the passion they used to share, but he hadn't.

"Go home, Liberty," Anthony ordered, walking her firmly to the front door, knowing if she stared much longer up at him, he would not be able to control himself. "Marry your Jarrett. Together you can start your *My Three Sons*. I don't care. Just go!"

She hesitated at the door. She knew he desired her, wanted her badly, judging from the bulge she felt pressed against her before he released her. She was thankful that he was keeping his self-control, yet afraid that the moment she was gone he would change his mind. His eyes narrowed and his hold on her arm tensed. She shrugged it loose and raced to her car. She wouldn't provoke him any further. Let him fume, she had gotten what she wanted. She was driving away before she got up the nerve to look back at him. She wasn't surprised to see that Anthony was still standing in the doorway watching her, his expression unfathomable. But she knew, he wanted her and even now he was probably regretting his accepting her engagement to Jarrett.

It was embarrassing to Liberty that she had been so blind before. How could she not have seen what kind of a man Anthony was? She could only be thankful that now she saw him for exactly what he was. There was a time when she would have died to be in his arms. Now his kisses turned her stomach. She felt unclean just being held by him. How she ever could have missed him, she didn't understand now. She was positive that she no longer had desire for him. Not even in the least.

Obviously, there was no hope, at least on Anthony's end, that they could ever be one big happy family. Again, Anthony had taught her a lesson about life, and being the apt student, she took heed. She would marry Jarrett and she would be happy with him, but she would never turn her back on Anthony. From now on, she would tread very carefully.

Chapter 9

Jarrett stared at the television set, watching *The Morning Show* without interest.

Liberty had awakened him early, just past seven A.M., to ask if he could watch Jamal while she ran an errand. He had agreed, still half asleep, his body sated from their passionate lovemaking. He hadn't bothered to inquire as to what errand she was running.

It was only after he heard the front door close that he glanced at the clock. Through sleep-blurred vision, he grasped that it was very early. Vaguely, he wondered where she was heading at such an hour. He had forced himself to wake up and shake off his lethargy.

As time dragged, Liberty's absence worried him. It was just yesterday that she had seen a person who had more than likely committed a crime. The man was still walking around free to do as he pleased and Liberty needed to be extra careful until the man was apprehended and the matter was cleared. She could very well be in danger, especially if the man had an inkling that Liberty had suspected him of bringing harm to Mrs. Wilkins.

Chastising himself for not going with her, Jarrett got dressed and began to pace the floor. Restless, he repeatedly peered out of the blinds for sight of Liberty's car.

It was nearly eight-thirty when Jarrett heard Liberty's car pull into the driveway. He glanced out the window and watched as she parked, then waited a moment before she left the vehicle. He stepped away from the window and hastened to the front door. He was about to open it when he hesitated, his hand on the doorknob. He didn't want her to think he was waiting for her like a parent.

Instead, he sat down and forced himself to be patient. He clasped his hands together in front of him, his elbows resting on his knees as he leaned forward in thought. He would talk to Liberty when she was settled and comfortable. Then he was going to have a serious talk with her about walking around so carefree without a worry in the world.

A few moments passed and Liberty had not gone inside. Jarrett wondered what was taking her so long. He stared at the door, apprehension slowly flushing through him. He set aside his pride and hurried to the door. He flung the door open and what he saw propelled him forward without thought.

Liberty was in a struggle. A short, stocky man was attempting to drag her into a long, tan Cadillac. His face was a mask of pain as Liberty kicked and clawed at him, her mouth covered by a dingy green cloth. The man was swearing and hissing and trying to pull Liberty into his car when Jarrett swung open the door and ran down the steps to help her.

The man saw Jarrett before Liberty did. He flung her away from him, causing her to roll onto the ground as he turned and jumped in his car. Jarrett was helping Liberty to her feet when the car sped out of the parking lot, nearly hitting them.

He ignored the car as he easily picked Liberty up and carried her safely inside the house. A quick glance inside the house and up the stairs indicated that the commotion had not disturbed Jamal. That was a relief; it was all Jarrett needed to have to explain to the boy what was going on.

Gently, Jarrett laid Liberty on the sofa. Glancing at scuff marks on her forehead, he ran to the bathroom and doused a cloth with cold water. He came back to Liberty and gently dabbed her face. She lay with her eyes half open.

"Liberty?" Jarrett whispered, worried by the look on her face.

"I was attacked," she murmured, her mouth feeling swollen as she spoke. Like a dream, she recalled that the man had held her mouth to keep her from crying out. His hold was very strong and abrasive and she felt bruised from her struggles.

"I know. He got away. Lie still," Jarrett soothed her.

"I think he tried to drug me," she said, fighting the strange desire to simply sleep.

Jarrett scowled, wishing he had been able to get Liberty out of the way and go after the man who had done this to her. He needed to call for help, but he was reluctant to leave Liberty's side.

"Are you breathing okay?"

"Yes, . . . I think so."

"I'm calling the police," Jarrett said grimly. He suspected the man who attacked her was the same one who had attacked Mrs. Wilkins. Keeping his voice low, he informed the police of the attack on Liberty. As he spoke, Jamal came down the stairs still wearing his pajamas. He went straight to his mother, who appeared to have fallen asleep. He crawled onto the sofa, snuggling up beside her, unaware of the tumultuous encounter she had just gone through.

Refusing to turn her son away, Liberty smiled at

him and held Jamal to her as tight as she could. As she did so, she and Jarrett exchanged worried glances. She wanted to make sure that Jamal was safe. And for some reason, the stranger she had seen at Mrs. Wilkins's had decided he wanted her. Sensing Liberty's concern, Jarrett stepped farther away, careful to keep his voice low and out of range of Jamal's hearing. All through the conversation, he kept his gaze on Liberty, watching her with a worried frown.

Jamal fell back asleep in Liberty's arms. To think that she could have been taken from him scared her tremendously. When Jarrett hung up the phone, he lifted Jamal and carried him back to his room.

"Was that the guy you saw at Mrs. Wilkins's?" Jarrett asked as soon as he returned to Liberty. She was sitting up now. He was relieved.

"I'm sure it was. It just happened so fast that I didn't get a look, but it was him; otherwise it wouldn't make sense. Would it?"

"No. I'm betting it was the same guy, too. . . ." Jarrett's voice faded into silence as he contemplated what the incident meant.

The stranger knew she had fingered him. He was trying to keep her from identifying him; Jarrett was sure of it. He had to get Liberty away from her house until the stranger was caught. It was obvious that although Mrs. Wilkins had survived the attack, the stranger regarded Liberty as a threat of some kind. If she stayed at home, there was no guarantee that Jarrett could protect her from further danger. And with Jamal, Liberty would be even more vulnerable.

"Call Anthony and get him to watch his son until we know—" Jarrett began urgently.

"No!" Liberty gasped, cutting Jarrett off. Anthony was the last person she wanted to call. Of course Jarrett wouldn't know that she had just left him and the warning he had given her.

"No? Are you kidding? Don't you realize that every moment Jamal stays in this house he's in danger now?" Jarrett argued, surprised by her vehemence.

"I can't give him to Anthony, Jarrett. You don't understand," Liberty said, slowly lying back in defeat. She couldn't stand the accusation that lit his eyes. She closed her eyes and shut out Jarrett's doubtful gaze.

"I think I do," he murmured, walking away from her.

"Jarrett." Liberty sighed, guessing that he was misunderstanding her fear.

"Don't Jarrett me, Liberty. You were attacked. The police are on their way and you're worrying about what Anthony Anderson thinks. How about worrying about what Liberty Sutton thinks and think about your son's safety?" Jarrett said.

At his words, Liberty's eyes flew open. She came swiftly to her feet, unexpecting the pain that shot through her at the rush of movement. Ignoring the pain, she moaned, "I am thinking of my son's safety. What makes you think that his being with Anthony is any better than being with me? That man could know everything about me by now, including that Anthony is Jamal's father. We don't know."

"That's ridiculous, Liberty," Jarrett retorted.

"It's not ridiculous. We don't know who he is, what he wants, and we won't know until Mrs. Wilkins is able to tell us," Liberty cried.

"Or until he grabs you again," Jarrett added dryly. "Look," he added at her grave silence, "if that's your concern, it's unreasonable. How would he know about Anthony unless you've gone over there since your encounter with the guy? And you haven't—" Jarrett paused in midsentence. He stared at Liberty in sudden understanding.

Flustered beneath his accusing gaze, Liberty lowered her eyes and sat back down.

"When?" Jarrett asked.

"Jarrett—"

"When, damn it, Liberty? When did you go see him? Was it before or after I asked you for the thousandth time to marry me? Or was it this morning when you disappeared? After we made love, for crying out loud." His voice was rising steadily. "That's where you went? To see him?" He was incredulous.

"It's not like you're thinking, Jarrett."

"And just how am I thinking, Liberty? Tell me, how would you see it? That you needed to see Anthony without Jamal, without me around? Why?" Jarrett demanded, no longer patient, her recent struggle forgotten.

"I went to see him to tell him I love you," Liberty insisted, close to tears.

"Oh, come on," Jarrett huffed, refusing to believe her tear-filled gaze. He wasn't going to fall for her look of pity.

"It's the truth! I went to Anthony to ask him to stop aggravating you."

"Thanks!" Jarrett stormed.

"And I told him that he was interfering with our relationship. For crying out loud, Jarrett, I only wanted to get him to understand that I love you and want to marry you." Liberty's voice wavered, then fell silent as she watched in growing uncertainty Jarrett's scowl only deepening at her confession. It was as if her words had not penetrated him in the least. She felt a pinch of humiliation at his response. He leaned forward, his gaze intense as he stared searchingly into Liberty's eyes until she lowered them in confusion.

"And did he agree to respect our relationship, Liberty? Did he agree to respect our marriage? Just what did you have to do to get him to agree? I wonder," Jarrett added softly, his voice barely above a whisper as his gaze roamed over Liberty.

She bristled in humiliation, then ire, angry that he could think so lowly of her. And even as she cursed Jarrett, she recalled with shame how Anthony had kissed her not once but twice. She flushed, mortified at the memory.

"You're being unfair, Jarrett. I do not want Anthony and he knows it. I didn't have to do anything, as you so cruelly put it. We just talked," she insisted, her gaze level as she spoke. He had to believe her or it was all for nothing and Anthony would have won.

"I—" The sound of police sirens made Jarrett pause. He went to the front door and glanced out the window. As the police car pulled into the parking lot, Jarrett considered Liberty once more. He was torn between his fear of her safety and his anger that she had gone to Anthony alone, regardless of her reason. Watching her, he felt a bout of guilt at accusing her of being with Anthony, because in his heart he could never believe she would make love to her son's father again.

"Jarrett—"

"We'll finish this conversation later. Right now, you need to tell the police what happened," he said firmly, halting her before she could speak. He opened the door before the officer could knock, hoping that by the time they were finished speaking with Liberty his own pain would have had a chance to heal.

* * *

"And you're sure it's the same man?" Officer Thomas asked, taking notes as he listened to Liberty recount her attack. Officers Proctor and Thomas had returned at getting the call. Liberty was surprised to see them. *Do they sleep?* she had wondered as they entered her home. Somehow, she wasn't at all reassured that the same officers were handling her problem.

"Absolutely. I am," Liberty confirmed, glancing at Jarrett as she spoke.

Jarrett had spoken barely two words since the police arrived. She wondered what he was thinking, if he was still brooding over her visit to Anthony. Or perhaps he was thinking about the man who had attacked her. She grimaced, realizing that she could have ended up just like Mrs. Wilkins or worse. Her whole world had been turned upside down in a matter of two days. And yet all she could wonder about was what Jarrett was thinking.

Jarrett paced back and forth, repeatedly glancing out of the window into the parking lot. He was worried sick. Here Liberty was nearly abducted right under his nose and all he could think about was whether or not she had made love to Anthony. He was acting like a fool. He loved Liberty and he certainly owed her his trust. He had demanded the same from her when Dominique had attempted to create a dissension between them. He trusted Liberty; it was that Anthony that he didn't.

Liberty had been through a lot and her experience in the last few hours was not making things better. Crossing his arms over his chest, he dismissed Anthony from his thoughts and began to consider what needed to be done to ensure Liberty's safety. He could bring her to his apartment, keep her there until the guy was caught. He would do anything to see to it that Liberty was safe.

"The description you gave fits Mrs. Wilkins's nephew, Mikel Wilkins," Officer Proctor stated, closing his little notebook.

"Her nephew?" Jarrett asked.

"Yes. He and Elizabeth Wilkins are her only surviving relatives," Officer Thomas explained.

"I see. Is he crazy?" Liberty asked softly.

"Crazy, maybe. Dangerous, without a doubt," Thomas replied. He stood up and closed his notepad as well. "We're going to have a detective stake out your home for a few days, Ms. Sutton, in case Mikel shows up here again. Of course, we ask that you take extra precautions. You may just be the only witness to see Mikel yesterday and he well knows it."

"Can't you relocate her or something until he's caught?" Jarrett demanded.

"I'm afraid not, Mr. Irving. We have no reason to believe the attacker will return."

"And why not? He did this morning," Jarrett snapped.

"We're going to have a detective come by the house," Officer Proctor reassured him.

"And what if this lunatic attacks your detective? What if he somehow gets to Liberty? What then?" Jarrett demanded, his dark eyes fierce.

"He won't get by our guy," Proctor stated confidently, keeping his gaze on Liberty as he spoke, trying to reassure her.

"Right," Jarrett mocked, disgruntled. He couldn't believe how lax the officers were proving to be. What was their problem? He walked to the front door and opened it, impatient for them to leave. They were useless.

"Ms. Sutton, you have my card," Officer Proctor said gently. "Call if you have any problems at all." With that encouragement, the officers left. Jarrett forced himself to remain composed, resisting the desire to slam the door behind them.

"Idiots!" He swore the moment the door was shut, then walked to Liberty. She was sitting on the edge of the sofa, her gaze at the window. It was as if she were alone in the room, and for a moment Jarrett felt the distance between them. He didn't like it. He wanted to hold her to him, to protect her, to love her.

"Liberty?" Jarrett called after a moment when she continued to stare at the window. Slowly she turned her gaze on him and he caught his breath. Silent tears were streaming down her cheeks. He had been watching her and not even noticed. It took no further prompting for him to go to her. She buried her face against his chest, basking in the comfort his arms brought her. He stroked her hair and softly consoled her.

"Hush, Liberty. It's going to be all right. I promise," Jarrett reassured her.

Liberty sniffed and mumbled in a forlorn voice, "He's going to take Jamal. He'll have an excuse now and I can't blame him or stop him."

Jarrett didn't have to question who *he* was. He knew she meant Anthony. He tensed, fully aware of Liberty's fear and how justified she was. Once the threat of Mikel Wilkins was gone, they would just have to make Anthony realize that Jamal belonged with his mother. One thing was for certain, Jarrett was not going to allow Liberty to be hurt again.

Chapter 10

"And what if they never catch this guy? What then? Jamal stays with me until he's caught and convicted!" Anthony stormed, refusing to bend. He stood glaring at Jarrett and Liberty. He resented Jarrett's possessive arm about Liberty's waist. He resented how natural she looked standing with him. How beautiful she still was. How much she obviously loved Jarrett.

"You're being unreasonable," Liberty snapped, moving Jarrett's arm from about her to step to Anthony. She had just left his house earlier that morning. Before she was alone, but this time she was confident with Jarrett by her side that Anthony would make no snide remark or try any sly moves with her.

"Unreasonable? Woman, you were about to be kidnapped right in front of my son and I'm being unreasonable to want him safe!" Anthony shouted. At his outburst Liberty glanced up the stairs, fearful that Jamal would hear them.

"There is no need to yell, Anthony. Jamal might hear you. He has no idea what's going on and doesn't need to know," Liberty scolded him firmly.

"He stays with me until the guy is found," Anthony said stubbornly but he lowered his voice.

"No!" Liberty insisted.

"He's my son and I know what's best for him," Anthony continued, ignoring her pain-filled outburst.

"He's my son and I don't want to. I can't let him go indefinitely. You are asking for too much, Anthony," Liberty moaned.

Jarrett considered Anthony behind a stoic gaze. He was inclined to agree, as much as he loved Liberty and sympathized with her need to be near Jamal. Sighing, he took Liberty's hands and waited patiently until she looked up at him with tear-brimming eyes.

"Liberty . . ." He paused and glanced at Anthony before continuing. "He's right. Jamal needs to be safe. Let him stay with his father until this matter is cleared up and then, when it's safe, Anthony will give him back."

"Yeah! Thanks," Anthony said sarcastically, taking a seat at the table with an envious glance about the room.

"I can protect him," Liberty whispered.

"With what? Come on," Anthony snapped, frustrated with her stubbornness.

"You can't protect him, Liberty. Send him to Anthony and then you need to disappear for a while as well. It's the only solution," Jarrett added firmly, his eyes locking with Anthony's in a moment of total agreement.

Liberty pulled away from Jarrett and wrapped her arms about her as if she were cold. She walked to the window and stared into the parking lot. They were right, of course, she knew. But she had lost Jamal once; she feared more than anything that it would happen again. It hurt to be separated from him for an hour, a day, or a week. There was no telling how long it would take before it would be safe to reunite with him. And would he trust her again? Would he tire of being out, then in, then out of her life again? Her head swam with the headache that had not gone away since her near kidnapping. She turned slowly and stared first at Jarrett, then Anthony. They were watching her, both expectant, as she slowly crossed the room.

"Two weeks, Anthony. Two weeks, then we can discuss what's happening," Liberty murmured.

Anthony didn't respond. He stared at her grief-stricken face and recalled that expression. He recalled how he had rejected her and the baby when she first told him she was pregnant and how again, when he told her that Jamal was in a near-death accident. And now, the thought of losing Jamal was wearing on her soul. A pang of guilt made him nod his head in agreement.

"Call me first. I'll bring him to you rather than risk that guy following you. Agreed?" Anthony suggested, coming tiredly to his feet.

"Agreed," Liberty murmured.

Anthony walked to the stairway and before Liberty could stop him, he yelled, "Jamal. Get down here."

"Wait. I need to get his things ready," Liberty said sharply, moving to run up the stairs. Anthony waved her suggestion aside, stating, "He has whatever he needs at my house. He'll be fine."

A few moments later Jamal came bopping down the stairs and at seeing his father immediately ran into his arms.

"Daddy! Did you see my Nintendo game Jarrett brought me? I'm racing!" Jamal gushed, taking his father's hand to lead him up the stairs.

Anthony frowned, the mention of Jarrett buying his son anything upset him to no end. He halted Jamal and lifted him to his shoulders. "Not today, son, next time. Right now we're going home."

"He is home," Liberty sputtered, incensed at Anthony's statement.

"He has two homes, Liberty. Mine and yours. He's going to mine. See you in a couple weeks," Anthony snapped, opening the door with one hand as he carefully balanced Jamal on his shoulders. Jamal ducked his head as they left the house. Liberty ran to the door and gasped as Anthony swung Jamal from his shoulders and caught him in his arms.

"Jamal!" Liberty cried. Jamal looked at his mother and without saying a word ran up to her, wrapped his arms about her neck and gave her a huge hug. Liberty's eyes watered as she returned his fierce embrace.

"Be good, baby. I'll see you soon. I love you," Liberty sobbed, kissing Jamal until he squirmed to escape her. When she released him he ran back to Anthony and she watched as they drove away.

"You should come inside, Liberty. It's not safe," Jarrett suggested, standing behind her, holding the door for her to enter.

Slowly she turned and with one last glance down the empty road, she sighed and went in.

"Do you want anything? Some coffee?" Jarrett asked, watching Liberty as she slowly passed from the dining room to the stairway.

"No," she mumbled, then slowly ascended the stairs. He watched as she went and with a sigh, he went about securing her locks and alarm. It was going to be a long night and he doubted if he was going to sleep much.

Chapter 11

Liberty awoke with a start. Her first thought was of Jamal and she caught her breath in a miserable gasp. It broke her heart to know he was gone. Each morning that he was away from her, she knew she would feel the sting of his absence. Glancing down, she considered Jarrett's soundly sleeping form. A frown creased her eyebrows. She had gone to bed as soon as Jamal was gone. She didn't recall when Jarrett had joined her. She only knew that it was hours that she lay staring up at the ceiling, feeling sorry for herself even though she knew the decision she made was the right one.

Through the thick coverlet of her curtains, she saw the hint of dawn. She quietly got out of bed, slipping into her slippers, and quietly left the room. Downstairs, her kitchen was bright from the natural morning light that spilled into the house from the skylights and large bay window. She turned on the faucet and placed her coffeepot under the running water. As the water filled the glass pot, she hummed a soft, sad melody.

She was reaching for the pot when a hand suddenly covered her mouth and a strong arm yanked her from the kitchen, down the stairs to her basement, and out the back door. Her arms were bound to her side beneath his fierce grip. Panic struck even deeper, as she was flung into the backseat of a black Lincoln. The moment she was inside the car it sped off and she realized that her attacker was not alone.

"Fight, scream, or even more and you'll regret it, lady," the man warned as he positioned himself more comfortably next to her.

Liberty looked up at him in mute obedience. Her heart leaped in shock and plummeted with revulsion at the sight of him before she realized the thick, lumpy skin and bulging eyes that were staring at her were in fact a mask. She glanced at the driver, not surprised this time when she saw that he too was wearing a mask, his long blond hair spilling out of the open back. The man beside her was huge, in sharp contrast to the driver, who seemed slight and delicate. Liberty suspected then that the driver was a woman.

"Slow down. Your exit is coming up," her attacker ordered the driver.

The car slowed considerably, so much so that Liberty wondered if she could possibly jump out and escape. The brief hope fled when moments later they turned and sped onto the beltway. Certain there was no escaping, Liberty finally found the courage to ask, "Where are you taking me?"

"You'll know soon enough. Who knows?" he added. His bulging eyes seeming to mock Liberty as he considered her. "If the kindness you have shown to Mrs. Wilkins pays off you may be found sooner rather than later."

"What do you mean? Is it money you want? I don't have any," Liberty added. He didn't respond. Liberty racked her brains for answers, then gasped and murmured in an accusing voice, "You're Mikel Wilkins?"

"No, I'm not."

He made no further attempt to enlighten her. Liberty swallowed, the absurdity of her situation frightening. If he wasn't Mikel Wilkins, then what did he want and why kidnap her? "This can't be happening," she murmured in bewilderment, her gaze forlorn as she stared at him. His eyes passed over Liberty once more, but he ignored her bleak comment.

She averted her gaze from her abductor, determined to remain calm and find a means of escape. But maintaining her sanity was a challenge as she stared out the window, fixated on the blur of trees as they sped by.

Liberty was stiff from having sat so rigid for such a long time. She didn't relax either when the driver steered the car off the beltway and headed down a long, dark country road. Instead, all types of bizarre, alarming thoughts invaded her mind and she could not help a visible shudder. She resisted the urge to look behind her. The unrealistic hope that somehow Jarrett had been able to follow was abandoned as panic finally sank in.

Jarrett was worried sick over Liberty's abduction and was plagued with guilt that he had not been able to save her. Not only had he been too slow to prevent Liberty from being taken in the car that skidded from the parking lot, but he couldn't get his own car to start, something that had never happened before. He was convinced it was a direct result of the abductors. And to make matters completely unbearable, it took some time for the police to arrive this time too. When they did, they wasted precious time searching the house, leaving Jarrett feeling even more helpless.

There were six uniformed officers, including

Thomas and Proctor. Shortly after the officers arrived, three more detectives arrived, ignoring the officers and Jarrett as they repeated much of the same steps as the officers before them. None of them seemed in a hurry to speed off after the kidnapper and he was baffled by their lack of action. He had insisted that they leave immediately to find the black Lincoln. They refused, insisting in turn that it would be better to wait for a phone call, since she was a victim of a kidnapping. *No kidding!* Jarrett huffed. Unable to contain his anger, he punched a frustrated fist into the wall of the kitchen. Immediately the house fell silent and the police watched him warily.

Jarrett was just about to storm from the house to search for Liberty himself when the phone rang. All activity stopped at the sound of the first ring, then Jarrett hurried to the phone. Before he could answer it, a policeman whom he recognized as Officer Proctor stopped him by firmly holding his wrist.

"It could be the kidnappers. We'll want to speak with them while we try and get a trace on the call, but we're not set up yet."

"I got it," Jarrett responded, visibly pulling himself together. He needed to keep a clear head if he was going to do Liberty any good.

"And, Mr. Irving, if it is the kidnapper, just give us the call. Don't provoke him," Officer Proctor warned.

"I won't," Jarrett responded. When the officer didn't immediately release his hold, Jarrett pointedly looked at his hand. With narrowed eyes, the officer released Jarrett, his hesitation communicating his doubt.

"Jarrett Irving?" the caller asked the moment the line was picked up.

"I am," Jarrett answered, amazed at how normal his

voice sounded when he wanted to rant and rave in agony over Liberty's disappearance.

"I have Liberty Sutton," the caller went on. At his words, Jarrett's eyes connected with Proctor's. He nodded and Proctor frowned. The other officers had crowded around Jarrett in hushed expectation. Proctor's partner, Officer Thomas, found another phone and picked it up the moment Jarrett answered the line.

"Tell me you didn't hurt her," Jarrett said without hesitation, not realizing he was holding his breath while he waited for a reply.

"No. We haven't hurt her, yet. But we'll have to see."

Jarrett inhaled sharply at that response. Ignoring Proctor, who stood so close he could hear the voice if not the words on the other line, Jarrett asked in a voice gone harsh from his fear for Liberty, "What do you want?"

Officer Proctor groaned at Jarrett's words. They needed to keep the kidnapper talking for a bit before asking his reasons for kidnapping Liberty; otherwise they had no chance to trace the call. They should have expected Jarrett to react just so. Proctor, annoyed, put his hand out to Jarrett, silently demanding the phone. But Thomas shook his head at both him and Jarrett, his calm assuring Proctor that in fact it was fine, the direction Jarrett was taking.

Jarrett breathed a sigh of relief at the silent countercommand. He would have gone crazy with curiosity if he had to wait for the officers to interpret the call for him.

"There's a letter in Liberty's mailbox with details you and the police need to follow," the kidnapper explained, unaware of the tension in the room. "Have you called the police yet?" the kidnapper asked as an afterthought.

"Yes," Jarrett answered. He might as well tell the truth. The man had Liberty and Jarrett wasn't about to play games with him.

"Are they there now?" he was asked. Thomas nodded at Jarrett.

"Yes," Jarrett responded.

"Are you listening, Officers? Have you got this call traced yet?" the kidnapper goaded.

Thomas frowned, then released a slow sigh.

"Not quite. I don't suppose you'll oblige us by staying on the line until the trace is complete," Officer Thomas retorted.

"Wouldn't dream of it," the kidnapper said with a sneer in his voice. "Now that we all know where we stand, you, Mr. Irving, and the police have until tomorrow morning to digest the list and respond. We'll contact you."

"We? Wait," Jarrett called, but too late he realized the man had hung up.

"There's more than one kidnapper," Officer Thomas stated the moment he hung up the receiver.

"Any demands?" another officer asked, sighing in exasperation at the tracer. As predicted, it had failed without more time to connect the call.

"Just that we check the mail. Wait, Mr. Irving," Officer Thomas called as Jarrett pushed past him to hurry from the house. They followed, stopping him just as he snatched open Liberty's mailbox that was outside her front door.

"We'll take it from here, Mr. Irving. There could be evidence all over the envelope," Officer Thomas suggested not unkindly as he reached inside the mailbox and removed the brown envelope.

"We were instructed to check the mail together," Jarrett pointed out.

"And so we did. Don't forget, you're not a police officer," the officer added, his voice edged with sympathy.

"And don't you forget that Liberty Sutton is my fiancée. I want to see her returned safely," Jarrett retorted, ignoring the sympathetic looks he was getting and resenting being shut out.

"So do we," the officer agreed as he carried the letter inside.

Officer Thomas handed the letter to the nearest detective, Detective Rohn, and waited while he carefully opened it.

"Well?" Jarrett asked impatiently, watching Detective Rohn and the two other detectives as they perused the letter.

"They're demanding five hundred thousand dollars in unmarked bills. They want a new car, a full tank of gas, and a private helicopter. Place to be determined," the detective explained, a grim frown creasing his forehead as he looked up.

"They have got to be joking!" Jarrett exclaimed, glancing from man to man in an effort to make sense of the situation.

"I don't think so," Rohn said.

"It's crap! Liberty doesn't have that kind of money and no one has a reason to think she does," Jarrett snapped.

"Nevertheless, Mr. Irving, it's what they want," Rohn insisted.

"It's crap," Jarrett repeated, then turned to the two officers who had been present the previous evening. "You know it's a sham. It's got to have something to do with the other night. And unless this Mrs. Wilkins is loaded, they have no hope of getting money from Liberty."

"The other night? Mrs. Wilkins?" Detective Rohn interrupted.

"Don't tell me you aren't even aware of the stranger that attacked my fiancée's neighbor the other evening?" Jarrett cried in disbelief.

"Wait a minute. I'm confused. Now Ms. Sutton is your fiancée? And a stranger was seen in this area? Officer Thomas, explain this and from the beginning," Detective Rohn said, his frown creasing his forehead again.

Jarrett looked away, slightly embarrassed by being called out on his claim that Liberty was his fiancée. It might not be a fact yet, but it was his intent. He didn't care what they thought as long as they got Liberty back. He listened in stoic silence as Officers Thomas and Proctor proceeded to explain the events that led up to Liberty's kidnapping.

"And no one saw fit to fill us in on this?" Rohn questioned, eyeing each officer in stern disapproval.

"Thought you knew." Thomas shrugged.

"We didn't get that far," Proctor added.

"So now you see why I know it was that guy Liberty saw," Jarrett interjected tiredly.

"I see that we have a complicated situation," Rohn said evenly. He began to pace back and forth. No one spoke as they waited for him to collect his thoughts.

"She was definitely kidnapped for money," he said softly.

"But she doesn't have any money," Jarrett insisted. "It makes no sense. Why would they think she's loaded like that?"

"Well, it certainly explains the ridiculousness to the

terms for her release," Officer Thomas commented dryly.

"So what now?" Jarrett asked, rubbing his head in agitation. He had to get it together, to think clearly for Liberty's sake. He stood with his legs apart, his eyes narrowed, as he forced himself to focus on the situation and listen to the officers.

"We agree to their terms," Detective Rohn said simply.

"Why?" Jarrett asked, dumbfounded.

"Either they are expecting a refusal, a plea for negotiations, or they really think we can get it. Mrs. Wilkins doesn't sound like your ordinary neighbor attack. She may have something she can add to this mystery," the detective continued. Turning to Officers Proctor and Thomas, he said, "Matter of fact, why don't you two visit the lady and find out what she knows about this, if anything?"

"Right," Thomas responded.

"What if you can't get the money? What happens to Liberty?" Jarrett demanded, hating to voice his misgiving but having no choice. Mrs. Wilkins could be broke and clueless as to where the kidnappers expected to get their money, and he was not happy with leaving Liberty's safety to chance.

Rohn paused at the front door and considered Jarrett with an almost sympathetic gaze.

"Off the record, my honest opinion is that Mrs. Wilkins will have an answer for us to piece this together. She may even lead us directly to the kidnappers. My gut instinct is it's not some random guys thinking it would be a lark to kidnap a woman and get paid. On the record, however . . ." He paused. "The truth is, Mr. Irving, we have a very small chance of finding Ms. Sutton on our own and especially if

Mrs. Wilkins proves to be no help. His eyes lowered slightly. "There's a small chance that we'll get Ms. Sutton back unharmed."

"What a hell of an optimistic attitude we have in the police department!" Jarrett huffed, so irate at the detective's words he could barely keep from clenching his hands in anger.

"Officers Thomas and Proctor will be here through the night, right outside. If you get a call before the morning, wave them inside before you answer. Got it?" Rohn said, ignoring Jarrett's outburst. There was nothing he could say to console the man and he knew it.

"Yeah, got it," Jarrett muttered, then slammed the door shut in a fit of frustration.

The house quiet once again, Jarrett sat down with a heavy sigh. He couldn't believe what was happening. Liberty's kidnapping was as bizarre as when he discovered, in the most preposterous and untimely moment, that she had a son. Ever since he met Liberty Sutton his life had become a whirlwind of drama, bafflement, and passion.

She was going to be all right, she had to be. And they would marry when she was returned to him. He couldn't bear the thought that he might never be able to apologize, to ask for her forgiveness for being a jealous fool.

Chapter 12

Liberty eyed her surroundings with controlled curiosity. The house was unexpectantly bright and cheerful, a home that characterized wealth, style, and warmth. Liberty hesitated for just a moment before following the woman fully inside. Without a word or another glance even, they left her unattended in what Liberty supposed was a family room. She sat near the unlit fireplace and looked around the room for a means of escape or a weapon. She had not been tied up, and from all appearances, her kidnappers had left completely, although she was certain they couldn't be far. She still found it odd that they didn't seem concerned that she might attempt to get out. Perhaps they thought she was too frightened to move.

Liberty stood and listened for any sounds. Hearing nothing, she took a wary step toward the window. She hesitated, peered over her shoulder, then took a deep breath. Carefully she moved the curtain to the side. She was surprised to find the house was not isolated; she could clearly see several homes nearby. For a fleeting moment, she wondered if the long drive had been a hoax and if she was still close to home. It would be too much to hope that she could leave the house and find her way to safety without being stopped.

She released the curtain and turned around. She

stared at the front door and gingerly tried to open it to no avail. She looked around the room again, searching for anything that could help her, until her eyes fell and froze on a sliding door that would lead to the backyard and freedom. She hesitated, then with her heart pounding so loud she was certain the kidnappers would hear it, she hurried across the room and tried the door. Could they have been so lax in their plans that they had left a means of escape unguarded and unsecured? She slid the door open fully. Two Doberman pinschers growled at her, their sharp fangs and bloodshot eyes causing her to shriek back in horror.

"Down, Flex. Down, Bruce," came a stern command from behind the dogs.

Trembling with shock, Liberty had all she could do not to faint and raise her gaze from the dogs to the short, balding white man standing behind the ferocious beasts. There was no question as to his identity. She knew the instant she laid eyes on him who he was. Mikel Wilkins.

"Lost?" he asked simply, his raised eyebrow a dry expression of amusement.

Liberty just stared at him in disbelief, barely aware that he had shooed the dogs away. He returned her stare, the searching examination of her face bringing Liberty out of her shock. *Why is he looking at me like that?*

Mikel started towards her, his eyes never leaving hers. Liberty took an unconscious step back. She was taller than him but his short, bulky form was no less intimidating. She swallowed when he finally pulled his eyes away as he closed and locked the door. With a wave of his hand, he silently commanded Liberty to have a seat. She complied.

"Do you know why you're here, Ms. Sutton?" Mikel asked, sitting across from her.

She wasn't surprised that he knew her name. She shook her head. Behind his cool demeanor she sensed an explosive temper and had no desire to test him.

He didn't enlighten her and Liberty held back a desire to demand he explain. She would scream if he didn't speak to her soon instead of watching her with his cold, calculating eyes.

"I—" Her words were interrupted at the sound of footsteps approaching. She looked up, seeing for the first time the man and woman who had abducted her earlier. She had no doubt they were the same pair, although now they wore no masks to disguise themselves. She was not so sure she was comfortable with the change.

Liberty came to her feet, feeling the need to protect herself at the sight of the slight blond woman and brown-haired, red-faced man. They appeared to have been arguing. Liberty was certain of it when the woman tossed her hair and moved away from the man when he appeared to reach for her.

"Veronica, Charles, you left the back door unlocked," Mikel reprimanded them the moment they entered the room.

"We weren't gone but a moment," Veronica said defensively.

"She was out the door in that moment," Mikel retorted.

"It won't happen again," Charles said quickly, his sharp glance at Veronica ending any reply she may have intended. She rolled her blue eyes heavenward in open annoyance before gracefully sitting on the edge of the sofa. Charles stood beside Liberty, his green eyes narrowed as he watched her, but it was an orange envelope held loosely in his hand that captured Liberty's interest. A tingle of suspicion shivered down her spine.

Mikel took the envelope and their eyes met once more. Liberty swallowed. Did he have to make everything so awkward and frightening? She wasn't sure how much more of the suspense she could take. As if reading her thoughts, Mikel gave her the envelope. Her hand trembled as she accepted it. She forced her gaze back to Mikel's and waited for his explanation. He nodded at the envelope.

"Inside that envelope is very important information. I need you to read it, study it, and become Elizabeth Wilkins."

An Important Message From The ARABESQUE Publisher

Dear Arabesque Reader,

Arabesque is celebrating 10 years of award-winning African-American romance. This year look for our specially marked 10th Anniversary titles.

Plus, we are offering *Special Collection Editions* and a *Summer Reading Series*—all part of our 10th Anniversary celebration.

Why not be a part of the celebration and let us send you four more specially selected books FREE! These exceptional romances will be sent right to your front door!

Please enjoy them with our compliments, and thank you for continuing to enjoy Arabesque.... the soul of romance bringing you ten years of love, passion and extraordinary romance.

Linda Gill
PUBLISHER, ARABESQUE ROMANCE NOVELS

P.S. Don't forget to nominate someone special in the Arabesque Man Contest! For more details visit us at www.BET.com

A SPECIAL "THANK YOU"
FROM ARABESQUE JUST FOR YOU!

Send this card back and you'll receive 4 FREE Arabesque Novels—a $25.96 value—absolutely FREE!

The introductory 4 Arabesque Romance books are yours FREE (plus $1.99 shipping & handling). If you wish to continue to receive 4 books every month, do nothing. Each month, we will send you 4 New Arabesque Romance Novels for your free examination. If you wish to keep them, pay just $18* (plus, $1.99 shipping & handling). If you decide not to continue, you owe nothing!

- Send no money now.
- Never an obligation.
- Books delivered to your door!

We hope that after receiving your FREE books you'll want to remain an Arabesque subscriber, but the choice is yours! So why not take advantage of this Arabesque offer, with no risk of any kind. You'll be glad you did!

In fact, we're so sure you will love your Arabesque novels, that we will send you an Arabesque Tote Bag FREE with your first paid shipment.

* Prices subject to change

THE "THANK YOU" GIFT INCLUDES:

- 4 books absolutely FREE (plus $1.99 for shipping and handling).
- A FREE newsletter, *Arabesque Romance News*, filled with author interviews, book previews, special offers, and more!
- No risks or obligations. You're free to cancel whenever you wish with no questions asked.

INTRODUCTORY OFFER CERTIFICATE

Yes! Please send me 4 FREE Arabesque novels (plus $1.99 for shipping & handling). I understand I am under no obligation to purchase any books, as explained on the back of this card. Send my free tote bag after my first regular paid shipment.

NAME _____

ADDRESS _____ APT. _____

CITY _____ STATE _____ ZIP _____

TELEPHONE ( ) _____

E-MAIL _____

SIGNATURE _____

Offer limited to one per household and not valid to current subscribers. All orders subject to approval. Terms, offer, & price subject to change. Tote bags available while supplies last.

Thank You!

AN064A

ARABESQUE

Accepting the four introductory books for FREE (plus $1.99 to offset the cost of shipping & handling) places you under no obligation to buy anything. You may keep the books and return the shipping statement marked "cancelled". If you do not cancel, about a month later we will send 4 additional Arabesque novels, and you will be billed the preferred subscriber's price of just $4.50 per title. That's $18.00* for all 4 books for a savings of almost 40% off the cover price (Plus $1.99 for shipping and handling). You may cancel at any time, but if you choose to continue, every month we'll send you 4 more books, which you may either purchase at the preferred discount price. . . or return to us and cancel your subscription.

THE ARABESQUE ROMANCE CLUB: HERE'S HOW IT WORKS

THE ARABESQUE ROMANCE BOOK CLUB
P.O. BOX 5214
CLIFTON NJ 07015-5214

PLACE
STAMP
HERE

Chapter 13

Liberty was stunned. She recalled instantly who Elizabeth Wilkins was. She gazed from Mikel to Charles, then back at the envelope

"We're depending on you," Charles said lightly. The brusque facade he had displayed when he abducted her was gone.

"I can't become Elizabeth Wilkins."

"Sure you can. You look like her, enough to have caused me to pause when I first laid eyes on you. You do remember, don't you, Ms. Sutton?"

"I remember," Liberty answered weakly. She didn't understand what insanity this was, but she could be no part of it.

"All you need is her ID, the key to her fancy car, and a sharp pantsuit. Elizabeth loves pantsuits. Of course, the folks in New Jersey won't know that as they may have seen her only once or twice in the last few years. But we can't take any chances. So you see, you can be Elizabeth," Mikel responded.

"And what will Elizabeth have to say to all of this?" Liberty demanded.

"She won't say a thing if she's silenced, of course," Veronica offered coldly.

Liberty had all but forgotten Veronica's presence. The woman was so small and fragile. Her thick blond hair did not help as it practically hid her beautiful features. Dark brown eyes stared into icy blue ones. There was a challenge in Veronica's eyes that Liberty couldn't ignore. It was almost as if Veronica was saying, *Don't let my five feet two inches fool you.* Liberty blinked rapidly, trying to compose her shattered nerves as she slowly turned to face Mikel.

"What do you want me to do?" she asked, unable to think of a way out.

"Tomorrow morning you will arrive in a small town just outside of New Jersey. The Wilkins-Zonnick trust fund is located there. The fund's vault is inside the Bank of Enterprise."

"Wilkins-Zonnick trust fund?" Liberty inquired, confused.

"That's not important. What's important is that I want those funds," Mikel said.

"I see. And here I thought you would rob a major bank," Liberty muttered, unable to contain her sarcasm.

"It's not a robbery," Veronica chimed in.

"Indeed no. Just a transfer of funds, rightfully mine, I might add," Mikel said, as if he could not resist. "Bank of Enterprise is no major bank but it was my great-grandfather's choice and that's how my aunt wanted it."

"Mrs. Wilkins?" Liberty asked, confused.

"You needn't worry about that," Mikel snapped. "We need you to be bright-eyed tomorrow morning, close out the Wilkins-Zonnick trust, and sign everything from Wilkins-Zonnick to Wilkins-Bronsini."

"Why should I do it? I don't understand any of this. I don't know Elizabeth Wilkins."

"But you know her grandmother, my aunt. And you

already know what I'm capable of," Mikel added. Liberty gasped, his insinuation alarming.

"You would attack Mrs. Wilkins again? But she's an old woman," Liberty protested, her eyes darting from Mikel to Charles and Veronica, then back to Mikel.

"I'll do whatever is necessary to get you to cooperate," Mikel insisted.

"It won't work. Mrs. Wilkins won't allow this. I'll get caught. This is insane," Liberty cried.

"It'll work. My aunt won't have any say in it. She's still in intensive care. At her age, they won't bother her until she's fully recovered. That only gives me a few days, two of which I've already lost. Plus, they'll have no reason to question you. Elizabeth will not be considered missing, because you'll be her. By the time anyone realizes what's happened, you will have been in and out of the bank and on your way home to that young son of yours and I'll have transferred my funds into my own accounts and be long gone," Mikel stated.

"No," Liberty blurted, her fear escalating at the mention of her son. Upset, she glared at them, ignoring their frowns. "I'm missing." She poked a hand against her chest. "It won't go unnoticed. Tomorrow morning when I don't show up, my job is going to call around. I never take off from work. I'm the office manager and everyone knows I take my job seriously."

"Ms. Sutton, relax. If you do as asked, by the time your job starts calling around, as you put it, you'll be on your way home or maybe even at work. All you need to do is cooperate," Mikel added, his voice almost soothing, the sharp edge gone.

"And my son? You won't bother him?" she asked hesitantly.

"I would never harm a child," Mikel said smoothly.

Too smoothly, she decided with a shudder. She couldn't trust him or a word he said. "And Elizabeth, do you mean to hurt her?"

"No. We are going to bring her here, hold her safely tucked away until you finish the job. Then we are going to release you and her," Charles answered before Mikel could reply.

"And what happens then? Mrs. Wilkins is going to be all right. What happens when she fully recovers? She'll know what you've done and you'll have to give the money back and this outrageous plan will have been for nothing."

Mikel laughed at her statement. Her eyes narrowed as she watched him. Charles and Veronica were smiling as well. Where was he finding humor? What were they planning now?

"Well?" she probed, unable to contain her irritation with the trio.

"I'm not worried about my dear old aunt. She won't be able to get one penny back by then," Mikel assured her. "We'll be long gone. So cheer up, you'll be home, Elizabeth will be home, and all will go back to normal."

"Why should I believe you and just do as you say?" Liberty blurted. Pointing to Veronica, she said, "You could silence Elizabeth the moment I sign those papers. And you could be planning to do the same to me the moment I leave the bank. Do you think I'm a complete fool?" Liberty hissed.

Mikel's dark green eyes narrowed. "We need you to get in there and get my money." His voice was like acid as he spoke, his sudden rage proving to Liberty that she had been right to assume he had a temper. "I have no reason to harm you if you do what I want," he continued. "Once you sign the funds to my account,

I'll release you. Of course, I'm going to make sure I'm long gone but you'll be released." Mikel added almost kindly, "If all goes well, you'll be safely home by tomorrow night."

"Fine." Liberty sighed. His rapidly changing moods were disquieting. She was certain that Mikel Wilkins was crazy and impersonating Elizabeth Wilkins an absurd request. She had to escape before they reached New Jersey, just how she was going to do it, she couldn't fathom.

She fingered the envelope, then slowly opened it and began looking at the papers inside. As she pored over the instructions, she saw they were written in big, bold letters as if designed for a half-blind or illiterate person. She became even more dismayed.

She looked closely at Elizabeth's license. There was no denying that she and Elizabeth definitely looked alike. They were very similar in features and age, although Elizabeth's hair was raven black where Liberty's was more of a brown black. Liberty's complexion was honey-almond, Elizabeth was much paler, appearing to have a very light tan. Other than those slight differences, their eyes, noses, and mouths could have made them sisters. As she looked at Elizabeth's pictures, she assumed they were in the folder to help her know how to act. She imagined that Elizabeth was a strong-willed, yet admirable woman. She was the type of woman that Liberty always wanted to be. It saddened Liberty very much to think that Elizabeth could be in serious danger.

"All clear?" Mikel asked when Liberty finally set the papers aside and looked up.

"Yes," she answered. It was perfectly clear that he was insane, but she kept that part to herself.

"Good. Charles, make sure everything is ready. I

want to be out of here in a few hours. I'm going to take a nap," Mikel ordered.

A man of few words, he left Liberty with Charles and Veronica, his attitude clearly stating he expected them to watch over Liberty. After the incident with the back door and the dogs, Liberty was certain they weren't going to leave her alone again.

At his exit, Liberty again took up the papers and slowly pored over the pictures and papers, amazed at the life of Elizabeth Wilkins.

"Watch her, I'll be back," Charles ordered Veronica, then hastened to ensure that everything was ready for their trip to New Jersey.

"Do you have any questions?" Veronica asked dryly.

Liberty looked at her for a brief moment before turning her attention back to the papers. "No," she answered evenly.

"Are you sure? I can be of assistance. Elizabeth and I were friends at one time."

Liberty was surprised by her claim. She dared to ask, "If she was your friend, why are you doing this?"

"Why not?" was Veronica's cocky reply. As an afterthought, she added, "Elizabeth became unpleasant to be around after she was appointed over Zonnick. Charles may not have gone to college but he was good with numbers. But Elizabeth had a plan to hire the best accountants and brokers with credentials a mile long. Charles didn't fit the new image she wanted to create. She fired Charles even though she knew I loved him."

"I see. Love has a strange effect on us, doesn't it?" Liberty murmured, surprised yet again by that little confession.

"Elizabeth loves no one. Just Elizabeth. And maybe her grandmother. That's it, I assure you. We are not going to harm her, if she doesn't give us any problems," Veronica stated with a heavy, weary sigh.

Liberty was quiet. How was she supposed to respond? she wondered as she set the papers aside.

"Are you tired? You can lie down if you like," Veronica suggested as if Liberty were a guest.

Liberty watched Veronica with wary eyes as the woman stood up and stepped aside, silently suggesting that Liberty take over the sofa. Thus far, no one had truly threatened her. She was in no immediate danger. Her biggest danger was reaching New Jersey and signing those papers. Who was to say that she had to cooperate once she was in the company of others? She could tell the bank personnel or security guards, the right glance, the right body language, and any sane person would know something was wrong. Someone could help her.

"Thank you," Liberty said, carefully scooting back on the sofa.

Veronica didn't leave, just stood to the side and stared at Liberty with an almost sympathetic expression. The silence grew between them to the point of discomfort for Liberty. Then Veronica stated in an almost tired voice, "Don't underestimate Mikel or Charles. They are both aware of all the things you could *attempt* to do to escape. They both agreed that if you make any attempts to escape them in New Jersey they may have to resort to desperate measures." Her voice trailed away with the implications of what that could mean before she continued. "I don't want to see you hurt, Ms. Liberty. Be careful. You do want to see your son again."

Veronica allowed a wry smile to spread over her thin lips. Her assumption was too accurate for Liberty's comfort. Then ignoring Charles's command that she watch Liberty, she left.

It was early, yet Liberty was exhausted, her body weak and trembling from the ordeal of staying alert from the moment she was abducted. The room grew dark with evening, and this time Liberty didn't wonder why they allowed her to have so much freedom. With their dogs ready to tear her apart, she didn't dare attempt an escape, at least not through the back door. And despite Veronica's casual disappearance, she had no doubt that they were nearby and would be ready to seize her the moment she even looked at a window or door.

Liberty's eyes closed but she was unable to sleep. She heard every sound, every movement. Her eyes popped open. She wondered what time it was. Carefully, she swung her feet onto the carpet and sat up. She looked around the room, allowing her eyes to adjust to the darkness. She was glancing from wall to wall when she spotted a clock on a counter that divided the kitchen from the breakfast area. But she couldn't see the time from where she sat. With a haste derived from fear, she went to the counter. Amazingly, it wasn't even midnight yet.

She sat on the bar stool and sighed. She was worried about Jamal and if she would ever see him again. Worried about Jarrett and what he must be feeling. Worried how she was going to get out of this mess. It was the oddest situation of her life. And she had certainly been in some bizarre situations.

She was staring into the kitchen, her gaze not focused on anything, when she saw it. Hope sprang up and guided her to her feet. She walked around the counter, her steps careful and quiet, until she approached the phone.

Mildly afraid she could be dreaming, she reached for the phone and picked up the receiver. Never did she expect to receive a dial tone. Never had she been so happy to hear one. Without hesitation she dialed the number to her house, certain that Jarrett would be there. She could barely breathe, barely release a sound, when she heard his voice gruff with worry and exhaustion.

"Oh, my God, Jarrett. Jarrett," she whispered, her voice so low he could barely hear her.

"Liberty, are you all right?" Jarrett whispered, instinctively lowering his voice in response to her hushed words.

"Yes." Liberty assured him hastily.

"Where are you? Did the police find you?" Jarrett asked hopefully.

"No, I'm still with the kidnappers," Liberty answered in a barely audible whisper. The house was so still, she was afraid they might hear her.

"It's that guy, Wilkins, wasn't it?"

"Yes."

"I knew it! Tell me where they have you and I'll get you out of there," Jarrett said firmly.

"You can't. But you have to tell Anthony about this. I don't want anything to happen to Jamal, and they did mention him," Liberty insisted.

"I will. Jamal will be kept safe," Jarrett responded, a lump caught in his throat. She sounded so final and he didn't like it at all. "Tell me where you are, Liberty," he repeated, keeping his panic at bay.

"I don't know but they're going to take me to New Jersey, an Enterprise Bank of New Jersey, I think. They're forcing me to pretend to be Mrs. Wilkins's granddaughter, Elizabeth. It's insane, but they expect me to impersonate her and sign Mrs. Wilkins's trust fund over to Mikel Wilkins. . . ."

"So that's why he sent that ridiculous ransom note demanding five hundred thousand dollars. To keep his real purpose quiet. Did they tell you about the ransom?" Jarrett asked.

"No. They haven't really told me anything accept they want to take Mrs. Wilkins's company or money or something from her."

"She's got that kind of money?" Jarrett asked incredulously.

"Apparently she's loaded, from what I can gather. But listen, Jarrett, I can't stay on this phone. I can't imagine how they could slip with something this important, but I need you to tell the police, get them to Elizabeth Wilkins's house before they take her, too. I wish I could help you more. I got to go. They plan to leave in a few hours and I . . . Jarrett, I'm scared."

"Don't worry, Liberty. We're going to get you out of there," Jarrett promised her, his throat constricted with emotion.

"I have to go. I think I hear something," Liberty said in a soft but serious panic.

"Liberty. When you hang up, dial any number, let it ring at least once, then hang up again. Okay?"

"Okay. And, Jarrett, I love you," Liberty murmured, holding back her tears as she carefully hung up the phone. Holding her breath, afraid that at any moment one of the kidnappers would discover her, she dialed 411, waited until the operator had finished her canned message, then carefully hung up, dreading even the lightest click of the receiver settling on the phone. Standing in alert, she waited again for a sound. When no one appeared, she made haste to return to the sofa and lay as still as she could. After several minutes had passed and no one came, Liberty's heartbeat finally eased to a more normal rhythm and at last she fell into a fitful sleep.

Chapter 14

Jarrett was torn between excitement that he had heard from Liberty and dread that he could not get to her. The police were outside, but he hadn't thought to call them in his excitement. The ransom had not been taken seriously. They all knew it was some kind of a decoy for Mikel. Her hurried explanation of why they kidnapped her was still baffling. They wanted her to impersonate Elizabeth Wilkins? The same Elizabeth that Jarrett had seen with the police? He frowned, coming to his feet. The police were waiting in an unmarked car in the parking lot. He didn't fully trust that they would secure Liberty's safety any more now than before they knew why she was taken. As far as he could tell, they were more concerned about capturing Mikel Wilkins than the welfare of Liberty Sutton.

He was not a policeman, he didn't own a gun, and as passionate as he felt about Liberty, he knew the situation was out of his control. Determined that he would not be left behind, he grabbed his car keys from the counter and left the house.

Officers Thomas and Proctor immediately sat up, attentive as they watched Jarrett approach them. Thomas rolled down the window, but Jarrett ignored it and opened the back door. Both officers turned inquiring gazes on him as he sat down and shut the door.

"Is there a problem, Mr. Irving?" Thomas demanded.

"Yes. I know where my fiancée is. Now, I will not get out of this car or inform you of anything until you say I can come along," Jarrett bartered.

"It isn't safe, Mr. Irving," said Proctor. "If you know anything, just tell us. We'll see that she gets back here safely."

"Can't imagine why, but I have little confidence that you will," Jarrett mocked.

"So where is she?" Thomas asked.

"Not until I know I won't be ditched," Jarrett insisted.

"We can't guarantee your safety," Proctor started carefully.

"Bull! I know how this works. If this was a stakeout and you needed an eyewitness to pull up on a criminal, that eyewitness would be right there with you. I'm going or I'll do this on my own."

Thomas retorted just as heatedly, "You are interfering with the police, Mr. Irving. We will not—"

"Fine," Proctor interrupted, his eyes never leaving Jarrett's face. "You can come along, Mr. Irving, but any interference from you at all and we will handcuff you to that backseat. Understand?"

"Understood," Jarrett readily agreed.

"So where is she?" Thomas asked after a few seconds of silence passed between them.

"I don't know where she is."

"Oh, come on," Thomas huffed, rolling his eyes in irritation.

"But I know where they are taking her," Jarrett continued firmly, ignoring Thomas.

"And that is?" Proctor probed, displaying the patience his partner sorely lacked.

"New Jersey, to a bank by the name of Enterprise. They want Liberty to pretend to be Elizabeth Wilkins. Oh," Jarrett snapped, recalling Liberty's warning, "and Liberty says Elizabeth is in trouble as well. You need to get someone to her place right away."

"I don't get it," Officer Thomas mumbled, considering Jarrett with a sullen gaze.

"The call could have been a hoax created by her kidnapper," Proctor suggested coolly.

"No. It was real. I could barely hear her. She was whispering. That idiotic ransom note was the hoax," Jarrett insisted, fully confident that Liberty's information was accurate.

Officer Thomas narrowed his eyes, looked away from Jarrett, then nodding, started the car.

"We'll get one of the officers to stay at your house, Mr. Irving, in case she calls again. In the meantime, Proctor, get Lieutenant Hoyt on the line. We're going to need help."

Jarrett sat back with his head resting upon the seat and closed his eyes. He could only pray that Liberty had not mistaken Mikel's plans and that they could reach her before she left the bank. He feared for her so much it hurt.

Liberty awakened to the sound of Veronica and Charles talking. She couldn't see them, but their hushed voices indicated that they were near and she could smell that they were drinking coffee. She peeped her eyes open. It was still dark inside the house. The curtains were drawn, but she was positive it was just before dawn. Mikel had said they would leave early. If she was going to swindle a bank, they would want her to arrive as soon as it opened.

She closed her eyes again, Veronica's anger unmistakable as she spoke.

"It won't make a difference," Veronica muttered.

"It will. You got to trust me on this," Charles said.

"Why? Because Mikel thinks it's a good idea? Even if she manages to get through signing the papers without being caught, who is to say that the fraud won't be discovered or the insurance company won't fail to notice that, surprisingly, the only heir to Wilkins-Zonnick received a trustee transfer while old Mrs. Wilkins is in the hospital? How convenient for him," Veronica stated, her flat voice never rising, never losing its monotone beat.

"It's not foolish. Mrs. Wilkins expressed concern over Elizabeth managing such a huge company. She was known to express her concern even when she gave Elizabeth controlling interest and placed her as chairman."

"Chairwoman," Veronica corrected dryly.

"Whatever. Mrs. Wilkins informed John Zonnick just two months ago that she was considering giving Mikel equal or more trustee obligations as Elizabeth."

"And who told you that, Charles? Mikel? If it were true, then why hospitalize her? Why not let her make it easy for him and give him the rights to the company the good old-fashioned legal way?"

"That was the plan, but Mrs. Wilkins found out about Mikel's partnership with me and all hell broke loose," Charles said in a bitter whisper.

"That doesn't explain anything."

"She thought I was some kind of gangster. At first it was funny because it was so ridiculous. But after Elizabeth fired me, Mrs. Wilkins had no doubt about my inabilities. She decided that there was no way she was going to allow the Wilkins name to be associated with the Bronsinis. Mikel and I agreed we had to take matters into our own hands." Charles paused and looked over at Liberty.

She lay still, amazed at the conversation, afraid to let them know she was awake and that she had heard so much. She found it hard not to swallow or take a deep breath.

"So, Mikel didn't like what she thought and clubbed the poor old woman," Veronica concluded.

"Mikel told you before, it was an accident. He didn't mean to hurt her. He was just trying to make her see reason. Hell, I'm not even sure if what he did is really a crime. In fact, from what Mikel has said, he was just defending himself from a crazed old woman. She swung a frying pan at him. Can you imagine that little old woman in a rage?"

"Charles, you weren't even there. And you don't know what I know about Mikel. Things Elizabeth shared with me about why he hates her so much."

"He doesn't hate her," Charles said.

"Yes, he does. And his anger extends way beyond Wilkins-Zonnick. He hates his grandmother, too."

"Like I don't know that," Charles scoffed.

"And the old woman knows it," Veronica continued. "Elizabeth told me that Mrs. Wilkins decided she didn't trust Mikel to head the trust fund. But she didn't leave him penniless. He's so ungrateful, Charles. Look at this house," she huffed. "She bought it for him, set him up with a nice Mercedes, fully loaded. She even ensured that he had a role with Wilkins-Zonnick."

"He deserved it," Charles said, defending him.

"Why? Because the trust was created by his great-grandfather? That doesn't give Mikel automatic rights. She told me that by the time Mrs. Wilkins married his great-grandfather's son, the man had all but diminished the value of the trust. You can imagine how his cousin Zonnick reacted to this. They wanted to cash out, sell the stocks, and sue her husband."

"All this from Elizabeth?" Charles discredited her story by that simple statement.

"She's her granddaughter. You don't think she would know her own family's history?"

"Fine, go on."

"Mrs. Wilkins is a very smart woman, Charles, regardless of what Mikel may feel about her. She restructured the company and eliminated any areas that were not cost-effective. She set up smaller secondary funds with aggressive shares and they grew, and grew and suddenly the fund was worth something again."

Liberty sat perfectly still, not wanting to distract Veronica from relaying her story.

"So his aunt was really smart," Charles said in disgust. "She was still a major bitch and so is her granddaughter."

"I think both you and Mikel hate the fact that she's black," Veronica suggested.

"Not me, and I never heard Mikel say a word about that fact either. But Elizabeth is one hard woman and that transcends any other issue. She deserves everything that's happening."

"I'm not so sure. Do you know who Elizabeth's mom is?" Veronica asked.

"A black woman?"

"Yes, but not just any black woman. Mrs. Wilkins's son fell in love with one of the maids on their estate. He got her pregnant and out came Elizabeth. What makes Mikel so frustrated is that he knows all of this and yet his aunt cared for Elizabeth as if she was more legitimate than he was."

"And he should be angry. While we're sharing, did you know that Mikel's mother was shut out from Wilkins-Zonnick at his aunt's insistence to the board? Her sister-in-law didn't matter, just Anne's granddaughter. Imagine where that left Mikel? Mikel's mother had as much right as Anne to sit on the board, make executive decisions."

"Is it Elizabeth's fault that Mikel's mom didn't protect his interest like Anne protected Elizabeth? I don't think so," Veronica retorted. "Besides, there is only Elizabeth and Mikel. Anne retired. He could have reasoned with Elizabeth, gotten a position on the board instead of taking these drastic measures."

"Well, it's too late. We've got Liberty Sutton now and we can't change our minds because you're having second thoughts," Charles scolded.

Though the story was intriguing, Liberty could not understand how she was involved. If Mikel wanted to keep her silent, he had made a poor choice in his associates. They were just standing there, telling his entire family history. Perhaps they weren't careful because he didn't plan to ever let her go. Her heart was hammering so hard against her chest, she could feel the blood rushing through her veins.

"I'm not having seconds thoughts. I just want you to see reason. I don't know why you are always so quick to believe him. You actually believe our Mikel was so weak that an old woman could beat him down, is that it?" Veronica mocked him.

"She swung her cane at him, too," Charles retorted.

"He should have ducked, then left the house," Veronica stated harshly.

"But he didn't and when he pushed her he had no idea she would take such a serious fall. It wasn't his intention. Believe you me, Mikel needed her with all of her senses. How else could he get the trust? Things would have been a lot better. It was only by a stroke of good fortune that he spotted Liberty Sutton when he left the house. Otherwise, Veronica, we would have no chance at getting Mikel's money back," Charles added.

"That's for damn sure," Mikel chimed in, walking into the kitchen. He had thrown on a T-shirt and jeans and looked much younger than his fifty-one years. He glanced over his shoulder at Liberty and smirked. "You can get up now, Ms. Sutton. We'll be leaving soon."

Liberty started to pretend that she was asleep, then sighed. Releasing a delicate yawn, she stood up and turned to face her captors.

"How much did you hear?" Veronica asked, her expression aghast that she had talked so casually with Liberty just a few feet away. Liberty was amused. Surely the woman hadn't forgotten she was there?

She shrugged and answered, "Just that it was a good thing Mikel saw me when he did."

They were all staring at her now. She hadn't really looked closely at any of them since her arrival, but now she decided they were an odd group of villains, almost comical in fact.

Veronica was short, but standing next to Charles, who must have been six three or more, she appeared even shorter. She was thin and muscular, as if she spent a great deal of time in the gym. Her thick, long blond hair was fascinating, appearing almost as a shroud around the petite woman. Her blue eyes were cold. In fact, Liberty found Veronica's gaze the most unsettling of the three; her eyes were so indifferent. Her beauty was sharp and cold and hard. Her features were pinched, too sharp from her finely plucked eyebrows to her thin pink lips. Liberty decided Veronica was not the kind of beauty that a person admired.

Charles was just the opposite of Veronica. Liberty was amused that for even a moment she could have mistaken him for Mikel Wilkins. Where Mikel was short, stocky, and balding, Charles was tall, lean, and had a headful of unruly brown hair. Charles's gaze was direct and unwavering, just as Veronica's had been; however, his eyes were far warmer than hers although they were just as determined. As she considered him, she realized her first impression was wrong. He was not the crazed monster she had imagined. His hazel eyes would not have been intimidating or unfriendly. Had it not been for where she was and why she was there, she would have considered him almost kind. But then he was a scam artist, Liberty remembered. He would have mastered the art of disguise and learned to show warmth and gentleness where there was none. How could he scam people if they were afraid of him?

And of course there was Mikel, appearing stern and very professional even in his attempts to act menacing. He was no common criminal. She was hard pressed to believe that he even knew what he was doing. But he was no innocent and she would serve herself well not to forget it.

"Are you hungry?" Mikel asked.

Liberty paused in front of him. "No." How could he expect her to eat.

"Coffee then?" he pursued, reaching into the cabinet to get a coffee mug.

"I don't think I can stomach anything this morn-

ing," she answered honestly. She hadn't felt well since
the kidnapping and with each moment that passed
she felt more and more nauseated.

"All right, then, Veronica will show you to the restroom."

"I showed her last night," Veronica interrupted.

"Go with her, Veronica. She will need your help to
look and dress like Elizabeth. I trust you won't try anything foolish like escaping?" Mikel asked, directing his
gaze to Liberty.

"No. I won't try to escape," Liberty confirmed. She
had no reason to try. She had already called Jarrett
and she knew he would be in New Jersey when she arrived. She was confident that he would make sure she
got out of this mess.

She and Veronica had just reached the stairs lead-
ing to the second floor when Mikel shouted in fury.
They both turned, nearly colliding into one another.

"The phone! Who left the damn phone?" Mikel was
so agitated he had turned beet red. Charles stopped
sipping his coffee to stare in dumbfound disbelief at
the offending telephone. Veronica rushed back to the
kitchen with a shaken Liberty a few steps behind her.

"Did you use this phone?" Mikel yelled, the words
more accusing than questioning as he eyed her.

Liberty shook her head, too upset to speak.

"Don't lie! Did you use the phone?" he hissed, picking up the receiver and waving it at her in a fit of rage.
Again, Liberty shook her head, too afraid to tell the
truth for fear that his anger would outweigh his
greed. Mikel scrutinized Liberty for what seemed an
eternity. A sweat broke out across her forehead, but
she refused to back down. She would never admit she
touched the phone, let alone called Jarrett.

Mikel swore softly, then turned to Charles. "Hit redial, Charles," Mikel ordered. Charles picked up the phone and pushed redial. He placed the phone to his ear.

Liberty held her breath. Jarrett's instructions were a blessing. She would never have thought of it and was thankful that she had not ignored him or forgotten in her haste to hang up. She prayed now that it had worked. Had she been thinking, she would have tested the redial herself.

"Information. It's information." Charles shrugged and hung up. Mikel frowned and glared at Liberty.

"You called information?" he asked.

"What? If I had known that phone was here I would have called the police," Liberty retorted calmly. She shrugged, trying to appear unaffected. She wasn't sure if it worked or not. Mikel's eyes narrowed into that now familiar suspicious gaze. Then he scowled and released a grunt.

"Get her ready." With that he turned from them and poured himself a cup of coffee, the stiffness in his back telling her he did not believe her, but she knew he was confounded on how to prove it. The man was no master criminal, he was a spoiled rich brat that never grew up, she decided. All he wanted was his aunt's money, and for that Liberty could only be grateful. Had he been a hardcore criminal, she didn't believe she would have a chance.

She knew he still believed she used the phone, but so long as he couldn't pinpoint where she called, she was safe or as safe as she could be under the circumstances.

Chapter 15

"She's been kidnapped, Carl. We have to do something," Brenda insisted, still incredulous over what she was hearing.

Jarrett had called her over, refusing to tell her what was going on but that it was urgent that she come to Liberty's house. When she arrived the police were outside again and Jarrett was in complete disarray. There was no doubt, in just looking at Jarrett, that Liberty was gone. He looked a mess. He hadn't shaved, his clothes were rumpled, his face a mask of uncertainty. The sight of him was enough to send her into shock.

"Don't worry, Brenda, We're going to get her back," Jarrett said firmly.

"Does Anthony know yet?" Brenda asked, surprised that Anthony wasn't ranting and raving about how irresponsible Liberty was to allow herself to get kidnapped.

"No. I haven't told him," Jarrett admitted.

"Well, why not?"

"Why should I, Brenda?" Jarrett barked in exasperation. "If I call him now, what's he going to do? Nothing. He doesn't need to get involved yet."

"But, Jarrett, he'll find out one way or another. You of all people know how he is. He'll blame all of this on

Liberty, including the fact that he wasn't informed about her kidnapping. Besides, he's going to find out when he brings Jamal back," Brenda insisted.

"I'm hoping Liberty will be safely home by then," Jarrett confessed, his tormented expression causing her to pause.

"Of course," Brenda murmured with a twinge of shame for her lack of similar faith. A brief silence followed before Brenda exclaimed, "I just don't understand, Jarrett. Why would they kidnap Liberty? She doesn't have any money. I mean, it isn't as if she can help them."

"She saw Mrs. Wilkins's attacker." The simple statement was filled with venom and frustration. Jarrett was angry with himself for storming off and not being at Liberty's side the day Mrs. Wilkins was accosted. Never mind that there had been no way that he could have known such an unpredictable event would take place. He should never have lost his temper and left her alone while he sulked like a child. He was angry even more so that he hadn't been able to protect her even when he was by her side. He felt completely helpless and frustrated.

"So they kidnapped her to keep her from talking? That's doesn't make sense. The old lady is going to be all right," Carl suggested.

Both Brenda and Jarrett stared at Carl, their inquisitive gazes expressing their concern. Carl shrugged, wondering why they were looking so confused. "Hey, I'm just saying, if you want to keep someone's mouth shut, you don't kidnap them indefinitely. You knock them off, you know what I'm saying?"

Brenda was furious. Her dark eyes clouded as she put her hands on her hips and, leaning forward, bit out, "Is this your idea of support? Is this how you console people when something happens? That was the poorest example of consoling I have ever, ever witnessed and I am ashamed of you, Carl Smith."

Carl could only gulp in embarrassment and look to Jarrett for help. Jarrett didn't respond. Defeated, Carl quietly walked to the sofa and sat down. It would be wise, he concluded, to keep his comments to himself.

Jarrett dismissed Carl's statement, refusing to believe the worst. He walked to the front door and as he had done so many times before, he opened it and peered into the parking lot. Officer Proctor and two other officers he had not seen before sat waiting in their patrol cars. Jarrett still hadn't heard from Lieutenant Hoyt. He was beginning to wonder if the officers took the information and ran with it. It would be like them to ignore his demand to help get Liberty back.

"We have to get her back, Jarrett. Unfortunately, Carl's words," Brenda said with a sharp glance at Carl, "are frighteningly true. What can we do? Carl? Can you do anything?" Brenda demanded, walking to him with determined square shoulders.

"I can't do anything, Brenda. I'm not an officer and I'm definitely not a federal agent," Carl answered carefully, worried about upsetting Brenda and Jarrett as he had earlier.

"You're head of security for First National Securities. There must be something that you can do. Can't you use your authority to get us into that bank?" Brenda insisted.

Jarrett stopped pacing and considered Carl, his eyes hopeful. It was Carl's turn to pace. He could possibly connect with Enterprise's head of security, convince them to allow him to watch out for Liberty when she came through, and get her out of harm's way once she entered the bank. It could work.

"Please, Carl, give them a call," Brenda pleaded, afraid Carl would refuse to get involved any further.

"Fine, Brenda. I'll call them," Carl relented.

"Will you call them now?"

"There's no time. We need to get on the road," Jarrett said hastily.

Carl frowned. "It's ten at night."

"All the more reason we should go," Jarrett said.

"You can call them while we're on the road," Brenda suggested.

"What can they do before the morning?" Carl protested, overwhelmed at the pace Jarrett and Brenda were making decisions for the three of them.

"Plenty. Let's go now, call your friends at the bank en route and be ready for the bastards when they check in tomorrow," Jarrett insisted, plotting as he spoke.

Carl glanced at Brenda knowing she was in complete agreement with Jarrett. He hesitated, logic causing him to resist their plan. "It's too crazy. We should just tell the police and let them handle this," Carl said.

"The police couldn't handle just watching the house. Had they been able to handle this, Liberty would be here right now!" Jarrett spat out, furious again at how the officers had let Liberty's abduction take place right under their noses.

"We should go then," Brenda suggested, noting Jarrett's fierce expression.

"I suppose we could get the police involved when we get there?" Carl asked, submissively.

"Is that how it works? Do you normally call in the police when you have a problem at the bank rather than use your own security?" Jarrett asked, following Brenda and Carl out the front door. He turned to lock the door as Carl answered.

"Depends on the nature of the problem. Robbery? Yes, we call the police. Fraud? Maybe, depends on the type of scam. Harassment? We handle. Large fund transfer and withdrawal? We handle or the individual will sometimes bring his own security. It just depends on the situation."

"I see," Jarrett said. "We can take my car." He was opening the door for the couple when Officer Proctor approached him. The officers had looked up in curiosity when Jarrett and the couple left Liberty's town house. With a glance at his watch, Officer Proctor said, "Can I help you, Mr. Irving?"

Jarrett paused, his door open. He considered the officer with a slow mocking smile before answering coolly, "Yeah, you can have one of your officers sit inside the house until I get back, in case Liberty calls again." Then he got in his car and shut the door.

Officer Proctor frowned, not sure if he wanted to detain Jarrett or not. He bent over and knocked on the window. Jarrett started the car, then rolled the window down, looking up with a mocking gaze. "Yes?"

"I need to know where you're going, Mr. Irving."

"We're hungry and I need to get a breath of fresh air. We're just going to get something to eat," Jarrett lied, looking directly into the officer's eyes.

Officer Proctor hesitated, then stood up straight and nodded, deciding there was no reason to suspect anything different. If Mr. Irving thought to find Liberty Sutton, he would be turned away, Lieutenant Hoyt had promised that. He shrugged. "Enjoy your dinner."

"We'll try," Jarrett said, then drove away, glancing through the rearview mirror at Officer Proctor.

"Carl Smith, chief security officer, First National Securities. Yes. Yes, six A.M.? Great. See you then." Carl hung up the phone. Jarrett glanced at him. When Carl didn't offer information, Jarrett grew inpatient.

"Well?" he demanded, glaring at Carl.

"Can you please keep your eyes on the road, Jarrett? It's bad enough, your speeding like a madman," Brenda hissed from the backseat.

"What did they say?" Jarrett barked at Carl, ignoring Brenda, although he followed her directions.

"Mark Schmidt will meet me at six A.M. at the bank to go over the situation. They have not heard from Maryland about this case at all," Carl answered, looking at the notes he had taken while on the phone.

"Do you think maybe we have the wrong bank?" Brenda asked.

"Not possible. According to Schmidt, Wilkins-Zonnick's trust is one of their largest accounts. Besides, there is only one Bank of Enterprise in New Jersey."

"You're kidding?" Brenda scoffed.

"No kidding. Schmidt also said he was unaware of any problems with the account."

"That's probably because there are no problems with the account. Mikel just wants the money," Jarrett muttered, glaring at the road as he sped through the night. He could only pray that he arrived at the bank before Mikel Wilkins.

Chapter 16

Liberty kept her face averted as she looked out the window. Her shoulders were sore, her back uncomfortable. She was tired, miserable, and scared, and the ride, although in a plush green Ford Expedition truck, was proving to be long and draining. She sat in the backseat thinking the vehicle was not exactly inconspicuous. Veronica sat beside her, Charles drove, and Mikel sat ramrod straight in the front passenger seat. They had repeatedly gone over what she was to say, how she was to act, and what she was to do the moment the bank doors opened.

Problem was, she was worn out. And she was beginning to feel hunger pains as well, but was too worried she would be sick from the nervousness in her stomach if she ate. How in the world did they expect her to pretend to be this woman Elizabeth and get away with it? It was daft, foolish, and completely unrealistic on their part.

She shifted her gaze to the back of Mikel's seat. He was obviously determined to see his plan through. He was a strange, frightfully ruthless man. This man had attacked his own grandmother for money and was planning or willing to bring harm to his only cousin. There was no reason for Liberty not to conclude that he wasn't capable of quieting her immediately after he received the trust transfer.

She closed her eyes again, imagining Jamal and Jarrett. Wondering what they were doing, if they were all right. She missed her baby. A spontaneous smile played at the corners of her mouth as she imagined Jamal laughing and running through the house.

"Looking forward to acting like a rich woman?" Mikel asked.

Liberty's eyes popped open. "What?" she stammered.

"You were smiling. Are you looking forward to our little tryst or was that a smile of expectant escape?" Mikel asked.

"I was thinking of my house," Liberty said, thinking it was better not to mention Jamal. She mentally thanked Anthony for insisting on keeping Jamal. Realizing now that if something was to go wrong, Jamal could very well be on their radar. She couldn't let that happen. Perhaps she would just cooperate fully and they would let her go. She sighed, not at all assured that it would be that easy, either pretending to be Elizabeth Wilkins or being freed once her signature was on the papers.

"Pull over at the rest stop, Charles. I need a cup of coffee," Veronica demanded, abruptly snapping Liberty out of her thoughts.

"No," Mikel said harshly, glaring at Veronica. "We will not stop until we get to New Jersey. You can get coffee in the city."

"Oh, great," Veronica mumbled. She crossed her arms and stared out the window.

Liberty didn't ask any questions and was careful to keep her expression bland, not wanting to draw Mikel's attention again. She stared at the back of his head much the same as she had earlier, thinking how it had already been a long night. Liberty was certain it was going to be an even longer morning.

"One more time," Mikel said sharply.

Liberty rolled her eyes, groaned, then went back into the bathroom. She stared at her reflection in the mirror. She couldn't believe how different she looked. Veronica had put a ton of makeup on her. Her hair was pinned up high in a tight bun. Her black formfitting skirt suit fit perfectly, the crisp white blouse accenting it well. She was wearing three-inch heels and had been given a black handbag. Veronica had even done her nails in bloodred polish. She was the image of a rich, sophisticated executive. Now she had to act the part.

Taking a deep breath, she put her hand on the doorknob. On the count of three, she swung the door open and strolled into the room. They were in a suite at the Marriott. Mikel had spared no expense in seeing to their comfort. He sat at the bar stool, his gaze expectant as he awaited her return. Charles and Veronica stood side by side, each drinking coffee, waiting.

Liberty walked gracefully and purposely across the room, not stopping until she was only a few steps away from Mikel. She tucked her bag under her arm and extended her hand to Mikel.

"I'm Elizabeth Wilkins. We spoke this morning," she began, her voice smooth and void of any hints of nervousness.

"Yes. Have a seat, Mrs. Wilkins," Mikel said, pretending to be a bank official.

"Thank you. Here is the information you will need.

Can you tell me how long this will take?" Liberty continued, sitting in the seat next to Mikel.

He accepted the envelope she handed him, opened it, looked it over as if he were thoroughly inspecting its contents, then placed it on the bar. "It'll only be a few minutes. I'll have to get you to sign a few papers."

"Wonderful." Liberty smiled.

"I'll be right back."

Mikel walked to the bathroom and went inside. He closed the door and a moment later opened it. He walked back to Liberty and sat down again. Then he pushed papers in front of her.

"This form is a transfer of the trust to your new account. Sign here."

Liberty signed Elizabeth's name to the blank paper, in big bold letters.

"And this form is to authorize your cousin's signature on all future transfers, withdrawals, and extensions. Sign here."

Again, Liberty signed, careful to keep the signature the same, conscious that her hand wanted to automatically sign Liberty Sutton.

"This form is authorizing the bank to automatically transfer trust deposits to your new account via old or outstanding securities. This will also ensure that you continue to gain interest on funds due the trust. Sign here," Mikel added.

Liberty leaned over, pretended to glance over the information, then signed again.

"Thank you, Mrs. Wilkins." Mikel stood and Liberty followed. He reached for her hand and shook it.

"Thank you." Then she walked away and went back into the bathroom and closed the door. A moment later she returned and waited for Mikel's response.

"Well?" Veronica asked when Mikel continued in silence.

"It was better," he muttered, not yet confident that Liberty was believable.

"Did I do something wrong?" Liberty asked.

"No. I just need you to be as thorough and tough as possible. Elizabeth is very, very thorough. And arrogant. Remember that," Mikel added with a disgusted grunt.

"I will," Liberty assured him.

"Well, let's eat," Mikel suggested.

Room service had delivered breakfast during the role-playing, but Mikel wouldn't allow them to eat until they had finished practicing. They sat at the table, weary and exhausted, not just from the long ride into the city, but the worry of what would happen in just a few short hours when they entered Enterprise. No one was more concerned than Liberty.

Chapter 17

Jarrett sat in front of the window, his chin resting on his fist as his eyes stared into the early morning sky. He had not slept since they checked into their hotel. He was fully dressed and ready to leave, to stake out Enterprise in case Liberty showed up early. He was worried and wondered for a moment if he wasn't being too reckless by not confiding in the police.

Holding his hands against the windowsill, he pressed his forehead against the glass and closed his eyes. He was willing to do anything to ensure that Liberty was unharmed. He had no confidence in the police and trusted his own instincts far more. Frustrated, he turned from the window and after a swift glance at the clock left his room. It was time to go.

Brenda frowned at the brisk knock. She glared at the clock and swore under her breath. It was just past five A.M. Carl's meeting wasn't until six. What did Jarrett expect them to do? They had arrived in New Jersey very late and she was exhausted. Another fierce knock and Carl jumped, disoriented and surprised, and turned in an agitated fog before he opened the door.

"You're not ready," Jarrett stated firmly, stepping inside with a disapproving glance from Carl to Brenda.

"We have an hour, Jarrett," Brenda said coolly, sitting up. Fortunately she and Carl had been too tired to do more than remove their shoes.

"We should get going now," Jarrett ordered.

"Why? It won't make time move any faster," Brenda said softly, feeling a rush of sympathy for him.

"How do you know that Mikel isn't sitting in front of Enterprise waiting anxiously for the bank to open? If he's there, I want to be there too."

"And blow everything when he recognizes you?" Carl chimed in.

"He won't see me. You're driving. I'll sit in the back and keep a very low profile. Please," Jarrett pleaded, the word a pitiful growl of desperation. It was enough to bring Brenda to her feet.

"Let's go, Carl. I can't stand to see a man cry," Brenda said lightly.

Jarrett didn't respond. He led them from the room and in subdued silence they left the hotel and headed for the bank.

Mikel didn't miss a thing. He watched with keen interest as the security guard and a businessman in a navy blue suit unlocked the doors to the bank. The streets were empty and the parking lot was void of vehicles, excluding one car that had been there since Mikel arrived with Liberty, Veronica, and Charles.

The doors opened and a moment later, the businessman disappeared, followed by the security guard, who swiftly glanced over the parking lot. Mikel sat up straight, his gaze burning into the door as if he could see inside. He waited, his eyes slowly roaming from the building to the sparse traffic that sped down the road. Finally, he saw what he was looking for. The arrival of Mark Schmidt.

"Wake up. He's here," Mikel hissed to Charles and Veronica. Liberty was awake, having remained in a mute alertness since they arrived two hours earlier. Veronica stretched, then sat back and looked out the window. Charles opened his eyes, having slept ramrod straight. Neither of them said a word as Mark Schmidt walked up to the bank followed by several other businessmen.

"Who are they?" Liberty asked, watching the elder white men form a polite line as the security guard unlocked the door from within.

"The gentleman in the gray suit is Mark Schmidt. He's your target. The other men are just bankers. You have about ten minutes to get confident because we're going in the minute the bank is officially open for business. Understand?" Mikel asked with a stern gaze at Liberty.

"That's why I'm here," Liberty responded flippantly. For a moment Mikel hesitated, his look unsettling. When he turned away, Liberty released a sigh of relief.

"Time," Mikel hissed barely ten minutes later.

Liberty gulped, then with a steady hand, opened her door. She was barely outside the car when Veronica and Charles came up behind her.

"Remember, stay calm. Keep eye contact. And having an air of haughtiness won't hurt," Charles suggested as they headed for the door. Two other customers were walking toward the building. As they reached the door, Liberty paused, uncertain how to proceed.

"Be haughty," Veronica hissed, irritated by Liberty's hesitation.

"Right," Liberty muttered. Then, unable to think of anyone else, she imagined Dominique Greggs, Jarrett's ex-girlfriend and the haughtiest woman she had ever personally met. Within moments she was acting as if she were truly Elizabeth Wilkins. For once, she was thankful to have met Dominique. As they entered the bank, Charles and Veronica casually walked toward the booth while Liberty paused. She looked around until she saw the gated entry near the back of the bank, and with a confidence born of a will to survive she headed over.

Charles and Veronica sat in the waiting area where they were promptly approached by one of the bankers. "Can I help you?" he asked with a bright smile.

"Yes. Can you explain the different savings options you have? I'm also interested in stocks and bonds," Veronica said sweetly, coming to her feet. Charles stood as well, disgusted by the excited gleam that entered the young man's eyes at her question. They both knew that it could take hours for him to provide detailed information on all of the options they could have if they banked with Enterprise. They would only need twenty minutes if all went well. With pasted smiles, they followed the young banker to his desk and sat side by side.

Liberty had not glanced back once they started. She repeated Elizabeth's name over and over until she reached the door. She was about to knock when one of the security guards stopped her.

"Can I help you, miss?" he asked, his old wrinkled face stern and disapproving of her presence.

It took all she had not to be intimidated by his stance and take a step backward. Instead, she put on her haughtiest air and said in a steely voice, "Yes, you can. I am Elizabeth Wilkins. I am here to see Mark Schmidt."

"You'll need to let them know that up at the front, ma'am. No one is allowed back here unescorted," the security officer insisted, unperturbed by her haughty demeanor.

"Excuse me? Escorted? I am the trustee for Wilkins-Zonnick. You open that door this moment and let Mr. Schmidt know I am here!" Liberty stormed.

The security guard didn't move. Instead, he narrowed his eyes, then reached out to grab her arm, intent on escorting her from the bank. Liberty was shocked, uncertain what to do. Mikel hadn't schooled her on the Gestapo security they were using. Just as she was about to open her mouth to protest, the office door opened and Carl appeared. Liberty's mouth fell agape. She was shocked and glanced fearfully around her.

Before she could ask Carl what he was doing in New Jersey at Enterprise, Mark Schmidt appeared. A glance at Carl and she quickly recovered. He winked at her and she knew that Jarrett had found her. She was ecstatic.

"Can we help you, ma'am?" Carl asked smoothly, his eyes burning into Liberty as he prayed she would follow his cue and ask no questions until they were safely behind doors. He had casually noted the white couple glancing their way and he was certain they were a part of the kidnapping.

"Yes, I am Elizabeth Wilkins. I am here to discuss the Wilkins-Zonnick trust," Liberty stammered.

"Right. Of course. Ms. Wilkins. It's wonderful to meet you at last," Mark Schmidt said coolly, his glance at the security guard a silent order to release Liberty. With a disgruntled look, the guard let go and watched as she followed Mark with Carl behind into Mark's office. She nearly released a yelp of joy when she saw not only Brenda but Jarrett standing by Mark's desk. She ran to Jarrett and held on to him with a grasp full of longing. "My God, Jarrett. You're here. I thought I was never going to see you again," Liberty cried.

Jarrett returned her embrace, his hold even firmer, leaving her breathless. But Liberty didn't mind.

"Are you all right? Did they hurt you? Where are they?" Jarrett burst out, holding her away from him so that he could stare into her face.

"They're outside. But I'm all right, just shook up. They didn't hurt me, although I'm sure they would have had I finished the job for them," Liberty answered.

"You'll finish the job, Liberty, but this time we'll be here to see you safely home," Carl said.

"What? Are you crazy?" Liberty retorted. She stared from Carl to Jarrett, then to Brenda, and shook her head. "I have no idea what the three of you are planning, but I am not going to go back now. I can't. You can't take my hope now."

"Don't panic, Ms. Sutton. We do have a plan," Mark Schmidt said soothingly.

"Really? And what could that be?" Liberty asked caustically.

"You are to move forward with their request, take them the papers, and we will be right behind you. You'll be safe," he said with an air of confidence that did not reach Liberty.

"No. I will not continue with this charade. Just arrest the creeps. I'll testify," Liberty insisted.

"We can't," Mark said.

"Why not?" Liberty asked testily.

"Because the real Elizabeth Wilkins is missing,"

Brenda chimed in, walking to Liberty and taking her hand.

Liberty shuddered, a ripple of shock staggering any retort she could think of. She had forgotten about Elizabeth Wilkins. Mikel had kept his word.

"Since when?" Liberty whispered.

"About the same time you called me, Liberty. We found out just after arriving here," Jarrett answered, brushing Brenda aside to hold Liberty. "And don't worry, Liberty. The New Jersey police are within the perimeter of the bank. Mr. Schmidt has informed them of the situation. I don't like the idea of you continuing with this charade any more than you do, but you are Elizabeth Wilkins's only hope. The police need you to throw off Mikel and guide them to Elizabeth."

"As if he would tell me what he did with her," Liberty muttered.

"Perhaps. But if he thinks he has won, his actions and maybe some information from you may lead us to her. We need your help, Ms. Sutton," Mark added.

"She's not far. If Mikel wasn't lying, she's at his home," Liberty said calmly.

"His home?" Mark repeated, incredulous.

"Yes. I don't suppose he thought I would have an opportunity to divulge his plans. I heard him talking about his intentions to hold Elizabeth hostage until I signed over the trust to him," Liberty stated. There was a strong chance that Mikel had not yet harmed her. After all, if Liberty failed in her fraud attempt, he would have little to no chance of ever getting one cent of his money, especially with a warrant out for his arrest for attacking his own grandmother. No, he needed Elizabeth alive for backup, if nothing else.

Knowing that Elizabeth's life could very well be in her hands gave her a sense of duty and courage.

"Carl's working with the bank security, Liberty. He won't let you get hurt," Brenda whispered, rubbing a reassuring hand over Liberty's back. She was slightly irritated that Jarrett wouldn't let Liberty go, although she fully understood his passion.

"You're only saying that because you're in love with him," Liberty huffed, standing up straight to look at Brenda. Brenda smiled, not offended by Liberty's accusation.

"True, but he's a great cop."

"Securities chief. I am no cop," Carl insisted, but then added at Liberty's aghast glance, "But I do work with law enforcement all the time—"

Mark interrupted, having shown patience as long as he could. "We don't have much more time. Ms. Sutton, I need you to do whatever it is you're supposed to be doing. They'll grow suspicious if you don't get back soon."

"Well, I am supposed to transfer the Wilkins-Zonnick funds to these." She handed him the transfer information that Veronica had given her just before leaving the hotel. "And I need to sign over transfer, withdrawal, and exchange signatures to Mikel. The insurance should also be handled by Mikel. I think that's all. Everything is in that folder. I need the entire folder back. I was given explicit instructions not to give it to you but to use it in order to know what exactly to ask for," Liberty finished breathlessly.

"Fine. Fine. This looks in order. I'll be right back," Mark said after reviewing the papers. He handed the folder to Liberty, then left them in his office.

The door had barely closed when Brenda walked over to Liberty and pulled her into a second hug.

"I was worried sick about you," Brenda whispered in her ear. Liberty's eyes watered, but she held back from crying. "So was I."

They both laughed. Jarrett stood aside, allowing Brenda her moment. But his eyes never left her. His searching gaze had hungrily etched over every inch of her since she arrived. He wanted nothing more than to race out of the bank and take Liberty safely back home. It was disheartening and frustrating to know that not only was another woman's life in danger, but Liberty would not be truly safe until Mikel Wilkins's plans were seen through and were able to be thwarted.

"I feel as if I am in a weird dream or daze. It's all so unbelievable. I can't believe people actually have the nerve to kidnap people and try something like this," Liberty confessed, slowly pulling away from Brenda.

"Oh, they do. And worse, I'm afraid to confirm," Carl chimed in. Brenda shot him a narrowed glance.

"I'm sure," Liberty agreed.

"It'll be over soon. You'll be under severe surveillance the moment you leave the bank," Jarrett said firmly, turning a warning glance on Carl. Arrangements had been made by Carl and Mark to ensure that Liberty's well-being was watched at all times. All Liberty had to do was remain calm and follow through.

"All is taken care of," Mark Schmidt said as he entered the office. He closed the door, then handed Liberty a manila folder. "All signed and legal transfers from Elizabeth Wilkins to Mikel Wilkins are done. All you need to do, Liberty, is give the folder to Mikel. Explain to him that everything went smoothly. He will need to meet with Enterprise Securities and the finance vice president within three days of the exchange to make it all legal and bonded. That should ensure his confidence that nothing is amiss."

"Then what? How do I get away?" Liberty asked.

"You'll be followed. Are you heading back to the hotel or Maryland?" Carl asked.

"I don't know. He never said. Although I am sure he plans to go back to his house. That's where she is," Liberty added.

"We'll be behind you, Liberty," Brenda assured her.

"What does that mean? How am I going to get away?" Liberty demanded, growing a little hysterical with their lack of clarity.

"Mikel will be arrested the moment we see Elizabeth."

"And what if you don't see Elizabeth before he—" Liberty couldn't finish. She was barely able to ask the question, so dreadful were her thoughts.

"We'll be there, for you and Elizabeth. Trust us," Carl insisted. She glanced from Carl to Brenda to Jarrett. Their eyes locked but she knew he too trusted Carl's plan. She was Elizabeth's only hope.

"Great plan," Liberty muttered at last, then holding the folder close to her chest, she took a deep breath and nodded at Carl. He opened the door.

Veronica released a heavy sigh of relief the moment she saw Liberty walk with a firm, bold strut from the banker's office. She and Charles watched, tuning out the clerk, as Liberty left the bank. A moment later, Veronica stood up, followed by Charles, and with a brusque thank-you, informed the clerk they would get back to him. With a disappointed gape, he watched as the couple left.

"How did it go?" Charles asked, barely having

closed the door behind him as he got into the backseat.

"Like I was Elizabeth Wilkins," Liberty answered calmly.

Mikel didn't fail to notice the shaking of her hand as she handed him the folder. Their eyes locked for a moment, then Mikel slowly opened the folder and perused the contents. His face remained expressionless as he shifted from one page to the next. When he was done, he closed the folder with a light snap. He tucked it on the side of his seat, then started the car.

"Everything in order?" Charles asked after Mikel failed to provide the information on his own.

"Looks like it," Mikel answered cryptically.

"Then we can let Elizabeth go?" Veronica asked carefully.

"Not quite. In three days. Then we'll see," Mikel added, glancing at Veronica through his rearview mirror.

Chapter 18

The police had been notified of Mikel Wilkins's expected exit from New Jersey and his impending arrival back to his suburban home. According to Carl, Mikel's fate was all but fulfilled. He had little to no chance of escaping the authorities.

Jarrett was not so confident. The woman he loved was being held prisoner by a madman. He was not feeling too confident about anything just yet. Now that she knew they were near, would she be able to pull through? Would her calm help her or make her kidnappers suspicious? His eyes flashed with worry for Liberty's safety.

He took a deep breath and tried to relax. It would do no one any good if he had a car accident and got himself or someone seriously injured. With a heavy sigh, he slowed down and attempted to have faith in the officers. But never for a moment did he lose sight of the Expedition. Just three cars ahead of him, he could clearly see Liberty sitting in the passenger's seat.

The mood in the car was surprisingly somber for a group who had just pulled off a scam worth millions of dollars. Liberty had a sense of unease. Why weren't they at the bare minimum smiling? she wondered. Refusing to look at any of them as they sped down the freeway, she felt her only consolation was in Jarrett's presence. Though she had not looked back, she could feel his presence a few cars behind them. She was confident that he had not abandoned her.

Time ticked dispassionately onward. Incredibly, what should have been at least a six-hour drive was a little less than four when the green Expedition pulled into the driveway of Mikel's home.

It was Liberty's first glance backward since leaving New Jersey. She remained carefully expressionless even as Jarrett's vehicle slowly passed by the house. She couldn't do a thing about the crazy pounding of her heart as she spotted Brenda and Carl slowly park a few houses away. Mikel opened the door, his lazy confidence surprising to Liberty. She would have thought he would glance around him before entering his home. He hadn't so much as looked back.

When they entered the house, it was cool and dark, although it was just past three in the afternoon. The heavy brown curtains and all of the shutters had been drawn closed. Veronica casually and with nimble familiarity opened the curtains and shutters as Charles escorted Liberty back to the sofa she had so recently slept on.

She sat still for several moments, watching as Veronica brought glasses from the kitchen and Charles began cooking. They weren't talking and she could only wonder what they were thinking. Mikel had disappeared, as had the folder. She began to worry.

Minutes ticked away into hours, and with a start, Liberty realized she had fallen asleep. She opened her eyes and Mikel, as if in a dream, was sitting across from her, his gaze curious as he considered her. Liberty sat up straight and returned his gaze, careful not to say a word, not sure what he was thinking.

"Tell me what happened in the bank," Mikel said finally.

"Nothing out of the ordinary that I could see. I went inside, informed the clerk that I needed to see Mark Schmidt, and they took me right to him," Liberty answered carefully.

"And?" Mikel prompted.

Liberty shrugged. "And I told him who I was and what I wanted and he readily agreed. No questions asked."

Mikel was silent. He continued to stare at her. Liberty returned his gaze although she was beginning to fear he knew or at least suspected that Schmidt knew everything. She would not divulge anything. Her life and Elizabeth Wilkins's life, depended on it.

Liberty anxiously waited as Mikel walked to the island in the kitchen. He opened the envelope and meticulously spread out the papers from the bank. He scrutinized every page, carefully analyzing the signatures. Liberty held her breath, praying that she had not somehow slipped up. The way he was looking at the papers she was beginning to feel he could have somehow discovered her secrets.

Mikel bent over the papers, his back to Liberty. Charles and Veronica stood to the side, waiting patiently for Mikel to finish. After a few minutes he finally raised his head. He glanced from Charles to Veronica, then slowly turned around. His eyes fell on Liberty. She caught her breath. His gaze left her cold. She couldn't read into his expression.

"You did good," he finally stated, his voice casual.

Liberty swallowed, the relief she felt overwhelming. He took slow deliberate steps toward her. When he was standing less than a foot away, he paused, shoved his hands in his pockets, and offered her a half smile that could only be described as a smirk.

"There's just one problem," he murmured.

Liberty's heart dropped. She knew it would be too easy for him to simply let her go. *What now?*

"There is?" she managed to gasp from her constricting throat.

"If we could trust you to just walk out of here and never look back, everything would be okay. But we can't, can we?" he asked, as if he were speaking more to himself than Liberty. "We can't take the risk that you will not run straight to the police and hinder our exit," he continued. He sat in the chair across from her. Leaning forward, he observed her behind a steely gaze. Charles and Veronica were watching her as well.

"Of course you can. I promise," she whispered frantically, not understanding his intent. Her eyes fluttered from Mikel's dubious gaze to Charles's and Veronica's sympathetic eyes. "I promise," she repeated.

"Well?" Charles finally demanded when Mikel remained silent.

"Exactly. Well, what now?" Mikel asked caustically. He had an air of controlled excitement as he stood and turned his back to Liberty. She could not see his face as he said, "We have what we want. It's over. Let her go."

Charles glanced at Veronica. Veronica frowned slightly but quickly regained her apathetic position when she caught Liberty's gaze. Liberty frowned without restraint. She wasn't sure if she trusted his carefree discharge. As she came to her feet, it suddenly dawned on her that he had not mentioned Elizabeth. What of her? Was she to be set free now, too? Liberty couldn't fathom that they would release one without the other.

"And Elizabeth?" Liberty found herself asking. The words were out before she could control them. She had to know. She couldn't just walk away, not without knowing Elizabeth's fate. Mikel had started toward the stairway when she came to her feet. He paused in midstride at her question. She waited, forcing herself not to hold her breath in her anxiety. He didn't turn around, and for what felt like an eternity the room was perfectly still. His back was stiff and with a growing sense of worry she watched his shoulders square even more as he continued up the stairs without responding.

"Is she here? In this house? You can't hurt her. You promised," Liberty called, furious that Mikel might harm Elizabeth after she had done everything he had asked. He turned and his gaze locked directly with hers. It was as powerful as actually being touched. She actually took a step back, then stilled herself, waiting determinedly for a response from him.

"Elizabeth is fine, Ms. Sutton."

"How can I believe you?" she whispered, unable to accept his answer as an honest one.

"Ms. Sutton, I suggest you accept your dismissal as your good fortune," Mikel said with finality. "Veronica, Charles, you know what needs to be done," he added coolly, dismissing any further conversation.

She barely had a moment to digest what his words meant before he disappeared down the hallway. She wanted to slap him silly, but instead she allowed her gaze to stray from him to lay warily on Veronica, who was easily approaching.

Liberty's eyes narrowed and her mouth opened in

an unspoken question. She was about to speak when Veronica murmured, "Now, just take it easy."

Charles grabbed her arms and with deft expertise, she was blindfolded. Liberty's protests were quickly muted as Veronica covered her mouth with a thick strip of tape.

Caught off guard and unprepared for the assault, Liberty felt her body go weightless as Charles lifted her from the floor. She felt trapped and wanted to thrash in a panic. She remained perfectly still, holding on to him. She wasn't sure but she felt as if they were going up the stairs. *But where?* she wondered wildly. In a matter of moments, she was set back on her feet. Just as quickly she was pressed downward until she was sitting on the floor.

"Remain calm, Liberty. Do not remove the blindfold. Mikel is going to send someone to get you and everything will be well. In the meantime, relax," Veronica whispered in her ears.

She heard Charles's loud footsteps leave the room, then the clicking of Veronica's heels as she followed. The door snapped closed and she heard the lock. Immediately she could sense that she was alone. She wasn't sure what frightened her more, the darkness behind the blindfold or the unknown. She was confused. Why had they blindfolded her? She had been in the house already, seen it clearly. Maybe they just wanted to intimidate her, make her too frightened to act. Well, it worked. She wasn't going to make a move until she was sure she was alone. Then she remembered the dogs and stiffened. Were those crazed dogs in the room with her? Fear made her bold. She snatched off the blindfold.

She looked around her cramped confinement and realized she was in another room. There was no window, not a single slit for light. She wasn't sure if it was kindness or forgetfulness on her host's part, but they had left the lamp on the nightstand beside the bed, a tray of crackers, cheese, and fruit on a platter, a pitcher of water, and a book. A book? How long did they plan to leave her in the room?

Her shoulders slumped, her legs were heavy with exhaustion and sheer defeat as she sat on the edge of the bed.

Veronica had whispered that they would send someone to her. It had only been minutes after Mikel left that she was blindfolded and brought to this room. She grimaced. The room was cozy enough but it was still a prison, not bigger than her son's room. Still, who would build a house with a room without windows on purpose? She would have not felt so helpless if there were a window. The only exit was the door and she suspected that if she were somehow able to get it opened, she would come face-to-face with either Charles or Veronica.

She stood up, pacing the small space in agitation. She wondered how long it would take before they left the house. And why leave her in Mikel's home? Suppose it was not his, but Charles's home or Elizabeth's? Maybe that was their plan. Send someone for her and maybe even Elizabeth. Maybe, she thought, feeling a surge of excitement, just maybe Elizabeth was also in the house, in a room similar to her own. Tentatively she walked toward the door. She took a deep breath, then slowly put her hand on the knob. She held her breath. No one came barging into the room. Ever so carefully she twisted the knob, turning it fully as she attempted to open it. It was locked. Her hand dropped away and she leaned her forehead against it.

She would have to wait and pray that Veronica's last words to her were the truth.

The police notified Jarrett that Mikel had somehow slipped through the airport without a trace; Jarrett didn't know what to think. After all, he had watched with his own eyes as Mikel, Liberty, and two other people, a man and woman, had left the house, gotten into Mikel's car, and headed for the airport. They had followed. In what was a deliberate attempt to create confusion, the unknown woman first got out of the car before they pulled into the parking zone. The unknown man got out of the car the moment they went through the gate to receive a parking pass. Finally, Mikel and Liberty parked, after circling the garage for several minutes. They got out of the car and walked casually from the parking lot to the airport ticketing center. They had just approached the ticket counter when without any warning, they made an abrupt turn and got out of line and hurried toward the exit.

There was a huge onslaught of arrivals. Jarrett had sensed with rising panic that Mikel was out for the slip. What he hadn't understood at the time was why Liberty was assisting Mikel's efforts, without any signs of resistance. When the couple was able to lose themselves in the crowd, they exited the main hall down the escalators. Jarrett was incensed.

He nearly created a scene, his emotions were so volatile and on the brink of exploding. Before he could react, Carl had raced up to him, pushing through the crowd, and whispered urgently, "It wasn't Liberty with him, Jarrett. I just spoke to the police on my cell phone."

"What?" Jarrett bellowed, his boisterous response

bringing a multitude of curious stares. He ignored them, his gaze full of disbelief as he stared at Carl.

"It wasn't Liberty with him. She was a diversion. Liberty is somewhere in the house. We need to get back," Carl added.

"How do you know? Have you lost your mind?" Jarrett demanded, frowning fiercely at Carl.

"The police found a note. She's somewhere in the house. They claim she's unharmed," Carl added carefully.

"The house?" Jarrett asked dumbly.

"His house. Mikel's," Carl responded. "His note promises she's alive and well. We need just find her and free her. She's warm and safe, the note said," Carl said reassuringly.

His words did nothing to relieve the cold chill Jarrett was experiencing. He was getting more and more frustrated. He must have been out of his mind. Of course he knew something wasn't right in the way Liberty was acting, but he had not gotten close enough to really get a good look at her. He turned around, looking for the nearest exit.

Carl didn't have to ask to know where Jarrett was racing off to. Carl shook his head. He recalled meeting Jarrett when he and Brenda first married. Jarrett was calm, suave even, never temperamental. Carl found Jarrett's fierce demeanor slightly unnerving and knew that if Jarrett got his hands on Mikel, no one would be able to pry him loose. Hastily he hurried after Jarrett. "Hey, Jarrett!" Carl called, but Jarrett didn't respond. He nearly knocked a couple into the seats as he pushed his way through the crowd of people. Carl grimaced, pushing past the crowd with an apologetic glance left and right as he raced to catch up. Huffing, he attempted to soothe Jarrett as they jogged the rest of the way to the parking lot. "The note says she's unharmed."

"Yeah, sure. Like Mrs. Wilkins? The man kidnapped her. Why should I trust his note?" Jarrett demanded.

"You know, police are already at the house. They left behind two officers when we followed Mikel here," Carl said carefully.

"The police are idiots. This whole situation should never have happened," Jarrett scoffed.

Carl held on to the door handle the entire ride back to Mikel's. Brenda had waited in the car and was shocked and worried to see Jarrett and Carl running back to the car. She reached in the front seat and unlocked the door, asking the moment they got in the car, "What? What is it? What happened?"

"Liberty was left at the house. We're going back," Carl explained as he snapped on his seat belt. Brenda had barely sat back when Jarrett jerked the car into gear and raced out of the parking lot.

"Be careful, Jarrett. It won't do Liberty any good if we get into an accident."

Carl looked back at Brenda, making sure she was buckled in. Jarrett ignored them both, his gaze straight ahead as he sped at eighty-plus miles per hour down the freeway. He was completely unaware of his frightened passengers' desperate hold on the doors as he weaved in and out of traffic. Brenda thought she was going to be sick by the time they pulled up to Mikel's house.

When they arrived, the police, as Carl had stated, were already in the house and there were shouts being called that they had found Liberty. Jarrett pushed his way through the crowd of officers.

"Liberty? Where is she?" Jarrett asked, running up

to Officer Thomas. The desperation on his face caused the officer to have mercy on him.

"She's fine. She was left in a pretty plush prison," the officer said, attempting humor.

His words did not sit well with Jarrett. *Prison! They had locked her away in a cell?* Turning from the officers toward the commotion coming from the stairway, he watched as Liberty was led down the stairs. When her eyes fell on him, they lit up and Jarrett felt a surge of pleasure and relief at her brightened expression. She paused as did he. It was as if they were the only two in the room. Then she broke into a wide smile and released a slight gasp as she brushed past the officers and ran straight into Jarrett's arms. He held her, his arms wrapped around her waist.

"Jarrett, I'm so happy to see you. I was so worried," she murmured. "He got away, didn't he?" she asked, pulling away to stare into his eyes as if she would discover the truth there.

"Don't worry about him," Jarrett insisted, gently laying her head back on his chest. "You're safe now and the police will find Mikel."

She sighed against him, closing her eyes as she allowed his warmth to soothe her.

"You're right. I'll let the police deal with Mikel. I just want to go home," Liberty whispered, his mouth softly grazing his neck as she spoke against him. Jarrett suppressed a need to kiss her then and there.

"Soon. Let the police do their job and then we'll get out of here," Jarrett assured her. He led her to the sofa, then sat beside her and waited for the police to finish their search of house. Holding her close to him, he gently caressed her arms as they waited, content to know that at last they were together and safe.

Chapter 19

Brenda leaned her head on Carl's shoulder. His arms encircled her waist, then he gave her a reassuring squeeze. He knew Brenda was upset about Liberty's state. But his Brenda would never show what she considered to be undignified emotions. What he loved about her also exasperated him. She was not inclined to hysteria or sudden outbursts. Even now, when her best friend lay weak and obviously exhausted from her long ordeal, Brenda remained calm and decisive.

He glanced at her and their eyes caught. Her tight expression was the only clue of what she was going through. She was worried about Liberty, and Carl wanted only to comfort her.

Brenda was grateful that Carl was there. She wanted to shake Jarrett. Throughout the entire ordeal of having to watch and follow Liberty, Jarrett had proven to be, not the sophisticated, calm, impressionable man Liberty claimed he was, but aggressive, irate, and completely out of control too. She understood his fears and worry, but he had nearly caused them to lose Liberty, and for that she was having a difficult time forgiving him.

Brenda didn't want to interrupt Jarrett but she wanted desperately to go to Liberty. She looked at

Carl and whispered, "I don't know whether to feel happy or sad right now. She looks so weak."

Carl patted Brenda's hand. "She's fine. It's been a long day for all of us," he said, consoling her.

"A longer day for Liberty, I'm sure." Brenda sniffed, fighting back tears of relief.

Carl heard her, but knowing his Brenda, he pretended not to notice the tears welling in her eyes. He said with what appeared to be a flippancy, "It isn't as if she didn't know we would find her. We told her we were following her."

Liberty sat with her head resting on Jarrett's shoulder. The police wanted to have her examined by medics. Why, she couldn't fathom. She was fine. No one had touched her, drugged or even tied her up, she informed them. They only wanted her to be an imposter and then they left her. Her biggest scare was not knowing if they would really leave her unharmed. Still, she allowed the medics to examine her and give her a clean bill of health. She was just plain exhausted and they suggested rest. She could have told them that. She only nodded in appreciation.

Now she stretched out on the sofa, her head resting tiredly against the pillows, Jarrett sitting beside her. The warmth from his body was comforting and she wished she could snuggle up beside him.

"I knew you would come, Jarrett," she said, forcing her eyes open as she spoke.

"I just wish I had been here earlier. They duped us," he added in an apologetic groan.

"It isn't your fault. Besides, you're here now," Liberty responded gently.

"No thanks to the police," Jarrett said, glancing at the officers in the room with disdain.

Jarrett held Liberty close to him, the thudding of

his heart a welcome sound from the hours of silence she had experienced. She was too exhausted and too relieved to move. Her only thought was that she was safe and back with Jarrett.

The next few hours sped by with a flurry of activities. Detectives were all over the house. Jarrett never left Liberty's side. He sat with her cuddled in his arms and gently stroked her shoulder as she answered question after question for the detectives, leaving a sense of déjà vu. Through it all, Jarrett watched with an impatient scowl as they searched the house over and over, looking at the same spots and repeating the same questions to Liberty. They were a mass of confusion, Jarrett decided.

Two hours later he had had enough. He was getting Liberty out of the house. He stood up and gently lifted her into his arms. She had dozed during a lull in the officers' questioning.

A detective halted Jarrett. "Just a moment, Mr. Irving."

Jarrett glared at the detective but did not offer a response. The detective cleared his throat and asked pointedly, "Where are you taking Ms. Sutton? We're not done yet."

"Home. She's tired and your questions can wait until she's rested," Jarrett answered in an authoritative voice.

"Sir, your interference is understandable but we need her to find out where Mikel has gone," another officer chimed in.

"And she will cooperate. But not right now." Without further delay, Jarrett strutted out of the house with Liberty clinging to him. The lieutenant kept the officers from stopping him. They knew where to find Liberty Sutton if they needed her help.

Chapter 20

Liberty awoke to a slight headache. Her eyes adjusted slowly as she sat up, covering her eyes from the midday sun. She realized she was at home, alone in her bedroom. She sat still, listening for voices or any sound. She heard nothing. Carefully she came to her feet. As she stood, she realized that she had been changed from the rigid suit she had worn as Elizabeth Wilkins into a comfortable pair of pajamas. A pleased smile curved her lips. Jarrett was loving to have changed her. She couldn't wait to see him, to finally tell him what she'd been trying to tell him for days. She would marry him. It was a long overdue yes, she knew, but better late than never.

She flung the bedroom door open and headed down the stairway. She was on the last step when she heard Jarrett's muffled but clearly angry voice. She peered carefully around the corner, expecting to see more police officers. The family room was bare. Not a soul in sight.

The kitchen was empty as well. *So where is Jarrett?* She frowned and turned in the other direction toward the dining room. She paused just inside the doorway, noting with growing alarm that Jarrett was swearing into the receiver of the telephone. Every instinct in her told her something was definitely wrong.

Mikel Wilkins had gotten away. They still had not found him, she was sure of it. Would he dare attempt to kidnap her again? She was about to call out to Jarrett when she heard Jamal's name. She froze. What about Jamal? She didn't move as she listened keenly to Jarrett's words.

"And tell her what? Jamal had not—" Jarrett cut off his next words when he felt Liberty's presence. He raised his gaze and looked with obvious distress at Liberty.

She shook her head and whimpered a desperate "no."

"Liberty." Jarrett whispered, standing up.

She took a step back and asked in a desperate voice, "Please, Jarrett. Tell me they didn't take Jamal? Tell me he's all right."

"We believe he is," Jarrett responded.

At his words, Liberty burst into frustrated tears. It was true. They had kidnapped Jamal, although she had done nothing wrong. She had done everything they ordered her to do. Why had they taken Jamal?

"Liberty, it's going to be all right. We found you and we'll find Jamal too," Jarrett tried to reassure her. He pulled her carefully from the floor and held her sobbing body close to him.

"Why?" she cried. "Why did they take him? Where was Anthony?"

"They have Anthony, too," Jarrett confessed grudgingly.

Liberty froze, then pulled free of Jarrett so that she could stare up at him. "What?" she asked in overwhelming disbelief.

"I don't understand," Liberty said softly, shaking her head in frustration.

Jarrett sighed and hesitated.

Liberty swallowed and considered him, waiting with forced patience as he found the words to tell her more bad news.

"I want to be the one to tell you why," he began carefully.

At his words, Liberty blinked, baffled by what he meant.

"Tell me what? What else is there, Jarrett? Just say it," Liberty insisted, losing all patience.

"We switched the papers before you left the office," he blurted, the pained expression on his face confirming he spoke the truth.

"You switched the papers?" Liberty asked. Exhausted with the shock of hearing that her son had been taken, then his father, and now that she had been duped by the very people who claimed to love her, Liberty walked slowly from the dining room to the family room. She sat on the corner of the sofa and stared in defeat at her clasped hands.

"Liberty, you've got to understand. It was the only way we could be sure that you didn't disappear without a trace. The papers were marked. Noted for forgery where only bankers would know the distinct mark. We had no idea that they would move so quickly. I warned Anthony to hide. He's such a fool," Jarrett added furiously.

"So am I. I trusted you," Liberty murmured.

"Liberty," Jarrett moaned, sitting beside her. He held her hand and whispered, "I knew the risk, I won't lie. I knew what could happen when they found out about those papers, but it was worth the risk to make sure you were safe."

"Worth the risk to whom, Jarrett?" Liberty bit out, turning her dark gaze on him. "He's my son, Jarrett. I would give my life for him. *My* life. How dare you *choose* to risk my child's life? How dare you make such a decision?"

"Liberty, you make it sound as if I don't care about Jamal."

"You only care about you. All of this is about you. Not me or Jamal. You had me fooled, congratulations!" Liberty snapped, then fiercely stood up and stormed away.

"You're wrong, Liberty. I love Jamal, believe it or not. I love him as if he were my own child."

"That's impossible. Your actions have proved otherwise. Just leave, Jarrett. Get out," Liberty hissed, then raced up the stairs before he could see the torrent of tears that spilled from her eyes.

Jarrett stared up the stairway, a look of pain and defeat weighing him down. He had known that Liberty would be angry. He never imagined she would want him to leave because of it. Sullen, he grabbed his keys and stormed from the house. Even in his frustration, however, he took a moment to note that there were detectives posted outside Liberty's door.

Jarrett drove recklessly. He wasn't even sure where he was headed until he unwittingly pulled onto Anthony's street. There were still several police cars parked in his driveway and in front of his house. Jamal's grandmother was standing on the front porch talking with one of the officers. Anthony and Jamal had been taken in early predawn hours. Jarrett whispered a desperate prayer that whatever happened, Jamal would be returned safely to Liberty. She had been through so much over her son, the last thing she needed was to lose him when she had only just found him.

"Jarrett." Jamal's grandmother called, a slight catch in her voice as if she had been crying.

"Mrs. Yogan," Jarrett responded coolly. He was no more fond of the stately Mrs. Yogan than he was of her son-in-law. Her light brown eyes stared up at him with the first sign of vulnerability he had ever seen in her. It was a bit of a shock to his system to realize that she was trusting him to see her grandchild returned safely. He felt a pang of guilt for allowing his own prejudices to blind him to her pain.

"They've heard from Mikel Wilkins. He's demanding money, Jarrett. He won't accept less than twenty-five million dollars. Is he insane?" she scoffed. The idea that anyone would actually expect to receive that type of money was preposterous to her.

"Yeah, he is," Jarrett answered flatly. "I believe," he added consolingly, "that that is the amount of the trust he tried to embezzle. He's expecting the police to give him money from the trust. So don't worry."

"Where is Liberty?" Mrs. Yogan asked just as Officer Proctor came out onto the porch.

"She's on her way here," Proctor answered, lighting a cigarette as he looked down the street.

"On her way here? Why?" Jarrett demanded, instantly riled by the officer's casual attitude.

"The lieutenant asked for her, Mr. Irving."

"Why?" Jarrett repeated.

"He wants to talk to her, ask her some more questions."

"And he just couldn't wait a few hours, right?"

"No. He can't, Mr. Irving. You see, Mikel wants the money delivered by Liberty Sutton only." Proctor confessed.

"What?" Jarrett shouted, enraged. He stormed into the house, Proctor behind him. "Where's the lieutenant?" Jarrett demanded.

"He's not here yet. Just calm down, Mr. Irving,"

Proctor advised. "The lieutenant won't let anything happen to Ms. Sutton. He'll make sure she's safe the entire time."

"No way!" Jarrett spat out, then shook his head emphatically. His eyes were dark with rage and frustration as he ranted. "There is no way I am going to let her walk into another trap with that madman. Forget about it, Proctor. She's not going to be used by you people."

"Do you mean in the same way I've been used by you?" Liberty asked sullenly as she entered Anthony's house.

Jarrett swiftly turned around at the sound of her voice, his rage immediately replaced with concern at her words. "Liberty, I won't let them put you in more jeopardy," he stated simply, his tone softer, his gaze searching.

"And I won't let Mikel hurt my son. I'm going, Jarrett," Liberty answered firmly.

Jarrett swore under his breath, his chest expanding in frustration. Liberty followed the officer who had picked her up and went into the kitchen where the lieutenant was standing in deep conversation with fellow officers.

"Ms. Sutton, how are you?" he asked the moment he saw her.

"As you can imagine, not well, Lieutenant Jefferson. I just want my son back, unharmed," Liberty managed to say.

"As do we. It would be nice if Mr. Anderson made it back as well," the lieutenant added, a poor attempt at humor expressed in the laughless faces of Liberty, Jarrett, and Mrs. Yogan.

"Well, please, have a seat," he said hastily after the uncomfortable pause fell over the room. He pulled out the chair for Liberty. She sat down with a heavy sigh. He then pulled out a chair for Mrs. Yogan, sitting only after she sat.

Jarrett continued to stand, staring down at the lieutenant like an angry bear. Jefferson ignored him as he began to earnestly explain to Liberty what needed to be done. "You actually expect Liberty to trust you guys after your last fiasco? Come on," Jarrett snapped.

Outrage filled him that they wanted Liberty to wait like a sitting duck for Mikel. The man was insane. He knew he could never say it, but at this point Mikel could very well have already seriously harmed Jamal and Anthony. After all, the real Elizabeth Wilkins had not been found and Mikel refused to say where she had been hidden until his ransom was paid. Jarrett was not going to allow Liberty to get hurt.

Mikel Wilkins's plans had all suffered poorly. His attempt to have full control of the Wilkins-Zonnick fund so that he could hastily swindle the funds into a secure Swiss account had failed. He had no choice but to demand money at this point. The man had already hurt his own aunt and possibly his cousin. Why should Jarrett believe that he would not harm Liberty or her son?

"When do I leave?" Liberty asked, although she could not control a hesitant glance at Jarrett's stormy face.

"Midnight," was the short reply from Jefferson.

Liberty gaped in surprise. She had expected to be asked to leave as early as this afternoon and as late as tomorrow morning. What was Mikel thinking?

"Why midnight?" Jarrett voiced the question that ran through Liberty's mind.

"My educated guess is that he's counting on darkness to thwart any rescue attempt. If I was going to demand a ransom I would want it delivered under the cloak of darkness too," the lieutenant said before divulging Mikel's directions.

"Let me get this straight," Jarrett began with unchecked annoyance. "You want my wife to carry millions of dollars in the trunk of her car. Go to an isolated parking lot at Dulles Airport. Get out of the car and walk back, alone, to the baggage claims depot and just wait. That's crazy."

Liberty was staring in wide-eyed surprised at Jarrett. He had called her his wife. Was he even aware that he had done it? Jarrett felt her gaze and turned to her expectantly. Misreading the confusion in her eyes, he suspected she didn't understand just how upset he was that she would have to again face Mikel alone.

"She'll be followed every step of the way," Jefferson responded

"What?" Jarrett stammered, glancing from the lieutenant to Liberty.

"You called me your wife, Jarrett," Liberty answered staring in wide-eyed confusion at him.

"I did? Yeah, I did," he mumbled, mulling his earlier words. It was a slip that would normally cause Liberty to become frustrated or even angry with him. Instead, she only stared at him tenderly. Had she changed her mind? Was she over her anger about Jamal? He couldn't fathom her response.

"She'll be safe, Jarrett," Jefferson insisted. "We're going to have a helicopter and unmarked cars at the airport and following her throughout the entire process. We will be far enough away to allow Mikel to have his comfort zone, but she will not be harmed."

"And what happens when she leaves the car?"

"They take it, supposedly. I'm betting that they'll empty the money into another car and pull out. It would make more sense than taking Liberty's car, as it will be wired."

"And when will the officers be posted?" Jarrett demanded, crossing his arms over his chest.

"They are being posted right now. If we wait until tonight, Mikel and his people will probably notice, no matter how smooth the transition. We post them now and just let them wait."

"What happens if Mikel's smart and changes his instructions at the last minute? Suppose he decides to send Liberty left instead of right and all of your men are posted right. Get my point? What then?" Jarrett asked.

"Then I'll go left. I'll do whatever it takes, Jarrett, to get my son back. Why are you fighting this so much?" Liberty demanded softly.

"Because I'm worried to death about you, that's why," Jarrett answered harshly. "I don't trust Mikel and I have no faith in these guys," he added with a disdainful wave over the room.

"You're going to have to accept that I'm doing it, Jarrett," Liberty insisted, coming to her feet and taking a few steps away from the officers.

Naturally Jarrett followed. He bent forward and whispered, "I'm worried, Liberty. Do you understand?" he asked, unwilling to explain his worst fears.

Liberty looked up at him with sympathetic eyes. She understood how he felt, she could appreciate his concern. She was no longer angry with him for Jamal's kidnapping. Jarrett could no more control that event than he could control what happened to her. But she wasn't going to leave her son's welfare to chance or in Anthony's hands. For all she knew, Anthony could be tied up and gagged somewhere, unable to do any more than she had been able to when she was kidnapped. She was going to see that her son came back home safely.

"Jarrett, I know these people. I spent a few days with them and I know how they operate. Jamal's a good boy. He's safe. Anthony, I don't know about. But even if there was only a one percent chance that Jamal would be returned, that would be enough for me to risk my entire life for him. I'm going to drop off the car at the airport and do exactly as Mikel instructed. At twelve-thirty I'm going back out to the parking lot and I'm getting my son from the waiting car. He will be there, Jarrett. I believe it. And I will come back to you and marry you, I promise," Liberty added softly.

So softly in fact that Jarrett wasn't sure he had heard her correctly. Releasing a sigh, he pulled Liberty into his arms with such fierce devotion that it left her gasping for air.

"I love you, Liberty Sutton," he whispered in her ear, easing his hold slightly.

Liberty closed her eyes, feeling blessed to have him, strained to have to leave him again.

Taking a deep breath, she murmured, "And I love you too, Jarrett."

He studied her as if he would find some great treasure that only she could give him. Drawn by his magnetic gaze, the heat of his breath caressing her face, Liberty leaned into him until his lips touched hers. Firmer, more demanding the kiss became as they both clung desperately to each other. Liberty moaned softly, feeling the familiar flame ravish her senses as she molded into his arms. She wanted to stay that way forever, to feel the strength of his body as he held her close to him. Then he groaned and pulled away, although most reluctantly.

Chapter 21

Brenda was worried sick over Liberty's decision to go meet her abductors. It was outrageous what the police wanted her to do. Yet, she knew that if she had a son in the same predicament as Jamal she would do anything to get him. She felt completely helpless for the first time. There was nothing she could do or say. She could only be there for Liberty if she needed her. She gazed at Carl and her brown eyes clearly showed her distress. Carl's arm around her waist squeezed gently, encouraging her that Liberty was going to be fine.

"Jarrett's not going to let anything happen to his woman," Carl whispered to Brenda.

"I know. But I just wish this was finished already. I want Liberty back home, safe and normal again," Brenda said, resting her head against Carl's shoulder.

"It'll be that way, Brenda. Don't worry," Carl insisted, his voice patient, his hold caring as he guided Brenda to a seat. She closed her eyes and tried to shed her fears; after all, Liberty was resourceful and spirited. If anyone could walk away from such a traumatic experience, Liberty could. Besides, Carl was right, Jarrett wasn't going to let anything happen to Liberty. His constant presence was testimony to that.

The lieutenant was finding Jarrett more difficult

to manage than he had first realized. Jarrett had proven to be arrogant or downright sullen at times. It was only because of Liberty's insistence that Jarrett be present that the lieutenant had given in and allowed Jarrett to ride with the officers.

Liberty took great pains to maintain a calm disposition. She drove as casually as she could, not pausing until she came to the designated area in the Blue Lot. It was only then that she panicked. There were no parking spots available. What was she supposed to do now?

She looked around in frantic expectation of finding a sign or a signal or something to direct her next move. Just as she was about to back the car up and go around the lot again, a yellow Volkswagen pulled out of a parking spot on the far end of the lot. Liberty halted, considered the exiting car with a suspicious gaze, then hurried to the spot before another vehicle attempted to seize it.

She backed into the parking space as she had been instructed. The car parked, she turned off the ignition and proceeded to wait, for what she was not sure. She sat rigid, her eyes alert to every movement, her ears sensitive to every sound as her gaze swept over the parking lot. There was no movement, no activity of any kind. She was extremely uncomfortable with the silence. Finally she heard a tap on the passenger's door. For a moment she panicked, then she swallowed and took a deep breath. She had to be brave for Jamal. It was the only way to make sure he wasn't hurt.

Cautiously, she turned her head toward the door. She had not locked it, based on the directions she had been given. A hasty look at the opening door caused Liberty to flinch as her breath caught in her throat. A masked person slid into the seat beside her.

Staring straight ahead, the masked person demanded in a husky whisper, "Where are the bags?"

"In the backseat." Liberty's reply was terse.

She was certain by the voice, though it was disguised as well, that it was a woman. She was dressed in black from head to toe, her mask the odd choice of an ugly old woman. Could it be Veronica? If it was, why was she hiding behind the mask when Liberty already knew what she looked like?

"Where is my son?" Liberty asked fervently, her eyes anxious as she scanned outside for signs of her son.

"No questions," the woman responded curtly, her voice husky. Behind the mask, only her eyes were visible.

Frustrated by her powerlessness, Liberty knew she had to pacify the woman who seemed on edge from the moment she had gotten in the car. Antagonizing her son's abductor would only endanger him, and she was not willing to test the resolve to carry out their threats. Compressing her mouth tensely, Liberty turned with her back straight and her hands on the wheel. She heard the woman huff and gave her a bewildered glance.

"Reach back there and get them," the woman ordered at Liberty's confused stare.

"The bags?" Liberty asked stupidly.

"Yes," the woman hissed.

Liberty hurried to do her bidding, carefully lifting the heavy bags into the front seat one at a time. The woman took the first bag, opened the door, and dropped it to the ground. Then she accepted the second bag and dropped it too. Liberty noted with little surprise that Charles was waiting outside the door, his frame mostly hidden in his hunched position. He traded the two bags tossed outside the car for two similar bags that the woman tossed into the backseat. Liberty wondered if they were sophisticated enough to realize they were being watched by the police. And if so, why wasn't Charles wearing a mask, too?

"Now, take the second bag, Liberty, go inside as Mikel instructed you," the woman said. The moment Liberty was gone, the woman slid into the driver's seat. Liberty walked away, never looking back even after she heard the car pull out of the parking lot.

Liberty hurried through the lot. By the time she reached baggage claim, her arm ached from the exertion of carrying the bags and the long walk she had to take. She placed the bags on the baggage claim cycle, then warily scrutinized her surroundings. There was a small gathering of individuals apparently waiting for their luggage. None of them seemed to notice that rather than picking up luggage she had placed it on the cycling bin. She stood back and watched as the bags slowly advanced around the cycle until they disappeared behind the aperture. She waited a few moments, watching as the luggage bin renewed its cycle.

Her bags were gone.

She wasn't sure if she should wait or leave. Why would they take the bags when they already had the bags with the money? Whatever Mikel intended, she couldn't fathom. She only knew that as of yet she had been given no sign of her son and she was growing more upset. A quick glance at her watch and she decided that no one was going to come to her. With tears of frustration in her eyes, she turned to leave.

She headed out of the terminal, sniffing back silent sobs as she hailed a cab. This too had been part of the instruction she was to follow, except she had thought to do so with her son in her arms. Her heart was

pounding wildly as she forced herself to remain calm.
She didn't know what to think. Had Mikel reneged on
his promise? Overwhelmed with disappointment, Liberty was caught off guard when a cab sped up to her.
She jumped back, her eyes snapping with anger when
the taxi driver got out of the car and hurried to open
the door for her.

"Ms. Sutton?" he asked.

Her anger instantly dissolved at his familiarity. She
looked around. Where had he come from? She faced
the cabdriver.

He grinned at her, nodding his head toward the
door he had opened for her. "Ms. Sutton, right?"

She nodded.

"I'm at your service, ma'am. And don't worry about
your fare, the cab's been paid for already," he added
in a thick New Jersey accent.

Most likely a hefty sum, Liberty thought. She hesitated, not sure what she should do. It was obvious that
he had been sent by Mikel but why? She certainly
wasn't about to get in his cab and go anywhere.

She started to turn away when she saw them. Anthony and Jamal, sleeping soundly in the back of the
car. She flung open the door and pulled Jamal to her.
He didn't stir. He felt warm to her touch. She could
feel his heart beating. She glanced at Anthony, reassured further when she heard a light snore. What had
Mikel done to them? They seemed well enough, except for the small bruise she was just now noticing
on Anthony's forehead.

She considered the cabdriver then. She wondered
if he was really a taxi driver, an unwitting part of
Mikel's plans. With his wide grin, the driver seemed
harmless enough. He was an elderly black man and
his eyes were gentle in his weathered old face. He still

had a full head of hair that was as dark as a newborn's, so dark she wondered if he dyed it.

He had already gotten back in his seat and was starting the engine, seemingly guileless in his efforts. His entire demeanor was natural, as if having two sleeping passengers in the middle of the night was normal.

"How did they get like this? Who helped them in?" Liberty asked, watching him carefully.

The driver glanced at her through his rearview mirror, then at the sleeping pair, and gave her another one of his wide grins. "Some white guys put 'em in the car. Said that guy had too much to drink and his kid there was exhausted."

"And you believed them?" she retorted.

The driver shrugged, gave a quirk of his eyebrows, then said, "Yeah. I've been a taxi driver for many a year, lady. I don't ask unnecessary questions about my passengers," he added at her increasing frown. "Like I said, they paid for the ride to get me here and take you three wherever you want to go."

"To the hospital," Liberty responded automatically.

The taxi driver continued rambling on even though Liberty was no longer responsive. She held Jamal close, rocking back and forth with him against her bosom as her gaze skimmed the airport lots. Her expression became increasingly baffled as she stared outside the taxi car window, perplexed by the absence of any police presence. She was certain they were somewhere near, they couldn't have abandoned her.

There was no telling what was going on and there was nothing she could do. Exhausted, she sat back against the cushion of the seat, closed her eyes, and fought back a wave of anxiety that threatened to explode within her. She had to remain calm. Jamal would be seen by doctors the moment they were safe

She glanced at Anthony and frowned again. He was going to be fine but she wondered how he was going to react to everything that had happened. Would he become more tolerable after his life-threatening experiencing? She could only hope.

"Which hospital?" the driver asked.

Liberty caught the driver's eyes in his rearview mirror. They were crinkled in what she was beginning to think was a constant smile he wore. Slowly she told him which hospital to go to, recalling the lieutenant's very specific instructions just before releasing her with the car and the money. If anything was to go wrong, she was not to stop or wait but was to immediately hail an officer, *as if any were in sight.* Otherwise, she was not to deviate from Mikel's plan.

Well, nothing had gone wrong. Mikel's plan included that she take a taxi back home. But the state her son and his father were in required her to deviate from the directions.

Chapter 22

Liberty closed her eyes once again, exhaustion and worry beginning to take their toll on her. She wasn't sure what emotion was stronger, her desire to cry in relief over finally having Jamal in her arms or her fear that he could actually be hurt and she was helpless to aid him without a doctor.

She gave him a gentle squeeze. He lay so still, his breathing so soft, that it took everything in her not to shake him awake. She was sure that he was only sleeping but she was afraid to try and awaken him if his condition was actually serious. She wished she had a better grasp on how to handle her current dilemma. She looked down at Jamal, wishing Jarrett was with her.

She groaned, thinking of Jarrett. How she had made such a mess of things, she wasn't sure anymore. She only knew that the experience left her realizing just how short life could be and that Jamal and Jarrett were both very important to her. She had allowed Anthony's spite to interfere with her life long enough. It was time that she reached out and accepted all that life had to offer. Happiness had come her way when Jarrett said he loved her and wanted to marry her, and she, like a coward, had almost rejected his offer. She wasn't going to allow fear of Anthony's repercussion to ever again hold her back from choosing her own way.

Jarrett's adoring smile flashed into her thoughts. She could imagine how he would respond to her newest revelation. Who would have thought such a harrowing experience could finally toughen her up so quickly? Well, she had Mikel Wilkins to thank for that lesson. She frowned, her eyes flying open at the thought of her abductor.

The darkness of the night seemed to be a flurry of blue-gray mist as they sped down the freeway. She leaned her head against the backseat and tried to relax, allowing the lull of the moving car to ease her weariness as she maintained a steady hold on her son. Even as she tried to ignore the thought, she wondered if Mikel had made it to safety. Would he call Mrs. Wilkins to at least say good-bye? Liberty doubted it and felt a pang of resentment that the old woman was being so abused.

She stared out the window, not wanting to think about Mrs. Wilkins or Mikel or anyone at all. Just Jarrett. Jarrett's kisses, his teasing caresses, his dazzling smile, his strong arms. She wanted to bask in his warmth, just the thought of him causing her to sigh with pleasure. Her disquiet was just beginning to subside a little when the sound of sirens zooming up behind the taxi caused her eyes to open wide in alarm.

She sat up, her son stirring from the sudden movement. She paused, staring down at him. He had moved, that was a good sign. She stared at him, waiting for him to move again. He stirred slightly and Liberty could have cried in relief. She was distracted with relief when a swarm of police cars swiftly surrounded the taxi.

A glance at his face and Liberty knew the taxi driver was startled and frightened at the presence of all of the police cars. Before Liberty could respond to the flurry of activity outside the car, two of the officers had their guns pointed at the driver and ordered him out of the car. He complied, glancing in apprehension at Liberty in the back. She saw his confusion and blinked in uncertainty. There wasn't anything she could do. Gently she laid Jamal against his father and quickly exited the car as well. The commotion surrounding the taxi was staggering. She glanced around, searching for a familiar face in the maze of activity, then she heard Officer Thomas calling her name.

"Ms. Sutton, are you all right?" he asked, walking toward her.

"Yes," she answered slowly.

"Get an ambulance. Two are unconscious," one of the officers shouted after checking the backseat.

"Ms. Sutton. It's all right, please stay back," one of the officers she recognized from Anthony's home instructed, his hand outward to her in an effort to keep her from approaching the taxi driver.

"No. My son," Liberty cried, trying to push past the officer blocking her way. She glared at him. "That's my son and Anthony. No one else is in the car," she pleaded when the officer didn't budge.

Before he could respond, Officer Thomas had already gotten to Jamal and was carrying him from the car toward one of the ambulances that had arrived. This time the officer didn't hold her back and she rushed past him to catch up with the policeman.

"I can carry him," she said, staring with worry at Jamal as he continued to stir.

"It's just a few steps," Thomas suggested, not releasing his grip. Jamal awakened, his eyes strangely alert and comprehending as he looked around and his gaze fell on his mother.

Liberty gulped, not certain why she stood frozen, but she couldn't move. Jamal smiled, then yawned, all within seconds of complaining he was thirsty. Liberty burst into laughter, her eyes tearful with her joy. She hurried to him and hugged him so tightly he squealed a complaint.

"If you can give us a moment," one of the paramedics asked mildly, gently nudging Liberty away from her son.

"Of course," Liberty agreed, wiping at the tears that she couldn't seem to stop. Sniffing, Liberty stepped aside. With her arms crossed in front of her, she ran an idle glance around her, then inhaled sharply before releasing an elated cry as Jarrett got out of the backseat of one of the police cars. Without hesitation, she hurried to him.

"Are you okay?" Jarrett whispered, his mouth brushing against her forehead as he spoke.

"Yes. Nothing really happened and Jamal is safe, too," Liberty murmured. "Come, I want to be near him," she added. Taking his hand in hers, she led him back to the ambulance.

The scene was a spectacle of police and ambulance lights. Liberty wouldn't have been surprised if the news media had come out as well. Drivers on the highway slowed their vehicles out of curiosity as they passed the scene. Liberty ignored it all as Jarrett held her close to him. They watched as the medics checked Jamal, amazed that one so young could behave so well under the probing and gentle questioning. Then Anthony was guided forward, stumbling as if he were drunk. Liberty tensed slightly as they helped Anthony to sit next to Jamal and began tending to him as well. Anthony looked up and his clouded eyes fell directly on Liberty. She didn't move, vaguely aware of Jarrett's reassuring squeeze. She needn't have worried. Anthony looked away and responded slowly to a question put to him by the paramedic attending him.

"They'll be fine," Jarrett murmured just for her ears.

"Yes, I know," Liberty agreed, relaxing against the strength of his firm chest. The paramedics began to guide Anthony and Jamal fully into the ambulance. Liberty took an anxious step forward and asked, "What's happening?"

"Oh, we need just a moment, ma'am, to get them settled in, then you can ride to the hospital with him, if you like," one of the medics responded. She had expected to take Jamal with her now that he had awakened and appeared unharmed.

"Is something wrong with my son?" she heard herself asking, her eyes sweeping over Jamal, then Anthony. Anthony lay with his head turned away from her and she could see that he was in discomfort. She had no doubt he was suffering from a headache, judging from the nasty bump on his head. But Jamal was not so unfortunate. He sat bouncing on the cart beside his father, unaware that each movement must be agony from Anthony. There was nothing wrong with Jamal.

"It's standard, Ms. Sutton. You'll want to have him looked at by a doctor before taking him home," Officer Thomas answered, coming to Liberty's side.

She wouldn't jeopardize Jamal's well-being but how she dreaded taking the ambulance to the hospital with Anthony inside. Jarrett sensed her distress and approached her again, placing his arms silently around her, his body cradling her as she watched her son. Liberty sighed, reaching up to place her hands over Jarrett's. He was always so reliable and she had almost given it all up for fear of Anthony.

The medics reassured Anthony that he would be all right. They had insisted that he sit up, though he wanted nothing more than to lie still. He complained that he was light-headed and had been hit in the head and couldn't sit up.

"Just try to relax, sir, we're going to take you to the hospital, but we need to get you strapped in first," he was told by the medic. Before Anthony could refuse, the medics forced him upright and pulled the straps that he had unwittingly moved during his examination.

In his discomfort, he never noticed Liberty standing just a few feet away from him, Jarrett's arms protectively about her. Had he noticed he would have flown into a fit of outrage at the fact that although he was a victim of some crazed guy angry with Liberty, she was coddling Jarrett.

"Wait," Liberty called to the medics. She groaned, turning in Jarrett's arms to face him. He looked crestfallen as if he knew what she was about to say. As much as she hated to do it because of Anthony's presence, she could not allow her son to ride off without her.

"I understand. Go to your son, Liberty," he said calmly releasing her.

"Jarrett . . ." She paused, not sure what to say. So much had happened. Now was not the time to talk. She loved him and she knew he loved her. Why did she feel that was not enough?

"I'll call you the moment Jamal is settled. I promise," she whispered. Then with an almost chaste kiss, she hurried inside the ambulance and sat beside her son.

Jarrett watched as Liberty climbed into the ambulance and took a possessive space next to Jamal. He watched as the doors were closed and his eyes narrowed when Anthony for the first time noticed Liberty was inside the ambulance. The angry stare was not missed by Jarrett. There was no way he was going to give Anthony a chance to hurt Liberty again.

Jarrett had no doubt that Anthony would stoop to any measure to get what he wanted. And now, after the abduction, Jarrett was sure Anthony would use it against Liberty at every turn. But he was not fooled by Anthony's spitefulness. The look on Anthony's face when had watched Liberty had said it all. Until that moment Jarrett had wondered if Anthony was only jealous over Liberty's affection for him or if Anthony in fact still desired Liberty. After seeing Anthony's expression, Jarrett had no doubt he wanted Liberty back. Jarrett frowned as his gaze followed the ambulance. He knew what he was dealing with now and he wasn't going to give Anthony the chance to gain Liberty's affection.

Chapter 23

Anthony sat grimly on the edge of the hospital bed. He was clothed in the shorts, T-shirt, and crumpled shirt he had worn when he was kidnapped. Hospital slippers covered his feet, his own shoes having somehow been lost in the tussle during his abduction, and he was in desperate need of a shave.

Liberty sat across from him, holding Jamal protectively against her bosom on the other bed. She was kissing the boy's forehead, smiling down at him in total adoration. The doctor's examinations indicated that Jamal was fit to leave. However, due to his age and the fact that they weren't sure just what the boy was given to knock him out so thoroughly, they decided to keep him for observation awhile longer.

Anthony had not fared as well as his son. He was experiencing nausea and a ferocious headache, an afteraffect from the drug, no doubt. Judging from the bump on Anthony's head and how he said he had struggled with Mikel and Charles, the kidnappers most likely gave Anthony a higher dosage of the drug, to be sure that he was knocked out, no doubt. Thus, Anthony was suffering with the worst hangover-like feeling he had ever had.

He was furious, too. Liberty barely acknowledged him. This entire affair was her doing, he fumed, yet she was unapologetic, even sulky when he asked that she not take Jamal from his room. He wanted to be near his son, he had claimed. He also liked having Liberty with him. He deserved a little pampering after all. He had fared no better with his mother-in-law. She had come and gone, her only concern for Jamal. When she saw Liberty, she became cool and aloof and immediately found an excuse to leave. She hadn't even bothered to ask if Anthony was all right. So much for family bonds. So now he was alone with Liberty and Jamal. A lovely scene, if it weren't for Liberty's determination to virtually ignore him.

He knew she didn't want to be in the same room with him. He didn't understand why he was torturing himself by having her so near either. He could still feel the softness of her lips beneath his when he'd kissed her just a few days earlier. She was no willing lover, he thought, hating the fact that though her body was soft and supple when he held her, she had not wanted him. Not even a little. She only remained in his room with him because of her fear of losing Jamal. He was not stupid. He knew her motive and he enjoyed worrying her.

He watched her, his gaze raking over her slightly disheveled ponytail to her crumpled clothes. Her eyes had mild shadows from exhaustion, he was sure. Her face was void of any makeup and her pallor wasn't as bright as he remembered her. Still, she was absolutely beautiful. It made him angry that in her ragged state she was able to stir him, to drive him crazy with desire. He groaned, the need to touch her fueling his ire.

Liberty heard Anthony's groans of pain. Unlike his father, Jamal was fairing well. He was cheerful, giggling and squirming in his mother's arms. His only complaint was that she would not let him go. She relaxed her grip beneath his fidgeting, but did not set him free. She needed him to keep from having to deal with Anthony. While she held him, she felt the distance between Anthony and herself could be maintained.

Liberty studiously avoided looking at Anthony, her attention captured by the sight of a few officers just outside the room. She strained to hear their conversation. Had they caught Mikel? She leaned forward, raising her eyes in surprise as she listened to the recount of events that took place after she had left the airport. Since getting into the ambulance, she had not received any additional information.

Apparently, the masked woman who had approached Liberty in her car at the airport had been followed to a private airport just outside of Annapolis. She had gotten out of the car and transferred the money into a waiting green Mercedes. Once the money was tossed inside, the driver pulled off. At the same time, another person had gotten into the vacant car the masked woman had gotten out of and driven off in the opposite direction. What was animating the officers' conversation, however, was that the woman had been left behind, stranded.

"She was just standing there, until finally the lieutenant said to bring her in," one officer said, capping off the conversation with an exasperated sigh.

Unable to remain quiet, feeling she had a right to know what happened, Liberty gently laid Jamal on the bed, whispering to him that she would be right back. Ignoring Anthony's curious gaze, she hurried to the door.

"What about Mikel, the money? What happened to him?" Liberty asked, not caring that the officers weren't aware that she had been listening to their conversation. The officers considered her with startled glances.

"He got away, Ms. Sutton," one of them answered.

"You're kidding," Liberty said.

"No. We are assuming that he was the driver that sped off in the Mercedes. Once downtown, he jumped from the car while it was still moving."

"He just jumped out of a moving car and left the money behind?" Liberty asked, disturbed.

"Not quite. The car was checked and the only thing inside were two empty suitcases."

"No way!" Liberty gasped.

"Yes, way," the officer mocked, laughing a little at Liberty's wide-eyed disbelief.

"And the other car?"

"They did the same thing. Drove in a mad race through downtown, slowed to a turtle's pace, then jumped out and ran, too," the officer responded, his awe at Mikel's creativity expressed in his voice.

"And the money wasn't there either, huh?" Anthony chimed in, rolling his eyes heavenward in frustration. He had gotten up moments after Liberty. He was curious as well.

"No money was found," the officer confirmed, turning his attention to Anthony.

"It makes no sense. How did they transfer the money then?" Liberty asked. She kept her back to Anthony but wished desperately that he hadn't chosen to stand right behind her. She hated his closeness and was certain that he was standing over her on purpose. He knew she wasn't comfortable. If she didn't have so much to lose, she would stomp on his foot. Careful to keep her discomfort out of her expression, she stared at the officers.

"We don't know but it wasn't found in either of the cars or at the airport. It's just gone."

"So that got away. Some police force," Anthony stated scathingly.

"Oh, I wouldn't say they got away. Not just yet. They're bound to show up somewhere," one of the officers said defensively.

"Yeah, but in the meantime we're glad that you and your family are all right," another officer offered consolingly.

At his words Anthony and Liberty glanced at each other. It was curious how so many people had just assumed they were a couple. If they knew how she despised him, they would be shocked. In fact, Liberty thought with amusement, Anthony would be a little surprised to know the extent of her disdain.

Anthony's eyes narrowed. He was not amused and was just about to comment on her unseemly humor when the doctor returned. Anthony followed the doctor from the room for more tests, surprisingly tame.

During his absence, Liberty discovered the reason for the three officers' presence. Lieutenant Jefferson had ordered the officers to watch and keep Liberty and her family at the hospital until further notice. The officers would be there until they were allowed to leave. Liberty found the news disturbing. What of Jarrett? Would he be allowed in? She did not want him in the same room as Anthony just now.

Almost grieving, Liberty sat on the chair that was placed between the two beds. Jamal lay on the bed nearest the window, after falling asleep again. Anthony returned, his face sullen as he entered the room and closed the door behind him. Without so much as a nod at Liberty, he headed straight for the narrow bathroom and shut the door.

Liberty was dismayed once more that she was stuck with Anthony indefinitely. Resigning herself to what

she hoped would be a short sacrifice, she turned on
the television set. She was settling back in her chair
when the door was flung open. She stood quickly,
jumpy with the knowledge that Mikel was not captured. She was instantly relieved to see Jarrett coming
toward her, Lieutenant Jefferson and two other detectives right behind him. Suddenly the room felt
crowded, cramped with the presence of burly men.
Liberty didn't mind. Jarrett was here and she wanted
only to fall into his arms.

She took a step toward Jarrett. As she did so, Anthony hurried out the bathroom, worried by the
commotion he had heard. He too was rattled after his
ordeal with the kidnappers. He froze when he saw
first Jarrett, then the officers who'd helped him out of
the taxi. No one seemed to notice him though. Liberty was wrapped in Jarrett's arms, smiling up at him
with such adoration that Anthony wanted to yank
them apart. He could sense the excitement in the
room and frowned. The officers' expressions were so
full of excitement that Anthony momentarily ignored
Jarrett to consider the officers. Whatever was going
on, he suspected it must be good news.

"They found her. The driver was Elizabeth. Can you
believe it?" Jarrett told Liberty, smiling back at her,
completely unaware of Anthony standing just a few
feet away from them with a scowl on his face.

The loud entry of the men had awoken Jamal. He
sat up and rubbed his eyes, looking at the new arrivals
in curiosity. Then he recognized Jarrett and his eyes
lit up. It was more than Anthony could bear. He
nearly snapped at his son to lie back down. He refrained, knowing everyone would look at him as if he
were a monster. It was just one more reason for him
to resent Jarrett.

"Jarrett!" Jamal called happily, then jumped from the bed and ran to him.

Jarrett laughed and without releasing Liberty, he reached down and, not missing the glowering gaze of Anthony, he picked Jamal up and gave him a gentle hug with his free arm.

"What a greeting." Jarrett laughed as Jamal's small arms firmly wrapped around his neck and returned the hug.

"Yeah," Anthony snorted. The three of them looked like one big happy family. He didn't like it at all. First Liberty and now his son. Anthony's gaze darkened as he watched them.

"That's amazing. But how did you find her?" Liberty asked, pulling free of Jarrett's hold to allow him to hold Jamal completely. Jarrett adjusted Jamal in his arms, gave him a firm squeeze, then carefully set the boy on his feet.

"The officers who caught her at the lot found out that she was Elizabeth Wilkins," Lieutenant Jefferson added, crossing his arms in front of his chest in frustration.

"Elizabeth Wilkins," Liberty repeated, still reeling at the good news that the poor woman was found.

Jarrett flung his arm over Liberty once more, his hold protective as he and Lieutenant Jefferson made eye contact.

"Apparently," Jefferson began slowly, "Elizabeth has been with Mikel, safe and sound."

"Who is Elizabeth, Mommy?" Jamal asked with wide-eyed curiosity. Blessedly, Jamal had very little understanding of what had happened that night. He had been in bed one moment and the next he just remembered being outside and falling. Apparently they had taken him out of the house after their scuffle with

Anthony and made sure he went right back to sleep. He didn't wake up again until he was with his mother. He only knew that his father was angry, they had been taken to the hospital in an ambulance, and his mother was with him. Liberty was determined to keep his understanding exactly where it was.

"She's just a lady, Jamal," Liberty answered blandly. She was trying to digest the lieutenant's statement. She considered the officer and repeated, "Safe?"

"Yes," Jefferson paused, careful not to accuse Elizabeth although his gut instinct believed she was involved. "We're not sure just yet but Elizabeth is co-operating with authorities, Ms. Sutton. One thing is clear: Mikel Wilkins can't be too far, not without that money. And now that Mrs. Wilkins is fully recovered, we'll find him. But until we do, we intend to keep all of you under our watch."

"What? I can't sit around in protective custody. I know what happened to Liberty and how they got me and Jamal. I might as well do what I normally do," Anthony scoffed. All of the resentment he had been feeling came to the surface as he spoke. He pointedly kept from looking at Jarrett and Liberty. He wasn't sure if he could refrain from attacking Jarrett if he had to look at the man caress Liberty one more time. "Besides, I've got a business to run. It's bad enough I missed this much time as it is. "

"It's not actually protective custody, Mr. Anderson. We'll have at least two officers, undercover of course, at your side wherever you go for the next few days or weeks, however long it takes to apprehend Mr. Wilkins."

"I can't have cops coming with me to work. They'll think I'm in trouble. No way," Anthony refused bluntly.

"We're doing this for your protection, Mr. Anderson. Until Mikel is caught, there is no telling what he may try next, and maybe next time you and your son won't be so fortunate as to walk away unharmed," Jefferson responded with a bluntness that was meant to make Anthony see reason.

Anthony groaned, glared at Liberty, who had gasped at the officer's warning, then briefly closed his eyes. He was exhausted.

"I can look after myself and my kid," Anthony retorted finally. He opened his eyes, his gaze on the lieutenant full of reproach for his scare tactics.

"How? By doing whatever it was that got you kidnapped in the first place, Anthony? For crying out loud, think about Jamal," Liberty cried, unable to remain silent in this new battle to protect Jamal. His ego would allow him to purposely put himself and, more importantly, Jamal in harm's way and she couldn't allow that.

"Hey, had I known that your friends were after me and my kid I would have taken protective measures of my own," Anthony responded defensively.

"Mikel Wilkins is not my friend," Liberty fumed.

"Let's not turn this into a shouting match. Everything is going to be fine, Liberty," Jarrett interceded before Anthony could fling another accusation. "Anthony is going to allow the officers to stay with him, don't worry."

"Yeah, right," Anthony huffed.

"And Jamal will be safe. I'm sure Anthony knows the importance of this even if he doesn't care about himself. No man would deliberately ignore the dangers that Mikel presents. Not when it's about his kid," Jarrett added with a calm that did not fool Anthony. He knew Jarrett was goading him and he wasn't going to fall for it.

Refusing to be set up as a tyrant, Anthony took the

remark in stride. "I'm not entrusting my kid to some cops that repeatedly prove they don't know what they're doing. I want Jamal where I can see him, with me. So," he added with a deliberate gloating glance at Liberty, "Jamal will stay with me during this time period. Liberty, you're welcome to stay with me, too," his meaning not lost on Liberty or Jarrett as he continued. "That is if you don't feel safe in your home under the circumstances."

"As long as you accept police protection, I'm just fine with Jamal being with you," Liberty responded smoothly. She was seething inside. He had insulted her, tried to insinuate that they had a more intimate relationship. She wanted to slap him. She didn't, holding on to her composure by a thread of determination born of an aching need to never lose her son again.

Jarrett eyed Anthony with a dangerous glint of warning. Just as quickly, his eyes widened at Liberty's cool rebuttal. He knew that Anthony's comment was meant to sting not only Liberty's pride but his as well. Had Liberty not turned the comment around so smoothly, Jarrett wasn't sure how long he could have maintained his calm.

"Suit yourself." Anthony shrugged. He was disappointed that Jarrett hadn't responded. It gave him endless pleasure to watch Jarrett sweat. He sat down on the edge of the bed and fell silent, though his eyes didn't fail to notice how Liberty gently took Jarrett's hand. The two of them stood holding hands like high school sweethearts. Anthony turned his gaze, staring at the lieutenant as if his words were extremely important.

"Then it's settled. We'll have officers at your house around the clock. Ms. Sutton, you will naturally have officers with you as well. In the meantime, could you all kindly stay here for the night?" Jefferson asked.

"In the hospital?" Anthony scoffed, infuriated. He tossed Liberty a bitter glance before he lay back on the bed and closed his eyes, cursing everyone under his breath.

Before Liberty could respond to the officer's request, his cell phone rang. Everyone was very attentive as the lieutenant answered the call.

"When?" Jefferson responded, his eyes falling curiously on Liberty. Anthony sat up, his curiosity overriding his pain.

"I'm on my way. Absolutely. She'll be with me," the lieutenant stated. He snapped his cell phone shut, then with a smile that seemed oddly off balance on his aged, slightly crooked face, he walked to Liberty and said, "We got Mikel Wilkins. Elizabeth confessed her role and gave them all up."

Chapter 24

Liberty was happy to leave the hospital. At least until she arrived at the precinct and sat for hours in a leather chair that had seen better days. Jarrett had gone with her. If it weren't for his presence, she wasn't sure if she could have managed another moment without falling over from sheer exhaustion. She identified Mikel Wilkins, Charles, and Veronica. When she was finished giving her statement, she and Jarrett returned to the hospital. She didn't want to go home without Jamal and she knew they weren't going to release him before morning. It wouldn't have made much difference if she had gone home; daybreak was coming and as exhausted as she was, she knew she would want to be at Jamal's side the moment he awoke.

"Jarrett, go home," Liberty insisted even as she snuggled against him in the backseat.

"No, I'm not leaving you. You're exhausted and I don't want you alone," Jarrett said firmly.

"I won't be alone. Jamal will be with me," Liberty responded, suppressing a yawn.

"Yeah, and Anthony. I'd say that's the same as alone," Jarrett retorted, unable to contain his jealously.

"Ah, I see. Don't be jealous, Jarrett. You should just

go home, get some rest, and come back as early as you can, maybe about ten or eleven. That way, Jamal will be released by then and I can leave with you, okay?" Liberty consoled him, her sleepy gaze probing his face for understanding.

Jarrett stared down at the beautiful face looking up at him. Her mouth puckered as if she was waiting to be kissed even though he knew she wasn't thinking about kissing at all. He couldn't help it though, she had that kind of power over him. He leaned in and before Liberty knew what his intent was, he kissed her. He was tired, but not too tired to give her all the passion that these days of chaos had created. He desired her, missed her beyond reason. He wanted her and his breathtaking kiss clearly told her just how much she was missed.

"Jarrett," she managed to breathe between kisses. He was pressing her against the seat, his kiss no longer ravishing her mouth. He was tickling her neck, tasting the sweetness of her flesh as he trailed kisses down her throat. She gasped, knowing she should stop here. They weren't alone. Two officers were in the front seat, no doubt grinning at the spectacle they were creating. But she felt helpless to push him away when all she wanted to do was melt against him, give herself to him without inhibitions.

Jarrett moaned deep in his throat, a husky sound that made Liberty's body weak with hunger. If she were standing she knew she would have fallen, so liquid had she become. His left hand held the small of her back as his right hand found an entry into her blouse and began to fondle her breast. She squirmed with pleasure, biting back a gasp of pleasure at his touch. He was bending his head, impatient with the blockage her blouse caused, when the car stopped.

The motion snapped Jarrett back to his senses. He looked up and saw that they were at a red light and the officers in the front were staring conspicuously straight ahead. His gaze fell back on Liberty with longing. She lay there, unwittingly seductive in her languid pose against the cushion of the seat. Her eyes were on him, still burning with desire even as she groggily became aware of their precarious position. He watched, mesmerized, as the fire he had ignited slowly cooled. She smiled, her gaze now teasing as she accepted his help to sit up straight again.

"That was close," she whispered, hiding her embarrassment behind her light laugh. She was trembling as she attempted to straighten her blouse. Jarrett noticed it and knew then that the flames of desire had not completely been extinguished. Somehow, it boosted his ego to see her wanting him, it comforted him knowing she was going to be with Anthony with the memory of their passionate kiss fresh in her thoughts.

"Yeah," Jarrett murmured, once again glancing at the policemen in the front. He knew they were grinning. He wasn't bothered by it. They had stopped before they were completely out of control. Besides, his body had hidden Liberty from their curious glances, he was sure of it. He was lost in thought, in agony over the memory of their kiss, when they arrived at the hospital. He hated the idea of leaving her with Anthony, but he knew she needed to see that he could trust her.

"You'll call me when you're ready to leave?" he found himself asking.

She turned to Jarrett, a bright smile curving her mouth. "You know I will," she said easily. With a shy glance at the officers, she shrugged. Then on tiptoes, she kissed Jarrett again. She stepped away and hurried inside the hospital, the officers accompanying her. Jarrett stared, his mouth feeling swollen from the light kiss she'd planted before leaving him. With a grimace, he leaned against the police car, waiting patiently for the officers to return.

Liberty entered Jamal's room as quietly as she could. Anthony was asleep, his snores soft and consistent. Jamal lay curled on the second hospital bed, his body half covered with the blanket. Liberty pulled the blanket fully over him, then sat in the chair beside his bed, taking his hand in hers, and closed her eyes. A few hours later she awoke, her head resting beside Jamal's as he still slept. She opened her eyes to bright sunlight and squinted. Blinking she looked across the room at Anthony's bed. He was gone.

It was with relief that he had not waited for her to wake up. There was no reason for him to stick around. Mikel Wilkins was in police custody. The thought of his capture left Liberty feeling free, elated, and able to breathe. Jamal would not need to stay with Anthony.

She felt a sense of triumph that just when she thought she would have to give up her son as a duty to him, he was given back to her. She was excited and hopeful that everything would be back to normal. She exhaled a sigh of relief when Jamal was given an official clean bill of health and declared fit to return home.

Anthony's moping the night before was forgotten. She reached over and gently awakened Jamal. He awoke after a few attempts. Rubbing his eyes, he sat up, pleased to see his mother.

"Mommy," he exclaimed.

"Hey, sweetie. Time to get up. We're going home,"

Liberty said, her eyes shining with happiness. Jamal was pulling on his jeans when Anthony stormed into the hospital room, mindless of how close he came to knocking Liberty down when he flung the door open.

"Come on, Jamal," Anthony barked, ignoring Liberty's presence. "Let's go."

"What?" Liberty cried, standing in front of Jamal protectively. "He's going with me, Anthony."

"No way. My son is going home with me. After the events of the last few days, I don't know if I trust you to keep my son safe." Anthony's tone was cold and cryptic.

He was hungry, tired, and uncomfortable. He felt cramped from sleeping in the hospital bed all night, and the drug he was given by that Mikel person hadn't helped him any either. He was frustrated, irritable, and wanted to get out of the hospital immediately. And after seeing Liberty's affectionate display with Jarrett last night, he was determined to get his son away from her. She wanted Jarrett Irving, she could have him. She just wasn't getting his son in the bargain.

Liberty was stunned.

"But just last night you said he could come back home with me," Liberty stated as calmly as she could.

"No. That's not what I said. I said I wanted Jamal to stay with me until that guy was caught. You agreed," Anthony corrected her.

"Yes, but he's been caught. This is crazy," Liberty said, irritation seeping into her voice.

"Oh, cut the crap, Liberty. I want Jamal safe, and right now living with you is not safe," Anthony snapped, grabbing his few items from the room as he spoke.

"It is safe. Mikel Wilkins is locked away," Liberty retorted.

"Yeah? And for how long. You nearly cost me and my son our lives. I'm taking him home," Anthony said with such a note of finality that Liberty could have fainted from dismay.

"Your lives were never in danger. He would not have harmed you," Liberty stated firmly as Anthony helped Jamal into his shirt and began buttoning the small buttons, his fingers fumbling through the process.

She stared at him, appalled at his animosity. He was blaming her for Mikel Wilkins's abduction of him and Jamal, but why now? What had changed?

"I had nothing to do with what happened, Anthony. You know that," Liberty argued. It was then that she saw Jamal's confused glances from his father to her. She didn't want this discussion to take place in front of Jamal.

"You got us caught up in this mess, Liberty. That's all I know. I'm not going to keep rehashing this. Jamal is coming home with me."

Without another word, Anthony moved Liberty aside and lifted Jamal into his arms. Jamal looked at his father as if he didn't know him, then turned his gaze upon his mother. Her heart was wrung with pain at the wide-eyed uncertainty she saw in his eyes.

"I'm his mother, Anthony. I have equal custody. You can't just do this," Liberty said desperately, her mind racing with dread. It was the past all over again. But back then she had been robbed and never had a chance to fight. It was not going to happen again. She was not going to lose Jamal on a whim. She put her emotions in check, aching to grab hold of Jamal and pull him away from Anthony.

"I know that. I'm not saying I'm taking away your custody, Liberty. I just want the boy safe, that's all," Anthony said firmly and began to walk out of the room. He had not expected Liberty's devastated look; her doleful expression nearly stopped him. She loved Jamal that much? He had thought it was just her hatred of Tina and her resentment of him that had driven her to want the boy. He realized now that Liberty's emotions for Jamal went far deeper. He didn't know Liberty at all, he thought, and the idea renewed his frustration with her. He kept walking.

Liberty's throat was tight with tears that she refused to release. She held Jamal's hand, following closely behind the pair as Anthony headed for the elevator. He knew she was holding on but strode onward as if she weren't there.

"Jamal, baby, it's okay," Liberty murmured after Anthony pushed the elevator button.

"Hell yeah, it's okay. He's my son, Liberty. He's fine. I'll call you," Anthony blurted, glaring at Liberty. She was behaving as if he were taking the kid into foster care, Anthony thought with resentment.

The elevator arrived and he pulled away from Liberty, the movement forcing her to release Jamal's hand. He heard her distressed gasp, but ignored it. What he was doing was best for Jamal, he convinced himself as he got on the elevator. Liberty probably thought it best for Jamal to be with her and *Jarrett*, but he had news for the both of them. He was Jamal's father and he wasn't going to lose control of that.

"Bye, Mommy," Jamal whispered, his small hand waving to her as he disappeared on the elevator with his father. Anthony's face was a mask of coldness as his gaze made one final connection with Liberty.

Liberty nearly broke down in tears after the elevator door closed. Refusing to lose her composure in front of the nurses and attentive patients, Liberty held her head high and walked purposely back to Anthony's room. She picked up her purse, glanced around the room to be sure she had left nothing else, then headed back to the elevators. With a steady gaze, she considered her options. She could act like a madwoman and go after Anthony or she could use logic. Even if it broke her, she was going to get the best lawyer in the state and get her son back. She wasn't going to waste any time doing it either. Anthony was not going to get away with taking Jamal from her again.

Her eyes were dark and she felt strangely calm. She was no longer a foolish young girl, lost and confused. That era of her life was over. She was going to set Anthony Anderson straight once and for all. It seemed it didn't matter what she did. He would find a way to hurt her. She was no longer going to allow that to happen.

Liberty entered the lobby, her expression set in a quiet resolve as she passed the nurse sitting at the front desk talking with two security guards. She barely noticed them as she headed for the exit. She wasn't aware of anything except her newfound goal to get Jamal back. She had been through too much to allow Anthony to win.

Chapter 25

Jarrett yawned as he pulled into a vacant visitor's parking space outside the hospital's main entrance. He still felt exhausted. He peered down at his radio clock. It was just past ten A.M. Liberty hadn't called him and he assumed that she had overslept. He didn't bother to call the hospital, knowing she would ring his cell phone if she needed him. He got dressed and hurried to the hospital the moment he awoke.

He was excited. At last their lives were normal again. He had bided his time long enough. It was now or never, he decided as he drove to the hospital. He was going to take Liberty home, give her time to settle Jamal back into his routine, and then he was going to let Liberty know that he still wanted to marry. But this time it would be different. This time he was going to be gentle, understanding, and no matter what her response, he was not going to lose his temper.

He swallowed uncomfortably at the idea that Liberty might still be determined to put him on hold. It was a painful but very real possibility that Liberty just might not want to get married after all she'd just been through. He glanced at his image in the mirror and smirked. Nah! She loved him and he was a catch. They belonged together. He was determined to make sure that Liberty knew it.

As he opened the car door, his eyes caught a glimpse of a young woman walking firmly down the sidewalk away from the hospital. With eyes grown bright from recognition, he realized it was Liberty. Her pace was brisk and set as if she had a very specific destination. He looked back at the hospital entrance and did not see Jamal or Anthony. Maybe she was angry with him for not having arrived earlier? She didn't state a specific time she wanted him to be there. It was something else.

He hurried from the car and ran up to her. She was so focused on catching a cab, on stopping Anthony from once again ruining her life, that she had completely forgotten about Jarrett.

"Jarrett," she gasped and before he could say a word she broke into sobs.

"Liberty, what is it? Is Jamal hurt?" Jarrett asked, pulling her to him in a comforting embrace.

Liberty shook her head in response as she tried to regain her composure. Jarrett fell silent and held her, using every bit of self-control he had to be patient and wait for her to tell him why she was crying and where she was going.

After a few moments, she got herself together enough to whisper into his chest, "Anthony took Jamal."

"What!" Jarrett blurted, shocked, pulling away from her to look into her face in disbelief.

"Anthony took Jamal," she repeated, her voice a little clearer.

"I'm sorry, Liberty. I should have been here. I should have been here." Jarrett grimaced, wishing he had not left her. He was a fool to turn his back on Anthony for even a moment. But then, he wondered honestly, how could he have stopped the man from taking his own son.

"It's not your fault. You couldn't have stopped him. He's worried about Jamal. He doesn't trust me now because of what happened with Mikel," Liberty said as if she read his mind. She pulled away from Jarrett's consoling hold and wiped her eyes. "I couldn't reason with him."

"Have you ever been able to reason with him?" Jarrett remarked cynically.

"No, I guess I never have," Liberty responded with a sigh.

Jarrett took Liberty's hands and gently squeezed them. "Let's go get your son, Liberty," Jarrett suggested.

Liberty stared at the ground, lost in thought, before she raised her gaze back to Jarrett. She swallowed, then said, "I intend to, just not yet. I'm going to talk to Tom, my lawyer, about this."

"And so you should," Jarrett agreed.

"Where's your car?" Liberty asked after a long pause.

"This way," Jarrett answered and led the way.

"I thought everything was going to be all right," Liberty murmured, pulling on her seat belt.

"It will be all right," Jarrett responded. Glancing at Liberty as he pulled out of the hospital parking lot onto the main road, he added, "Whatever happens, Liberty, just don't lose your temper. That won't do you any good."

His comment upset Liberty. She stared out of the window resisting a tart retort. Jarrett had been so good throughout everything, standing at her side, keeping her strong when she felt she couldn't give anything else. And now he was scolding her as if she were a volatile child. She was holding on to her temper by a thread.

"I only meant that Anthony has a way of riling you up. I don't want your temper to work against you," Jarrett suggested softly. He knew he had upset her but he also knew he had to make the statement. If history had proven anything, Anthony and Liberty did not get along and the last thing she needed was to lose her temper while trying to prove how wonderful a mother she was.

"I'll try to remember that," Liberty hissed, unable to keep the resentment from her voice. She crossed her arms over her chest, refusing to look at him. Jarrett sighed, glancing at her for a moment before turning his attention to the road once more. He found it hard to believe that the stiff, obstinate woman across from him was the same woman who lay soft and yielding in his arms just last night.

"I wasn't trying to upset you. I only want to help," Jarrett began. It was a mistake. A torrent of words flowed from her like a dam that had been aching to burst.

"Well, you aren't succeeding, Jarrett. I know how to behave, thank you very much. I would think after what I've been through you would know that I am capable of managing complicated matters. I'm not a child. But I am going to get *my child* back and it won't be through a temper tantrum. I am going to get a lawyer of my own and request a review of my custody status and my rights. I am going to talk to Anthony after I see a lawyer, of course, and put an end to his tantrums and threats for good. That is how I plan to handle this situation, Jarrett," Liberty stated firmly.

She fell silent and he didn't say a word for some time.

A few minutes later, he glanced at her. She had relaxed her arms and was leaning her head against the window. He felt confident to speak then.

"I apologize for worrying about the way you would handle Anthony," Jarrett said humbly.

"Thank you," Liberty muttered, a quick glance at him enough for him to know she wasn't as angry as before.

"I wonder if we can go just one day, Liberty, without a misunderstanding? I don't know what to do anymore," Jarrett said, his gaze falling on Liberty as he stopped at a red light.

At his comment Liberty frowned but she didn't respond. She waited until they reached her house before she said in a soft, contrite voice, "I don't know what to do either, Jarrett. I only know that I love you and I love my son. What would you do?"

Jarrett parked the car, turned off the ignition, and turned to Liberty, his eyes dark with unexpressed emotions. "I'd marry me . . . or you, I guess." He laughed then. "Choose me, Liberty. I can help you. I want to help you. Let me go through this with you. I want to. I need to," he said in a torrent of words that he hadn't planned. He regretted them the moment he said them, certain she would not say yes. She was too emotional over Jamal to think clearly.

Liberty stared into Jarrett's eyes, torn by his words, hurting over what she must do. Instead of answering him, she leaned forward and kissed him. He pulled her to him and their mouths locked in a passion that overwhelmed both of them. When Liberty pulled away, she murmured against his mouth, "I've always chosen you."

Amazed by the passion that flared in her eyes, that made her voice low and husky, he allowed her to guide him into the house, up the stairs, and into her bedroom. He closed his eyes, reveling in the feel of her as she drew him to her.

Liberty lay staring at the ceiling in deep thought. She breathed lightly, no longer furious with Anthony. She and Jarrett had made love the moment they arrived at her home. When it was over, all of her anger had faded. Instead she felt calm, rational, and confident that she would turn the morning's disappointment around.

Jarrett had fallen asleep and was snoring lightly. They were both exhausted, not just from making love but from the crazy events over the past week. Still, she could not rest or fully relax, not while Anthony had Jamal.

It was still early, just past eleven o'clock in the morning. She wondered if Anthony had taken Jamal to his home or somewhere else. Anthony may have decided to keep Jamal out of her reach to be sure that she didn't throw a tantrum, something she knew he would expect of her.

She swallowed and turned her head to stare at her shimmering blue curtains. The sun barely penetrated the drawn draperies and it would have been easy to forget that it wasn't even noon yet. She wondered if Jamal was sleeping or if he was wide-awake. He would be hungry, she was sure of it. He probably wanted to play his Nintendo. Anthony didn't have any games at his home for Jamal.

Her throat had a lump from her efforts to hold back tears that threatened to consume her. She wanted to call Anthony, to plead with him to return Jamal, to beg him to stop being so cruel. But she knew that would not work. He needed time, she decided. Time to realize that Mikel Wilkins was not only an isolated incident that would never repeat itself, but that she loved Jamal and would never allow harm to come to him.

Not wanting to awaken Jarrett, very carefully she turned onto her side, tucked her hands under her cheek, and closed her eyes. Anthony would get over his anger and frustration with her, she was sure of it. Earlier she had felt that the world was coming to an end, defenseless and forlorn against Anthony's wrath. She knew now that he was scared for Jamal. That fear, she understood. She knew too that he had been given a reason, however irrational it might be, to lack faith in Jamal's safety within her home. She understood his concerns and doubted that she would not have responded the same way if the tables had been turned and Anthony had been the one who was kidnapped first.

It didn't matter. She was going to put things straight between them and establish her parental rights.

Jamal was her son, she had rights, and no matter how worried Anthony was about his son, he had no more right than she to take Jamal away. She needed to make Anthony understand that. The only way she knew she could get him to respect her position, her status, her role, was to get a lawyer involved. She had allowed Anthony's lawyer to handle her initial custody because she was so thankful and grateful. She was also so naïve. This time it would be on her terms, with her own lawyer, and Anthony Anderson would never threaten to take Jamal from her again.

Secure in her decision, confident that she was going to get Jamal back and more, Liberty was finally able to relax. She closed her eyes and finally drifted off to sleep.

Chapter 26

Jarrett awoke to the sound of hushed voices. Groggy, he blinked and glanced around the room. Liberty had left. He sat up, yawned, then came to his feet. He heard the voices more clearly now. Oblivious of his nakedness, he walked to the door and peeked outside the room. He frowned and took a startled step back. It was Lieutenant Jefferson. Now what?

He hurried back to the bed, searched the floor for his clothing. In haste he tried to pull on his pants and nearly fell. He zipped his pants, found his shirt, and pulling it on, left the room, forgetting to button his shirt.

"Don't tell me that Mikel got away again," Jarrett blurted, beginning to button his shirt at Liberty's surprised glance from his face to his shirt.

Lieutenant Jefferson had been sitting across from Liberty on the sofa. At the sight of Jarrett, he stood and faced the man, his face an unreadable mask.

Jarrett was smirking at him as he spoke. "If he did, I got to tell you, your police department is a joke! It doesn't make any sense how many times this man has gotten away from you people—"

"Mikel confessed. So did Veronica and Charles," Liberty interrupted with a big smile at Jarrett. Her words stilled Jarrett's rampage. He paused, hesitated on his last button, then dropped his hands to his sides.

"Really?" Jarrett said, dumbfounded. It was the lieutenant's turn to smirk.

"Yeah," Jefferson confirmed before sitting back down beside Liberty. "Mrs. Wilkins is awake and healthy as ever. He had more to lose by fighting it. Three kidnapping charges, embezzlement, you name it, he's been charged with it."

"And by confessing he gets time off, is that it?" Jarrett asked.

"Something like that. He's going to be behind bars for a long time either way."

"It's such a shame. I truly believe he was probably not that bad if he wasn't so angry with his aunt for leaving him out," Liberty said, amazed at how much trouble Mikel had caused only to confess to everything in the end.

"Apparently Mrs. Wilkins left him nothing, not even a patch of grass off of her estates. Mikel couldn't accept that Elizabeth was going to get off without so much as a slap on the hand for her part in it. So he confessed and told her part as well. The girl was up to her neck in the scam. They'll both be doing a lot of prison time."

"But how, why would she help Mikel when he hated her? Could she have been tricked into helping him?" Liberty wondered.

"Who knows?" the lieutenant agreed.

"So that's why you're here? Because Mikel's pretty much sealed all of their fates with his confession?" Jarrett asked.

"That's right," the lieutenant answered easily. "I wanted to personally inform Ms. Sutton."

"Does this mean that the others will confess too?" Liberty asked, concern creasing her forehead.

"Not necessarily. Elizabeth is denying it to the end. Veronica and Charles, as I said before, confessed even before Mikel did. But don't worry, Ms. Sutton, you don't have anything to be concerned about. Mikel was the mastermind and the strength behind this whole affair. Elizabeth just agreed to help him out. The others are nothing without him."

Liberty was relieved. She didn't care if she never set eyes on any of the Wilkinses again. Well, maybe except for Mrs. Wilkins. Liberty would have to remember to visit the woman at the hospital soon.

After the lieutenant left, Liberty leaned against the front door and closed her eyes. The Wilkins problem was over. Now she just had to get Anthony to believe the same. Then perhaps she wouldn't need a lawyer, at least not as quickly as she needed one right now.

The thought of getting Jamal back without a court battle brought a small smile to Liberty's face. Lost in thought, she was completely unaware of Jarrett's observing gaze. Determined to contact Anthony without being impulsive or unprepared, she went to sit on the sofa and reached for the phone. She needed to talk to Brenda, who was always good for offering a neutral point of view. It was a quality Brenda had that Liberty both dreaded and admired.

"Are you all right?" Jarrett asked, his eyes falling on her hand that was paused on the telephone.

"What? Oh, yes," Liberty responded, looking up at Jarrett with eyes that seemed surprised to see him. Jarrett frowned at her expression, but said nothing.

"I'm still digesting everything the lieutenant told us," Liberty added, uncomfortable beneath Jarrett's silent scrutiny. She didn't want to tell him that she was going to call Brenda for advice. Brenda was protective of her like Jarrett, but she didn't allow her ego to get in the way of her opinions. Liberty didn't need Jarrett to be big and strong, she needed him to be understanding.

"Me too. It's been crazy," Jarrett finally said, his eyes deliberately falling on the telephone.

When Liberty moved her hand away from the phone and carefully placed her hands in her lap, Jarrett sighed. He sensed Liberty wanted to call Anthony. He also sensed that Liberty would never believe that he actually understood how she was feeling. She was excited that she could tell Anthony there was nothing to fear now and that Jamal could come home. He wished that Liberty was not so naïve as to believe that it would be that simple.

With Mikel locked up, sealed by his own confession, Anthony had no excuse to keep Jamal, Jarrett knew that, and so did Liberty. Under the circumstances, Liberty's anxiousness was understandable. Still he wanted to advise her not to call Anthony but to wait until she got a good lawyer and could handle matters in court, once and for all, as she had said earlier. He knew that any comment he made would appear jealous and impatient, not logical and tolerant. Determined to bring up the subject of marriage again, and not wanting to be rejected flat out—something he knew Liberty was capable of when she was angry—he decided to stay calm and allow her the room she needed to handle Anthony in her own way. He would just have to keep his eyes open and watch for any manipulative move Anthony might try. So he simply inquired, "Calling Anthony?"

"Anthony?" Liberty whispered. What would it take for Jarrett to realize just how unimportant Anthony was beyond his role as Jamal's father? But contrary to Jarrett's earlier behavior, he didn't appear angry or agitated at the idea that she may have wanted to call him. His expression was warm and even understanding. Liberty flushed beneath his gaze. She was ashamed that she wanted to cry on Brenda's shoulder instead of Jarrett's. Right now, she needed a sister, a girlfriend to share her burden, unabashedly and without carefully chosen words, and Jarrett could never be mistaken as that.

She smiled, relieved by his patience, amused by her thoughts. "Actually, I was going to call Brenda," she said honestly.

Jarrett hesitated, watching her with his hands tucked into his jeans pockets. He knew Liberty needed to talk, wanted to express her emotions that she held on to so precariously at times, but he also sensed she didn't want to talk to him. It hurt but what could he do? He watched as she picked up the phone and raised a finely arched eyebrow at him. She didn't say a word but waited patiently for him to say whatever was on his mind. And there was obviously something on his mind.

"Call Brenda. I'm going to take a shower," he finally said.

Liberty was surprised. That was it? No accusations, no anger, just *I'm taking a shower?* Now she was really confused. She hesitated. She knew as he turned away that he wanted to say more but he was holding back. A little baffled by his behavior, Liberty sighed. She couldn't tell what was going on in his mind when he was staring at her in suspended silence. She cocked her head to the side in deep thought. Did he perhaps not believe she intended to call Brenda? She shook her head. That was not Jarrett's way. He might be stubborn and despise Anthony, but he believed in her. Something else was bothering him. What exactly she just couldn't fathom. Putting aside Jarrett's inexplicable behavior, she dialed Brenda's number.

Jarrett walked up the stairs to Liberty's master bathroom. He pulled off his pants and shirt and stepped into the hot shower. He allowed the heat to smother his frustrations. He leaned with his hands against the tiled walls and let the water drown his head, his eyes closed, his tension washing away with the soothing pelting of the water.

He was going to marry Liberty. Of that he was determined. To his credit, he had learned the valuable lesson of patience when he nearly lost her.

He had been so hurt by her last refusal that he returned the ring to the jeweler. It was a stupid and rash decision that he regretted. The last time he proposed to Liberty he had been cocky and overconfident. Her rejection had humbled him but not deterred him one bit. It had only delayed the engagement. With Mikel's untimely arrival, his affection had been put to the test and he learned just how much he actually loved Liberty and Jamal. They were his family, just as much as his two sons were. He didn't want to lose her. So if taking it slow, waiting for her signal to propose was what he needed to do, then he would. After all, she chose him, she told him so.

In the meantime, all he could do was prove to her that he got the message. He was going to back off of pushing that they get married and accept deep down that she really loved him. He sighed, backing away from the water. He wiped his eyes and stared into his fuzzy image in the fogged mirror. Liberty Sutton loved him, she just needed her memory jogged.

* * *

"I know what to do, I just don't know which one to do first," Liberty moaned. She was leaning back on the sofa, her eyes closed. She laid her left arm over her forehead as if she had a headache.

"You said it best, Liberty, you need to get a lawyer. Your own lawyer this time. And set the record straight once and for all," Brenda said firmly.

"So I'll get a lawyer first. That's what I'll do," Liberty said. She sat up and glanced up the stairs. Jarrett had not yet come down.

"And Jarrett?" Brenda asked as if she could read Liberty's mind.

"I love him but he's too emotional about Anthony," Liberty responded.

"I don't agree, Liberty. I think you are the emotional one."

"Brenda—" Liberty groaned.

"Now wait, you called me. Let me finish," Brenda insisted. "Jarrett was the one that insisted that Anthony legally give you custody in the first place. Remember? Anthony had no intention of making sure your rights were taken care of, he was just feeling bad because he lost his wife. And Jarrett never turned his back on you, Liberty. You kept him in the dark about everything, even the fact that Anthony's come on to you on more than one occasion. So let's be honest. Jarrett's been pretty admirable in how he's handled all of the drama you've brought into his world since you began dating. I think you need to rethink how you respect his role. You either love him or you don't."

"I said I love him."

"Then trust him, Liberty. For crying out loud. The

man asked you to marry him. He wants to be a part of your life, for good or bad, forever. He's proven himself over and over, through your child custody battle, your association with Anthony, and even this horrendous experience with Mikel Wilkins that he would not let you down. Why can't you trust him to help you this time?"

"I'm scared," Liberty admitted.

"Of what?" Brenda scoffed.

"Of losing him, I guess."

"You guess? If he wasn't trying to stick around, Liberty, he's been given plenty of reasons and opportunities to let go. If I had to guess, I suspect you have Jarrett on the edge and he's afraid of losing you. Give him a break. He'll take Anthony and put him in check, get you the custody rights you deserve, and ensure that Anthony stays in check."

"You're right."

"And Jamal loves Jarrett. I think Anthony's afraid of that. Let's face it, Jarrett's a great guy, a great catch. . . ."

"I can't believe you're admitting that." Liberty laughed. Brenda had never given Jarrett credit for how wonderful he'd been to Liberty.

"Well, yeah, I had to be sure before I said it," Brenda insisted. "I think you need to be aware that even the great ones get burnt out. Don't push him away. Let him help you and it will work out."

"I just don't want to be dependent on him or any man. I don't want to be hurt," Liberty muttered.

"Who does?" Brenda said scornfully. "I'm sure Jarrett had worries about being hurt, too. He's a divorcee. He's been through a painful breakup and has kids to boot. Stop just thinking about yourself for a change. That man's put himself out there. Don't lose him because you were hurt by an idiot like Anthony. You're really upsetting me with this nonsense," Brenda added sternly.

"Thank you, Brenda." Liberty whispered. She stood up, excitement warming her from head to toe. She was going to confide in Jarrett and trust him the way she used to. She was going to stop worrying that he would hurt her as Anthony once had.

Brenda laughed. "Call me later. I want to hear the romantic details when you two finally get over your issues."

"I will. Bye, Brenda," Liberty said, hanging up the phone as she stared up the stairs.

Chapter 27

Jarrett stepped out of the shower and paused.

Liberty was standing in the bathroom doorway. She leaned against the door, her eyes roaming freely over him, a smile curving her sensuous mouth. Jarrett tilted his head and considered her, returning the smile.

"We need to talk," Liberty said, her gaze never leaving his face as he reached for the towel and wrapped it around him. Walking barefoot over the cold tiled floor, Jarrett came to stand in front of Liberty.

"About?" he inquired.

Liberty took a deep breath, enjoying his freshly washed scent. He was overwhelmingly masculine and handsome as he stared down at her.

"I've been unfair toward you," Liberty began.

Jarrett narrowed his eyes, then his smile widened into a grin. He crossed his arms across his bare chest and raised an eyebrow. "Yeah?" he probed.

"Yes. Well, I think we need to have dinner," Liberty concluded. She had no idea what she was doing when she started her speech, but as she spoke she knew. She was going to propose to Jarrett! She would take him to the same restaurant where he had originally proposed to her. They would have a lovely dinner, then she would propose to him over wine. And he wouldn't say no. She knew he still wanted to marry her, he had asked her again just that morning.

"Dinner?" Jarrett repeated. Was this her cue? Was she hinting that she wanted him to propose to her again? His grin widened more.

"Yes. Tomorrow night."

"Tomorrow? I see, and in the meantime?" Jarrett asked.

"In the meantime, I need you to help me get no less than a hundred percent equal custody of Jamal. I don't want Anthony to ever have the right to take Jamal from me again, not even for a night," Liberty added, her smile gone as her tone turned serious.

"Are you trying to take away his custody rights?" Jarrett asked, careful not to sound doubtful or incredulous about her ability to take full custody from Anthony.

"If that's what it takes. I want full rights to my son. I'm not trying to keep Jamal from his father, no more than Dana's trying to keep your sons from you. I simply do not want to feel so helpless and at his mercy whenever he's angry," Liberty explained. She sat down on the bed, stilling herself from a wave of self-pity that threatened to overwhelm her.

"I see." Jarrett nodded. He fell silent for a moment as he considered her. He knew she had talked with Brenda. He wasn't sure if he was hurt or happy that it took Brenda's opinion to get Liberty to trust him. He decided it didn't matter. He had her back and that was what was important.

"I didn't want to burden you," Liberty began, his silence making her uncomfortable.

"You could never burden me, Liberty," Jarrett interrupted, then he hastily passed her and went into the room. Lost in thought, he dressed.

"I need you, Jarrett."

Jarrett laughed and walked purposely over to Liberty. His shirt was unbuttoned; his hair still had beads of water on it. He looked totally relaxed and Liberty wondered what he had been thinking.

"No, Liberty. I need you," Jarrett said with his usual calm reserve. His gaze was direct and Liberty felt a flutter of butterflies in her stomach. She had to take a deep breath to collect her thoughts.

"Okay," she said and felt utterly foolish afterward.

Jarrett smiled, swept an admiring gaze over her, then turned away and continued buttoning his shirt.

"I'm going home. I need to take care of a few things. I'll call Tom and we'll get the ball rolling. I'll set up a meeting for this week. We can go over the details of what you want to accomplish tomorrow at dinner. Don't worry, Liberty," Jarrett said as he put on his shoes. When he was done he stood up and gazed down at her.

She stared up at him, oblivious of how youthful and vulnerable she looked to him. He gave her a reassuring smile and offered his hand. She accepted and came to her feet.

"I won't let you lose Jamal," Jarrett whispered as he pulled her into his arms.

"I know," Liberty said into his chest.

Jarrett held Liberty for a moment longer, then with a sigh that came from far away, he planted an almost fatherly kiss on her forehead. Liberty was surprised by the patronizing kiss. Checking her watch, she saw it was just past four o'clock. Jarrett's eagerness to leave confused Liberty further. He hadn't even made an attempt to stay. The entire day had gone by with little accomplished. And though she was utterly confident that Jarrett would help her, she did find his exceptionally patient demeanor odd. She trusted him but that didn't mean he wasn't up to something. Just what she couldn't guess.

"I'll call you when I get home. We will have an appointment before the end of the week with Tom. Okay?"

"Okay," Liberty agreed.

She walked slowly from the room, trailing slowly behind him as he hurried down the hall. He was on the bottom step when he realized that Liberty had stopped on the top step. He looked up and paused.

"You all right?" he asked, his eyes full of concern.

She gave a small laugh, then nodded. "Yes. Are you?" she asked, tilting her head to the side waiting for his response.

"I feel great. I'll see you tomorrow," he answered.

His wide grin baffled Liberty even more. Could he be that happy that she had opened up and allowed him to help her? She was incredulous that it was possible for such a simple act on her part to make him behave so lighthearted. She was confident that it couldn't just be that he was pleased to be able to help her. It had to be something else distracting him. Deciding she was being silly to worry over a sudden mood swing, she hurried down the stairs and locked the front door. After her experience with Mikel, she was careful to make sure her home was secure. She glanced around the house that she had once loved so much. Too much bad had taken place during her short stay and she couldn't live her life feeling uncomfortable in her own home.

It didn't matter really, she thought with a light smile. If she married Jarrett it wouldn't matter. Naturally with her son and his two sons, they would need more space and they would have to move.

"I'm already thinking like a wife," Liberty said aloud, though she was alone. She laughed and began to think about what her wedding dress would be like.

Jarrett grinned all the way home.

Patience, he thought smugly. His Liberty was back! He felt relieved, as if the weight of the world had been lifted from his shoulders. Liberty was like no woman he had ever known or certainly ever dated. She kept him on edge, that was for sure. But he wouldn't trade her for anyone else. She was tough and independent even as she was vulnerable. She was beautiful and he was so thankful that he had not given up. Besides, with the turmoil Anthony put her through over Jamal, what kind of man would he have been if he had walked out on her?

Jarrett thought of his own sons as he pulled up to his apartment. He hadn't seen them since summer vacation began. He was upset when his ex-wife first told him she wanted to take them to Connecticut. Normally he would miss them terribly, but with all that had happened, he had not had a moment to worry about them. He had to admit that with all he and Liberty were going through, he was not ungrateful to Dana for insisting they visit her parents. After all, it was only a few hours away if he wanted to visit them.

Jarrett's daydream immediately ceased the moment he entered his apartment. Someone was in his home. He hesitated, debating between entering the apartment fully and surprising the burglar and immediately exiting and calling the police. Before he could come to a decision, the choice was made for him. The shadow hit the doorway before the slender figure of his ex-wife became evident.

"Jarrett," she greeted him, a plate of food in one hand, a glass of water in the other. She was heading for the sofa and did not pause at his presence. Jarrett considered her, then fully entered the apartment. His frown spoke volumes although he did not say a word as he locked his door. He walked up to her, jingling his keys. Dana looked up at him with smiling eyes and with feigned innocence sipped her water.

"I don't eat in my living room, Dana. You know that," Jarrett said casually. He sat in the chair across from her. Dana crossed her legs, put her plate on her lap, and considered him again with smiling eyes.

"I promise not to make a mess," she stated as he picked up a broccoli spear, dipped it into her dressing bowl, then took a delicate bite.

Jarrett couldn't help but grin. Shaking his head at her audacity, he leaned forward and said, "You scared the hell out of me." He sighed. "What are you doing here? Why aren't my sons with you?"

"They're still at my mom's, of course," Dana answered, setting her plate aside.

"Uh-huh, and you're here because?" Jarrett prodded.

"Because, Jarrett, love, I have wonderful news," Dana began. She sat up straight, cleared her throat, and then for once gave him a serious gaze.

"Yeah?" Jarrett inquired, raising his eyebrows, curious despite himself.

"I'm getting married," she blurted out as if she were about to burst.

Jarrett stared at her, surprised. Then he grinned and released a whooping laugh. It seemed marriage was in the air for all the women he knew.

"What's so funny?" she demanded, standing up in irritation so that she could stare down at him. Jarrett tried to stifle his humor and stood up as well.

"Nothing, Dana. Congratulations," he added, then gave her a gentle hug. Cautiously she returned the hug, then sat back down. "So you came here to tell me?" he asked, sitting down again as well.

"Yes. Paul, that's his name, he asked a while ago. He wants to get married right away. Next weekend, in fact. I was going to just do it. Have the kids there and everything. But I couldn't do that to you. We may have our differences but I thought it only fair to let you know that I'm getting married again."

"It's very considerate of you. I guess I never saw it that way. In fact, I have news to share with you, not as good, but similar," he added quickly at her surprised gaze.

"Yeah?"

"I'm asking Liberty to marry me. I plan to buy the ring this evening, in fact." Jarrett sat back, digesting his own words in wonder. Dana stared at him with a frown. Jarrett cocked his head to the side and, leaning forward, said, "What?"

"Asking her? You don't sound too confident, Jarrett. That's not the man I used to know," she added dryly.

"I'm not confident," Jarrett admitted with a frustrated shrug. "I hate to admit this to you, of all people," he added with a tense laugh. "I've already asked Liberty to marry me. She wasn't sure then. I think I nearly blew it. These past few weeks have been crazy, just enough to distract her and me from my earlier anger that she wasn't elated to marry me."

"Are you're asking her to marry you because it's a

challenge, Jarrett, or because you sincerely love her?" Dana asked, eyeing him doubtfully.

"I sincerely love the woman," Jarrett answered instantly and adamantly. "In fact, I'm asking her again to start over, to show her that I can accept no like a man should. I'm buying a new ring, and at dinner Thursday I plan to ask her to forgive me, to do what she will so long as she is happy."

"Wow," Dana murmured, in awe by his sincerity. He had changed. He was no longer the brooding, self-absorbed man she had married nearly ten years earlier. She was almost regretful. But then she thought of Paul and how happy he made her. She loved him and she wished the same happiness on Jarrett.

"Tell you what," Dana said, coming to her feet. "I'll help you pick the ring and even coach you a bit on what you should be saying. But," she added, pointing her finger at him like a scolding schoolteacher. "If I help you, you must promise that you'll come to my small but very dear-to-me wedding and that Paul and I are invited to yours."

Jarrett laughed. "It's a deal."

"Good. Let's go." Dana laughed, coming to her feet.

"Wait a moment, I have to make a phone call to my lawyer," Jarrett said.

"Why? Are you making her sign a prenuptial?" Dana laughed again, sitting back down as he walked away.

"Hardly," Jarrett guffawed as he picked up the phone.

* * *

"All taken care of?" Dana asked, standing and picking up her purse.

"All done." Jarrett sighed, proud of himself. Liberty was going to be excited. Tom felt confident that Liberty would be able to solve her custody problems with little to no problems. They were to meet with him Friday.

"All right then, Jarrett Irving. Let's get your fiancée's ring." Taking hold of his hand, she led Jarrett from the apartment.

"How about dinner afterward. I still can't cook. That mess you saw me eating was awful," Dana said as they walked together from his apartment.

Jarrett laughed. "No, love, you never could really cook."

Dana snorted.

"Sorry. So, are you in the mood for Legal Seafood?" Jarrett suggested.

"Seafood is always a good idea." Dana laughed, her voice fading away as they got on the elevator. "We can go to the one at the mall."

Neither Jarrett nor Dana noticed Anthony's sudden retreat down the hall as they exited Jarrett's apartment. They didn't see him peeping down the hall as they talked while entering the elevator. The moment the elevator doors shut, Anthony walked back toward Jarrett's door and paused, then released a low whistle. He couldn't believe what he had just seen. He had come to Jarrett expecting to clear up some matter, never dreaming just how everything would become.

The man was playing Liberty after all. Anthony didn't know whether he was pleased with his discovery or genuinely disappointed in Jarrett Irving. Liberty loved Jarrett and completely trusted him, of that Anthony was sure. To see him walking hand in hand with another woman amazed him. He could only imagine what the news would do to Liberty. He was only half sorry to have to tell her what he had seen.

Chapter 28

Anthony drove with a broad grin curving his mouth.

So Jarrett was a player. Here he had chided himself all day thinking he was a cad for the way he had treated Liberty, Anthony thought.

Anthony shook his head, amazed. Jarrett had played his part well. Anthony was certainly fooled. The man acted as if he were a saint, and frankly that was why Anthony had gone to see him. He thought that they could talk man to man. He had kicked himself all day about how rash he had been to take Jamal from Liberty. The expression in her eyes had haunted him. He couldn't blame himself for being angry, he reasoned. He had been hit over the head, kidnapped, had his son kidnapped and their lives put in danger. He had blamed her for it, including the fact that he was helpless to do anything about it. And the ultimate insult and pain was seeing her so lovey-dovey with Jarrett while he was still suffering a raging headache like he had never experienced before. And, he admitted too, he had been jealous. So he punished Liberty the only way he could, but he had been wrong.

He wanted to straighten matters out between them, but he knew that he and Liberty could not do it alone. He was loath to acknowledge Jarrett's strengths, but the fact was, Jarrett was reasonable and rarely lost his head in a heated argument. If Jarrett wanted to be in Jamal's life, then Anthony wanted to set the rules straight. And he wanted Liberty to know that no matter what went down between them, past or future, he was and would always be Jamal's father. Sometimes Liberty gave him the impression that she forgot who he was. She was so enamored with her lover, Jarrett, that she took Anthony's role as father lightly if not completely dismissing it.

"I'll like to see how enamored she is now," Anthony said aloud, turning onto Liberty's street.

He was certain Liberty wouldn't believe him. But he had heard the pair talking about dinner and he was prepared to call his trump card if he had to. It was an opportunity to get Jarrett out of the picture, and Anthony was determined to use it. He took a total about-face having gone from wanting to enlist Jarrett's help to clear the air between him and Liberty and start fresh to seeing an opportunity to possibly get Liberty's affection back.

Liberty was shocked when she answered her front door to find Anthony on her doorstep. A quick glance around him and her heart dropped with disappointment. Jamal was not with him. Sad, hating Anthony for coming to her home without Jamal and unannounced to boot, she opened the door.

Anthony's smile turned into a grin as Liberty blocked him from entering her home.

"What do you want, Anthony?" Liberty asked sharply.

"I'm hurt, really," Anthony said woefully.

"Sure you are," Liberty said with scorn.

"Liberty, are you going to keep me standing at the door like a salesman?" Anthony retorted, feigning hurt at her lack of hospitality.

"Yes, I am. Where's Jamal?" Liberty demanded, ignoring his glance over her shoulder into her home.

"At home with his grandmother."

"I want him back, Anthony. You should know that I am not going to dismiss what you've done. It won't be like last time," Liberty added, her voice void of emotion.

Anthony hesitated and considered her with an admiring gaze. "Wow, how calm you are," he said softly.

"And how wrong you are if you think I'm going to sit back and be treated like an adolescent while you dictate when and how I can see my son," Liberty retorted.

"You nearly got him hurt," Anthony stated, his jovial demeanor replaced with a stern stance.

"No. Mikel Wilkins did that. I was a victim, Anthony Anderson, not a culprit. How dare you treat me with such disregard after what I've been through!" Liberty stormed, her anger growing with each word.

"I see your temper is still as hot as ever," Anthony commented dryly.

"Yes, it is. And you will feel the full brunt of it when I get done with you," Liberty blurted. She instantly regretted her reckless threat at the darkened expression in Anthony's eyes. She could have kicked herself for losing her cool.

"Really?" Anthony said, then took a step back. He considered her with a smile that was taunting and belittling all at once.

"Yes, really. Now go home, Anthony. If you're not here to give me Jamal, then you and I have nothing to say to each other," Liberty said coldly, then stepped back to close the door.

"Sure we do. I think as a friend . . . I am your friend Liberty, believe it or not," Anthony added at Liberty's raised eyebrow. "As your friend, I am telling you that Mr. High and Mighty is not so high and mighty anymore."

"What are you talking about, Anthony?" Liberty asked impatiently.

"Jarrett's cheating on you, sweetheart," Anthony said easily. His words spilled out so smoothly that Liberty was not sure she had heard him correctly.

"What?"

"That's right. You heard me. He's cheating on you," Anthony repeated, barely able to conceal his pleasure in bringing Jarrett down.

"You're a liar!" Liberty stormed, then slammed the door. Anthony was surprised. He glanced around him and considered leaving. Instead he knocked on the door.

Liberty's heart was pounding. She hated herself for listening to Anthony. She hated herself for believing him. He was a snake! She leaned her head back against the door. She jumped when she heard Anthony's knock.

"Go away!" she shouted.

"Okay, babe. But I'm not lying."

"You are. You and I both know it. Just go home, Anthony. Get out of my life," Liberty sobbed.

"You don't want that. It would mean getting Jamal out of your life. Besides, I can prove that Jarrett's seeing someone else," Anthony added.

"I don't want to hear any more of your lies," Liberty scoffed through the door.

"You know I'm not lying or else you would not be so

upset," Anthony hissed, his voice lowered as a couple pulled into the driveway and glanced at him. "Come on, open up and let me give you my evidence."

Liberty hesitated. She didn't want to give Anthony any more room to hurt her heart. Just the thought that Jarrett was seeing someone else, even as a date, stung. For Anthony to be the one to discover Jarrett's two-timing secret hurt even more. Yet, curiosity compelled her to hear Anthony out. Collecting her composure, she opened the door and with her hands on her hips, she glared at Anthony.

"What proof do you have?" Liberty asked softly, all signs of being upset hidden behind her cool facade.

Anthony grinned. "Jarrett's my proof."

"Oh, this is ridiculous. Just go home," Liberty muttered, relieved and irritated all at once that Anthony was continuing to play games.

"You won't think it's so ridiculous if you get yourself down to Legal Seafood. He's having dinner with her right now," Anthony added, unable to conceal his glee as he disclosed his information.

Liberty didn't respond. She stared at him, unable to conclude if Anthony was telling the truth. As she stared at him the events of the last twenty-four hours played themselves over in her mind. Jarrett had behaved rather peculiarly all day, especially after he got out of the shower. He did not seem himself. She remembered thinking he was just excited that she had confided in him, but now she realized it was that he was anxious to get away, to be with his other woman. What a fool she had been. Again.

"You're cruel, Anthony," Liberty whispered, holding fast to her tears, wishing she didn't have a lump in her throat from wanting to cry. She would not cry, not in front of Anthony.

"No, I'm a good friend. I'm making sure you don't make a mistake with the rest of your life or Jamal's just because some guy has got you panting."

"I'm not panting. I thought he loved me," Liberty blurted.

"Yeah, so did I," Anthony scoffed.

"I tell you what, Liberty," he added after a long silence passed between them. "If it makes you feel any better, I had changed my mind about Jamal. I was wrong and I originally went by Jarrett's because I wanted to make amends. I thought talking to him would help before seeing you. Then I saw him with that woman and—"

"And so you came by to break my heart. Again," Liberty added in a painful whisper.

Anthony considered her, and for the first time since he had arrived he felt a moment's regret. Perhaps he was being cruel. Ah, to hell with Jarrett. All was fair in love and war. He didn't tell Jarrett to go running off in another woman's arms.

"Hey, if you don't believe me, that's fine. But check out the evidence. Legal Seafood is where they were headed. I bet if you left now you would likely find them there."

"I would never hunt him down to prove you right," Liberty said, rebuking him.

"Suit yourself. I think you know in your heart already that I'm telling the truth. That's why you're afraid to prove it to yourself," Anthony suggested.

"Jarrett would never cheat on me, Anthony. He's not like you!" Liberty hissed before once again slamming the door.

"I'll send Jamal over tomorrow. We can talk then when you've gotten over the bad news," Anthony said, then left the doorway.

Liberty stared through her peephole and watched as Anthony paused at his car door before getting inside and driving away. The moment he was gone, Liberty began pacing.

It explained a lot, Liberty thought bitterly. Jarrett had met someone else. But when? she wondered. Perhaps he just met her when she had left him at the hospital. No, that was too soon and all was well between them. It must have happened much earlier. When though? Before he proposed, after he proposed? Oh, she was going to go crazy. But she mustn't. It was exactly what Anthony was striving for. He wanted her to fall and run to him for comfort. It was not going to happen.

She needed to ease her mind and discover the truth for herself. She picked up the phone and dialed Jarrett's number. He didn't answer. She dialed his cell phone. Still no answer. She set the phone down and swallowed hard.

There was no way that she was going to listen to Anthony. She was not going to Legal Seafood. She was not going to search for Jarrett like some lovesick puppy. She was not going to fall into Anthony's trap. Oh, but what else could she do? Furious with herself for having so little self-control, Liberty picked up her purse and left her house.

Chapter 29

The moment Liberty pulled into the parking lot of Legal Seafood, her heart dropped.

There was no mistaking Jarrett's car. It was parked in clear view right in front of the entrance. Slowly she parked her car and a wave of sadness overwhelmed her. She leaned her head on the steering wheel, feeling defeated and rejected. It was her fault, she moped. She had allowed the shadows of the past to interfere with her future and pushed Jarrett away, right into someone else's arms.

Wallowing in self-pity, she grew more and more frustrated. She should just leave, she reasoned. It wouldn't help anything if she confronted Jarrett this way. She had already proven herself a fool by losing him; she didn't want to be an even bigger fool by making a scene. She sighed, thinking she could wait until their date tomorrow and then ask him what was happening. Besides, if she went inside and he wasn't with another woman, then what? But, she reasoned, lifting her head and staring at the restaurant, what if Anthony was right and Jarrett was with another woman? Jarrett would be able to lie if she confronted him tomorrow. If she went inside now he would have no choice but to tell the truth. And then it would be over.

She got out of the car and headed for the entrance.

If Jarrett was not with a date she would simply say she was hungry and on impulse decided to stop in. She was driving past, after shopping, she thought, making up her excuse as she went inside. *My, what a coincidence to run into you,* she would say.

The moment she went inside she was overwhelmed by the crowd of people. There was a bar in the center of the restaurant, every seat at it taken. It seemed as if every table was taken as well. Liberty felt a little relieved. Jarrett was probably with a few of his buddies. It was certainly not the type of place a man took a woman on a date, at least not a first date. There was no romance here, and Jarrett had proven himself to be the romantic type.

She paused and looked around the expanse of the space. Her eyes roved over head after head. She started to think that perhaps the car she thought was Jarrett's was not. She was beginning to feel more and more relieved when a familiar deep laugh caught her attention. She searched the back of the restaurant until her eyes fell on Jarrett. Beside him was an attractive woman.

Jarrett was engaged in an animated conversation with her, laughing, leaning forward so close that Liberty could barely see the other woman's face. It didn't look as if they were eating, Liberty thought. A few packages were on the table, feminine packages, which were likely the woman's. He had bought her gifts? Liberty groaned, feeling a sickening pain in the pit of her stomach. She couldn't believe this was happening to her again. There was no way he could deny he had a relationship with the woman sitting across from him.

She took a step toward the couple.

"Just one, ma'am?" the host of the restaurant asked, a menu in his hand, his tall body blocking her view.

Liberty gaped up at him, bewildered. "What?" she asked, peering over his shoulder to continue watching Jarrett.

"Will you be dining alone?" the host asked.

"No. I'm not dining. I'm meeting someone. Excuse me," Liberty said sharply, then moved around the host and headed toward Jarrett. Her precise movement, her direct gaze upon him was fully intended to give him the intuitiveness to look up and notice her. It worked.

As she moved toward him, he paused with his drink in midair, his eyes holding her as she approached. She could see him gulp. He set the glass down, looked at the woman across from him, and clearly swore under his breath. His disappointment at seeing her hurt as much as the discovery of his affair. He stood up before she had actually reached the table. He began to walk toward her. Before she could say a word he said, "Liberty, Liberty, it's not what you're thinking."

"Oh, yes, it is," Liberty said calmly, willing herself not to cry as she turned her gaze from Jarrett's puzzled face to the serenely pretty woman still sitting at the table. The woman seemed surprised to see Liberty, and that created another sharp pang of misery. He hadn't told his new girlfriend about her. Hadn't she been through enough? She didn't deserve this betrayal. She itched to slap Jarrett. Instead she stood stoically waiting for his explanation. Her only pleasure was that he was caught and just as miserable as she was.

"Liberty, don't let your imagination get the best of you. She's my—"

"My imagination!" Liberty hissed, his first words cutting deep. Was it her imagination that he was sitting with another woman, his face so close they could have been kissing? "I hope you are not letting your imagination get to you, Jarrett. It's only in your mind that I was here," Liberty mocked, then mustering all of the dignity she had, she ignored the curious glance of the woman with Jarrett and stormed out.

"Wait a minute!" Jarrett shouted, oblivious of the stares he created. "Liberty!" he called, hurrying to his feet to race after her.

She kept going, trying to rush away before Jarrett could stop her and humiliate her further. She was not only embarrassed that she had followed him, but she knew her eyes were brimming with tears. This time she would not be able to stop them. She was ashamed when large pools of tears shimmered in her eyes. She reached up to swipe at them but was detained when her arm was grasped by Jarrett. He stopped her in midstride and swung her around.

Liberty swallowed, unable to speak her rage and overwhelming humiliation in the face of his betrayal. She hated Anthony for being the one to discover Jarrett's affair. Was she so caught up in her own world that she had failed to see the signs? How had this happened and when?

"Listen to me, Liberty," Jarrett hissed.

"No. It's just like Anthony said and I will not listen to your lies," Liberty sobbed, unable to control her emotions any longer. She stared at the floor, feelings of helplessness washing over her.

Jarrett was confounded. Anthony had told her he was here with Dana? How Anthony knew where to find him was beyond him. He had done nothing wrong. If she would just hear him out she would know that he had not betrayed her.

"This is Dana—" Jarrett began, refusing to release Liberty even as she tried to pull her arms free.

"Oh, how dare you try to introduce me to her!" Liberty retorted, so caught up in her self-pity that she didn't recognize the name.

"Just wait a minute, Liberty. It's not what you think. This is—" Jarrett tried again. He released one of her arms to point to Dana. Dana stared up at the couple, amusement written on her face. Jarrett frowned at her half smile as Liberty interrupted him once again.

"It's every bit what I think. I can't believe you could do this, Jarrett," Liberty groaned in misery, beginning to notice several of the patrons turning curious glances her way.

"Oh, for crying out loud," Jarrett stormed impatiently. "Dana, meet Liberty. Liberty, this is Dana. My ex-wife," Jarrett blurted, bringing Dana to her feet as he spoke.

Liberty was stunned. She felt completely foolish. She immediately recognized Dana's name. She had even spoken with her on the phone on several occasions. But she had never actually met Dana as there had never been a reason to or an opportunity to meet.

Dana smiled and, ignoring Liberty's stiffness, gave her a consoling hug. Feeling utterly stupid, Liberty shook her head and took a deep breath.

"I'm so sorry," she murmured.

Dana shrugged. "No reason to be. Have a seat, we were just talking about you."

"I can't. I have to leave," Liberty said, wishing she could hide from Dana's knowing gaze.

"It's all right. These things happen. I'm just tickled to have finally met you," Dana chided as she slowly sat back down and waited for the couple to come to terms with their misunderstanding.

"Sit down, Liberty. Let's talk," Jarrett offered, guiding her toward a seat. By now the patrons realized the scene was over. They went back to their private conversations, ignoring the couple.

Liberty took a step back, confused and mortified. Anthony had successfully set her up. He had made her look like an immature fool and she fell for it. She swallowed, then shook her head, saying, "No. No, I can't. I have to go," before she pulled away from Jarrett and hurried from the crowded restaurant. Jarrett stared after Liberty's retreating form, dismayed and frustrated by her behavior.

"What are you waiting for, Jarrett Irving? Go after her," Dana scolded Jarrett.

Dana's words propelled Jarrett into action, waking him from his baffled stupor. "Thanks, Dana. I'll make it up to you," he said quickly, then hurried after Liberty.

Liberty was just reaching her car when Jarrett caught up to her. He stood in front of her door, moving her to the side as he refused to let her open the car door.

"Where are you going?" he asked, breathing heavily from his chase.

"Home. I can't stay here. I need to think," Liberty muttered.

"What happened back there? What are you doing here?" Jarrett asked, watching her closely.

"What are you doing here?" Liberty shot back. "And with your ex-wife. I thought she was in Connecticut," she added.

"She came back to tell me that she was getting married. She wanted to make sure I heard it first and that there were no hard feelings between us," Jarrett explained hastily.

"And are there any hard feelings, Jarrett?" Liberty asked.

"No. I'm happy for her. She found a new love, and so have I," Jarrett added pointedly.

Liberty paused for a moment, uncertain what to say. "Have you?" she whispered.

Jarrett stepped away from the car and moved within inches of Liberty.

"Yeah, I have," he breathed, taking her hands in his. "Liberty, I think I loved you from the moment I met you. With all that's happened, I have only grown to love you more. I need you and it drives me crazy when I think you don't feel the same way. I think now you do," Jarrett added with a laugh.

"Of course I feel the same way, Jarrett. I've been telling you that for years," Liberty muttered, unable to hold his gaze.

"Then, Liberty Sutton, will you please, please marry me?" Jarrett asked. He dipped his head, trying to capture her gaze.

Liberty refused to look at him. Her gaze fell to the ground, her breathing became ragged as she thought of all she had been through and all she had nearly lost. She wasn't going to be foolish again. Finally, just when Jarrett thought she was going to reject him again, she raised her eyes to his and answered, "Yes."

He released a relieved laugh and pulled her to him, kissing her passionately.

Dana stood at the entrance of the restaurant and smiled when the couple finally kissed. Feeling proud of Jarrett, she turned around and went back inside.

"I can't believe you would ever think I wanted someone else," Jarrett murmured against Liberty's mouth.

"I can't believe I thought it either," Liberty responded, laying her head against his shoulder.

"What happened? How did you know I was here?" Jarrett asked as they walked back toward the restaurant.

Liberty stopped just outside the door. A wave of shame came over her. She looked away from Jarrett as she responded, "Anthony."

Jarrett frowned. "Anthony?"

"He came over, all excited about his news, his bad news," Liberty admitted. She was leaning against the wall, her arms crossed in front of her chest as she stared at Jarrett. She felt guilty, as if she had done something wrong. How could she have been so stupid as to believe Anthony Anderson of all people?

"No wonder," Jarrett mumbled. He looked at Liberty and laughed.

Liberty pouted. "What is so funny?"

"Anthony. He set us up, and in his goal to hurt you, he helped me," Jarrett stated. "Remind me to thank him for that."

"Really?"

"Yes, really," Jarrett said. He pulled her to him and wrapped his arms about her waist. "I was going to propose to you again and again until you said yes. But, if you hadn't come here I would never have known just how much you love me."

"I tell you all the time," Liberty replied. "I'll throw a drink in your face every day if that's what I need to do to prove it," she suggested flippantly.

"No. Don't do that." Jarrett laughed, then he gazed at her, saying softly, "But I do need a little confirmation every now and then. Tonight I got it. I admit, it was a little embarrassing back there, but to know you truly love me, Liberty, it was worth it. Like I said, I'll thank Anthony the moment I see him."

"You'll get your chance soon. He's letting me get Jamal. He's backed off of his custody issue. He said he was going to talk to you about it instead of me. Imagine that."

"Well, good for him," Jarrett huffed. "But I still think you need to get your custody straight through the courts. No more of this courtesy of Anthony Anderson and dealing with his mood swings."

"Whatever you say, Jarrett." Liberty smiled, then laid her head on his chest.

"Whatever?" Jarrett probed.

Liberty giggled, gave him a coy smile, then nodded. They stood there, locked in a warm embrace, oblivious of the customers coming and going from the restaurant. Finally, Jarrett whispered, "Then let's go home."

Liberty looked up at him. "What about Dana?"

"She'll be fine," Jarrett murmured.

"No, you drove. I saw your car," Liberty insisted, pulling away.

"Yeah. Then I'll give her my key and take your car. I'm anxious to get you home, Liberty Sutton. Soon to be Mrs. Irving," Jarrett muttered, pulling her back into his arms.

"Mrs. Irving sounds so sweet," Liberty murmured, once again swept up in his arms and his kisses.

"Then let's get her my keys and go home," Jarrett urged.

"Your place or mine?" Liberty flirted, pressing her body closer to his.

"Our place," Jarrett said firmly, capturing her lips in a passionate kiss once more. Liberty encouraged him, not caring one bit who saw them or what they thought. This man was soon to be her husband and she was going to enjoy all the rights that brought her, including kissing in public. When he finally pulled away from Liberty, the small crowd that had left the restaurant clapped, cheering the couple on. Grinning, a little embarrassed by the knowing glances cast at them, Jarrett wrapped a possessive arm about Liberty's waist, they went back inside, both lost in thoughts about making up later.

I hope you enjoyed *Encounter.*
As a special treat, a preview of *Intuition,*
the haunting sequel, is included for your pleasure.

Intuition is due in stores October 2005.

Chapter 1

"Did I hear you right?" Elizabeth asked, her eyes round with disbelief.

Her lawyer's grin was followed by, "Yes, Ms. Wilkins, you did."

"I can't believe it," Elizabeth murmured, stunned by the news. Her eyes fell to the floor as she fought for control not to sob out her relief. She had cursed her cousin for his lies. She had wanted to die with mortification that everyone had believed her guilty. But she had fought instead because she was innocent and knew that she would somehow prove it. She never dreamed that it would be done for her, that her prayers would actually be answered. And in only a few days. The fact that it had not taken the many months or even the years she had feared was a miracle.

"Believe it, you're free to leave," her lawyer repeated, smiling across his desk at Elizabeth.

Elizabeth looked up, her brown eyes shimmering with unshed tears as she smiled at him. Henry McMinster returned the smile, his pale blue eyes twinkling with delight to see the beautiful young woman smile at last. He never for an instant believed that Elizabeth was anything but an innocent victim of Mikel Wilkins's schemes. Her conniving cousin was a cunning thief and had so thoroughly implicated

Elizabeth in his plans to steal the family's trust funds that there was little to no hope that Elizabeth could ever prove she wasn't guilty. That reality had saddened him even as his gut instincts told him she was not involved.

If it wasn't for Mikel's real partners and their outraged admissions, in the face of Mikel's betrayal of them as well, there was no telling when or if Henry could ever have fully absolved Elizabeth's name. He was staring at the written confessions of one Veronica Mitzer and Charles Bronsini, and there was nothing the police could do with such compelling statements except release the woman immediately.

Henry suppressed a chuckle as he considered Elizabeth's shocked expression. He fully understood her disbelief. The poor woman had spent three days behind bars. They wouldn't even let her out on bail, claiming she would run. She had been forced to wear the unflattering jail uniform of faded blue jeans and the discolored blue shirt. It was a pity that she had had to suffer even if it was a relatively short period of time.

Henry admired Elizabeth, too. She was twenty-nine, but he could see her strength and depth even beyond the prison outfit. She just looked so much younger with her flawless complexion and clear, brown eyes that she could easily have claimed to be eighteen years old.

But Elizabeth Wilkins was no child and she was no fool. One would have to sense that she was a well-educated, slightly arrogant woman. It was in her sharp eyes, the proud lift of her chin. If Mikel Wilkins wanted to implicate anyone in his schemes, she was the right choice with her perceptiveness and her excellent credentials. She made for a perfect partner—until you met her and knew instantly that this woman would never involve herself in such an outrageous plan.

Henry sighed wistfully. If only he was a young man again. He was fascinated that she could sit so serenely in the face of all that she had experienced. He knew she was stunned, and he also knew she was quickly digesting and pondering the information he had just given her. She was the most interesting and delightfully intelligent woman he had met in some years.

Patiently he leaned back in his high-back leather chair and waited for Elizabeth to respond to her good fortune.

Elizabeth was no longer able to sit still. She came swiftly to her feet and began to pace back and forth in the small space that Henry's office allowed. She had all but given up hope that she would ever be proven innocent of any involvement in the abduction of Liberty Sutton and the impersonation scheme that Mikel had concocted. The nightmare was finally over.

"Can I leave now?" Elizabeth finally asked, pausing in midstride to trap Henry with her gaze, her eyes challenging him as she waited for his response.

Unperturbed by the abruptness of her question, Henry tapped his pen on the yellow legal pad in front of him. "Absolutely. Just as soon as you sign a few papers you can go to the front desk. It's just down the hall by the way, and they'll give you your things. Then you're free to leave."

Elizabeth hesitated, her brown eyes drawn to the pen and pad he was tapping before she noticed the papers neatly set aside. Her eyes narrowed suspiciously.

"What kind of papers?" she demanded, her arms crossed in front of her chest.

Henry held a grin in check, amused by her battle

stance. "Your release forms. Normally, the officer releasing you would do it. Did you think they wanted a signed confession?" He laughed, unwittingly stumbling on the truth behind Elizabeth's wariness. He didn't really blame her for being cautious after what Mikel had put her through with her signature, even if her signature was forged.

"No, what sense would that make?" Elizabeth asked in all sincerity, unaware that Henry was only teasing. He sighed. She was far too serious. He hoped that her sense of humor would not be damaged by her traumatic time spent defending her innocence.

Henry was unaware just how serious Elizabeth had always been. She rarely got the punch line in a joke or she was always the last to get it when she got it. She knew she didn't have a good sense of humor, but she prided herself on her intelligence, which amounted for an occasional bout of dry wit.

"Then I would like to sign your papers and leave now. I have much to do and can only imagine how crazy things have gotten," Elizabeth said regally.

"Of course," Henry agreed, coming to his feet to join her. He walked around his desk, sat in the chair beside the one Elizabeth had recently occupied, and waited until she sat down again. He handed her a pen.

"Sign here," he said. "And here." She complied, her signature swift and sure. "And here," he finished. When she was done, he carefully set the pen aside, picked up the papers, and walked to his small copier machine and made a second set for Elizabeth.

She waited, barely able to contain her agitation as he placed the papers inside a folder before finally, with excruciating slowness that Elizabeth was hard pressed not to believe was deliberate, handed her the file.

"Ms. Elizabeth Wilkins, it's been my greatest pleasure knowing you. Take care of yourself," Henry said, then stuck his hand out to shake hers. Elizabeth looked at his pale wrinkled hand, then impulsively ignoring it, came to her feet and gave him a huge hug instead.

"Thank you, Mr. McMinster. Thank you," she breathed, then flung open the door, a lump in her throat as she kept happy tears at bay. She would not cry. She stepped outside his office, closed the door, and immediately leaned against it, her eyes closed, her lips parted slightly as she took a deep breath, her body trembling with relief. She was free.

"Ms. Wilkins?" a deep, masculine voice inquired.

Her eyes flew open and she was startled to see the most handsome man she had ever seen leaning against the wall directly in front of Henry's office. She was speechless. Utterly annoyed at her schoolgirl reaction at seeing him, she found herself unable to speak, so she nodded in response to his question. Did he always have such an affect on women? she wondered in awe as she continued to stare at him.

He was tall, at least six feet three, and obviously nicely muscled beneath his starched while short-sleeve shirt, if his rippling biceps were any indication of the rest of his body. His hair was cut close to his head but she could see that he had a fine, wavy grain that could be unruly if he allowed it to grow out. His coloring was softly tanned, almost olive, and accentuated his oddly beautiful, heavily lashed dark eyes that gave him an exotic look. In fact, everything about him spoke of the islands, his chiseled jawline, his full mouth. He was like a bronze statue come to life, and

Elizabeth could imagine being swept away to the Caribbean, lost in his gaze.

His eyes caught hers and she paused. He wasn't smiling. In fact, she was certain she saw a spark of amusement as he returned her stare.

Where she was assessing him in admiration, he was watching her with barely concealed curiosity. What he must think of her, she thought in dismay. She was not normally so taken by a man's looks, but he was devastatingly good looking. It was his fault that she had gawked at him. Why couldn't she have already gotten out of her prison uniform and back in her black suit and high heels before she saw him? She groaned, wanting to dive back into Henry's office.

Propelled by her dismay at both her reaction to him and his lack of reaction toward her, she walked away. She had to get her property, and after that she was determined never to see the precinct again. If this man worked here, then he was just one more embarrassment she was going to have to put behind her.

"Ms. Wilkins at last," the man drawled, catching up to her. She glanced at him but kept walking. She had moved as quickly as she could without appearing to flee. It should have been a hint to him that she was not interested in whatever he wanted. He caught her arm when she didn't pause in her escape. Surprised, by both his touch and the jolt it sent through her, Elizabeth came to an instant halt. She turned to him then, her face a mask of coolness as she regarded him. Still she didn't speak.

"I was hoping to have the pleasure of meeting you before you left," he said as he released her arm and extended his hand toward her. Elizabeth frowned, tearing her gaze from his eyes to his hand. What *did* he want? She looked up again, accepting his hand, wishing she didn't feel a thrill at the mere touch of him, especially when she glanced sharply at him and noted with disappointment that he didn't share the current that ran through her body when their hands met. All the more reason to maintain her cool, she thought grudgingly.

"And you are?" she asked softly, her demeanor nonchalant and disinterested as she removed her hand and firmly stood her ground. It took all of her self-control not to take a step back, not to look away as he continued to stare at her with his magnificent eyes. Did he know how mesmerizing his gaze was? He was almost beautiful he was so handsome. She promptly broke into a smile, certain he would take offense at such a description. He was just too masculine to ever worry that someone might question his appeal, she decided, unable to control the twitching of her mouth.

Her smile caught him off guard, especially after the greeting she had given him. He frowned. "I'm Gavan T. Ward," he answered.

"Gavan T. Ward, the author?" she exclaimed with an incredulous laugh. She swallowed her laughter, noting with chagrin that a smile touched neither his face nor his eyes at her outburst. He was obviously not amused.

"The one and only," he confirmed. "I was hoping to talk to you about Mikel Wilkins. I was speaking with a friend of mine who works here and he was telling me about your situation. I found it intriguing," he added, his explanation ending with such a hint of sarcasm that caused her to wince in embarrassment.

His mocking response sobered any trace of humor she had. She wasn't sure what reaction she felt more strongly about, the desire to run from his derision or to set him straight on his assumption that she was a con artist. She chose neither option.

"I'm not interested in speaking with anyone about my ordeal," Elizabeth said firmly, seeking to dismiss the man with her disdain.

He grinned and Elizabeth was insulted that he seemed to find amusement in such an awkward moment.

"I can certainly understand that. Actually," Gavan continued, "I didn't intend to burden you in that way. I was interested in speaking with Ms. Sutton, Liberty Sutton. The woman who was forced into impersonating you," he clarified, his emphasis on the word *forced* stinging Elizabeth's ears. She flushed, feeling the heat in her cheeks, praying that he didn't notice. He might be handsome but he was not kind or mildly considerate. His looks couldn't hide that fact.

"Oh," was all she could think to say.

Gavan grinned, delighted that he had succeeded in flustering her. He could see in her eyes that she wanted to ditch him. He had not intended to show animosity to the Wilkins woman, but she was not what he had expected. His friend, one of the detectives who had helped to bring Mikel Wilkins in, had never once described Elizabeth Wilkins as beautiful. Tearful and ignorant to Mikel Wilkins's scheming, yes, but never once did he mention what she looked like. The woman was a knockout from head to toe. It was in her demeanor, the steadiness of her eyes, the lift of her chin. To his chagrin, her disdain for him was very clear, too. It goaded him that even in her blue denim uniform that fit poorly, she was gorgeous and unruffled.

She was no schoolgirl who played naïvely into the hands of her cousin, and he knew the moment he saw her that he should stay away from her. He was a serious, award-winning author. His collection of true-life stories had won him much acclaim, and he knew that this woman would sway him on the subject of the Wilkinses. But when she had walked away from him, left him standing gawking at her like a fool, he had impulsively gone after her. He wasn't able to leave well enough alone. As he watched her struggle to keep her composure, he knew he wasn't going to be able to ignore the feelings this woman stirred in him.

He was an idiot to be so fascinated, but he was enchanted the moment she had breathlessly exited the lawyer's office. She had appeared so stunningly beautiful. Her eyes were a rich depth of brown, her mouth pursed as if waiting for his kiss. And he would have kissed her too if she hadn't promptly run away from him.

Never mind that she didn't like him and that she could very well be guilty of fraud, he knew in that moment that she was more than a story and he was not going to be dissuaded by her indifference. Besides, Gavan thought, grinning, he had never had a problem being charming before and he was going to lay it all on Elizabeth Wilkins until she was begging for more.

Dear Reader,

Liberty Sutton is one of my most exciting characters. When I first introduced her to readers in 1999, she was young, immature, and well, *Impetuous*. I never expected to write a sequel about her life. Yet, like many of you, Liberty was one character I could not dismiss or forget. The heat of her romance with Jarrett Irving and the drama of her relationship with her son's father were lingering issues that I was compelled to bring to closure.

This, the second novel in the saga of Liberty, is a thrilling mixture of hot romance, intrigue, and personal growth. After a heartbreaking experience, it's never easy to let go of our past and accept the future with open arms, but Liberty learns that if we are to survive life's ups and downs, then we must let go of the past and we must embrace the future.

I bring you *Encounter* and hope that you'll enjoy reading the twists and dilemmas that Liberty and Jarrett experience as they prove that love can indeed conquer all.

Sincerely,
Dianne Mayhew

ABOUT THE AUTHOR

Dianne Mayhew was first introduced to readers in the early 1990s. Her first romance novel was *Secret Passions*, followed by her second novel, *Playing With Fire*, which was adapted into a made-for-television film. Dianne followed *Playing With Fire* with *Dark Interlude*, *Impetuous*, and *Stolen Moments*. Her newest novel, *Encounter*, is the continuation in a saga of love, triumph, and personal growth.

A native Washingtonian, Dianne is married with two children and lives in Maryland. Her greatest joys are her family, reading a good book, and of course, writing.

BOOK YOUR PLACE ON OUR WEBSITE AND MAKE THE ARABESQUE ROMANCE CONNECTION!

We've created a customized website just for our very special Arabesque readers, where you can get the inside scoop on everything that's going on with Arabesque romance novels.

When you come online, you'll have the exciting opportunity to:

- View covers of upcoming books

- Learn about our future publishing schedule (listed by publication month and author)

- Find out when your favorite authors will be visiting a city near you

- Search for and order backlist books

- Check out author bios and background information

- Send e-mail to your favorite authors

- Join us in weekly chats with authors, readers and other guests

- Get writing guidelines

- AND MUCH MORE!

Visit our website at
http://www.arabesquebooks.com